DOUBLE DOWN

Books by Fern Michaels

Perfect Match
A Family Affair
Forget Me Not
The Blossom Sisters
Balancing Act
Tuesday's Child
Betrayal
Southern Comfort
To Taste the Wine
Sins of the Flesh
Sins of Omission
Return to Sender
Mr. and Miss Anonymous
Up Close and Personal
Fool Me Once
Picture Perfect
About Face
The Future Scrolls
Kentucky Sunrise
Kentucky Heat
Kentucky Rich
Plain Jane
Charming Lily
What You Wish For
The Guest List
Listen to Your Heart
Celebration
Yesterday
Finders Keepers
Annie's Rainbow
Sara's Song
Vegas Sunrise
Vegas Heat
Vegas Rich
Whitefire
Wish List
Dear Emily
Christmas at Timberwoods

The Sisterhood Novels:

In Plain Sight
Eyes Only
Kiss and Tell
Blindsided
Gotcha!
Home Free
Déjà Vu
Cross Roads
Game Over
Deadly Deals
Vanishing Act
Razor Sharp
Under the Radar
Final Justice
Collateral Damage
Fast Track
Hokus Pokus
Hide and Seek
Free Fall
Lethal Justice
Sweet Revenge
The Jury
Vendetta
Payback
Weekend Warriors

The Men of the Sisterhood Novels:

Double Down

Published by Kensington Publishing Corporation

FERN MICHAELS

DOUBLE DOWN

KENSINGTON PUBLISHING CORP.

http://www.kensingtonbooks.com

KENSINGTON BOOKS are published by

Kensington Publishing Corp.
119 West 40th Street
New York, NY 10018

All Kensington titles, imprints and distributed lines are available at special quantity discounts for bulk purchases for sales promotion, premiums, fund-raising, educational or institutional use.

Special book excerpts or customized printings can also be created to fit specific needs. For details, write or phone the office of the Kensington Special Sales Manager: Kensington Publishing Corp., 119 West 40th Street, New York, NY, 10018. Attn. Special Sales Department. Phone: 1-800-221-2647.

Library of Congress Card Catalogue Number: 2015934121.

ISBN-13: 978-1-61773-265-2
ISBN-10: 1-61773-265-6
First Kensington Hardcover Edition: June 2015

10 9 8 7 6 5 4 3 2 1

Printed in the United States of America

Table of Contents

Upside Down

Upside Down

Chapter 1

Jack Emery propped his chin on his cupped hands and looked out the window of the Bagel Emporium at the blustery weather outside. His thoughts traveled back in time to a year ago, to the last day that Emanuel Macklin was seen. A lot had happened in the past year. Much of his life, and the lives of his friends, had been turned upside down. And sometimes he had a hard time coming to terms with the way all of it had happened at what seemed to be the speed of light.

He was a free agent these days. Right after the first of the year, he'd left his wife's, Nikki's, law firm, with her reluctant approval, supposedly to write a book. It was something that never happened. He'd done some consulting work for a few months, but that hadn't worked either. He'd then stepped into his old shoes at the district attorney's office, prosecuted two cases, and walked away. He'd won both cases but they were both on appeal. Some smart-ass defense attorney would come up with some frigging loophole, and the bad guys would be right back out on the street. So, disillusioned, he'd thrown in the towel and walked away, frustrated and angry at a criminal justice system that seemed to coddle the criminals and leave the good guys, the victims, to fend for themselves.

Jack's eyes were glued to the redbrick building across the

street from where he was sitting. His building. Well, not totally his. He, along with Ted Robinson, Joe Espinosa, Harry Wong, Bert Navarro, and Jay Sparrow, owned the building. They'd invested the bonus money they'd gotten years ago when they worked for Hank Jellicoe, money that none of them had ever touched until a few months ago, when he convinced his little band of avengers that this was what they needed to do. *This* meaning buying the six-thousand-square-foot brick building, refurbishing it, and going into business together. Into a business that was completely off the grid. And today was move-in day.

In a shopping bag at his feet, he had a bottle of champagne, crystal wine flutes, and a jug of tea for Harry so they could christen their new business in—he looked down at his watch—ten more minutes. Next to the shopping bag was Cyrus, a huge, sleek, 140-pound black German shepherd, who was his new best friend forever. Cyrus was two years old and, as far as Jack was concerned, half human and half dog. Cyrus was so in tune with Jack, he knew what Jack was going to do before Jack knew himself.

Four months ago, he had stopped in for his morning bagel while Cyrus waited outside. While he waited in line for his coffee and bagel, the door opened, and a man bellowed, "Everyone on the floor!" As he was dropping to the floor to obey the robber's orders, Jack saw a black streak clear the door with inches to spare. In the blink of an eye, all 140 pounds of ferocious dog propelled the robber to the floor, then sat on him. Jack, in a lightning move, scooped up the gun the man had been brandishing while Domingo Lopez, known to his patrons as Ding, called the police. Cyrus was the hero of the day, and, as Ding said, "I don't care what the Health Department's rules are, Cyrus can come in here anytime." His patrons agreed, and everyone else looked the other way. Jack reached down to pat the magnificent dog on the head. Cyrus nuzzled his hand.

Jack returned to his thoughts as he stared out the window. The weatherman had predicted a possibility of snow flurries later in the day. It was, after all, December, so snow flurries were to be expected. Just like last year, when the same prediction led to three weeks of arctic air and so much snow that the District had to shut down because there was nowhere else to move the white stuff.

So much had happened during that short period of time. Charles Martin had flown the coop, Jack and Nikki had hit a rough patch, and he'd resigned, to her initial chagrin. But in the end, she agreed because she just wanted him to be happy with his life. During the past year, her twelve-member all-female law firm took on six new associates and seven new paralegals. The expansion was needed to deal with three class-action lawsuits that would make the firm *kazillions* of dollars. If the workload didn't kill everyone first. All they had to do was work twenty hours a day to make it happen. Sometimes, he didn't see or talk to his wife for days at a time. What the hell kind of life was that? Things were still sticky between the two of them, but they were both trying to work it all through. Alexis Thorn, Joe Espinosa's significant other, had given Espinosa the boot shortly before Valentine's Day, saying she preferred her job to a relationship, and she hoped that he understood that she couldn't do both. Espinosa did not understand, any more than Jack did. They'd cried into their beers way too many times the last ten months.

Maggie Spritzer was back at the *Post* as the EIC after John Cassidy resigned because he didn't have enough time to go fly-fishing. It had taken a lot of sweet-talking on Annie de Silva's part to get Maggie back in harness, but, finally, all the perks Annie dangled in front of Maggie won her over, and she was once again calling the shots at the *Post*. Not a bad thing, Jack had decided at the time. Or as Ted put it, "She's out of our hair for now."

Jack's little "guy group," as he called it, had three new exclusive members and one long-distance member. The other members referred to it as "an off-the-grid spy group," whatever the hell that meant. The name conjured up all kinds of weird images and possible scenarios. Bert Navarro was the long-distance member. Dennis West, cub reporter and Ted Robinson, hero worshipper, as well as a new billionaire, Abner Tookus, hacker extraordinaire, and Jack Sparrow, who out of necessity was called Jay for a little while, were the latest recruits to the off-the-grid avengers club.

Jack let his thoughts wander to Myra and Annie, who had settled in for the long winter ahead. The last time he'd checked with Myra, she was knitting. *Knitting.* She'd said she was making a scarf that was two miles long, and she needed a wagon to carry it in. Or, as Annie put it, one long line of colored yarn filled with sloppy stitches. Annie said she was taking cooking lessons and brushing up on her pole dancing. She had mumbled something about feathers on shoes, or maybe it was her white cowboy boots that she always wore, but he hadn't understood a word of what she was saying. What he did understand was that, unlike the others, who were running themselves ragged, she and Myra were bored out of their minds.

Women! He would never understand them. Never!

Isabelle Flanders Tookus was still in England, designing a new-age city, and had no downtime available for Abner, which pretty much left him at loose ends and ready to dive into the guy group. Yoko, it appeared, at least according to Harry, was happier than a pig in a mud slide with her plant nursery and raising Lily, which left precious little time for Harry, who these days was meaner than a wet cat on a treadmill.

Kathryn Lucas, fiancée of Bert Navarro, thrived on driving the open roads in her eighteen-wheeler, making two stops a month in Las Vegas for, as Bert put it, booty calls. He also said theirs would be the longest engagement in history because

Kathryn had no intention of ever marrying again. Bert said he was okay with the engagement because he had no other options, and he loved Kathryn heart and soul.

Cyrus raised his head, then reared up. He'd heard the sound of Harry's Ducati before Jack had. "Okay, big guy, do your thing while I pay the bill." Doing his thing meant going from table to table to offer up his paw and, with luck, get a little treat from his friends at the other tables. When he finished his rounds, he barked, and Ding came out from behind the counter and handed the big dog a monster dog treat. Cyrus barked, offered up his paw, and waited for Jack to open the door. Ham that he was, Cyrus turned and bowed. The patrons loved it and always clapped. Jack said, "You are the biggest ham I've ever seen, Cyrus. Hero worship is a sin. Do you know that?" Cyrus barked, waited for a break in traffic, and raced across the road to greet Harry, who obligingly ruffled his ears.

"Hi, Harry!"

"Hi, Jack!"

"Let's walk around back so we can all go in together. I want us all to oooh and aaah at the same time. Ted just turned the corner, and I think I saw Sparrow come in from the other direction. Haven't seen Abner yet, though. Oops, there he goes. How's it going, Harry?"

"It's going, Jack. You?"

"It's going, Harry. You up for this gig?"

Never long on words, Harry said, "I'm here."

"Let's do it!" Jack said as he picked up his feet and raced to the back alley behind the newly remodeled property, where the guys were waiting for them. Cyrus barked a greeting, then offered his paw. It was a ritual that had to be observed, or Cyrus would bark relentlessly until the others made it happen. Satisfied that he had all the attention he needed, the big dog stood back while Jack allowed the retina scanner to check his eyeball, then listened for the hydraulic hiss of the door opening at their new, off-the-grid digs.

Chapter 2

One by one, the men entered a small eight-by-ten room that was totally empty except that it contained a good-sized state-of-the-art kitchen, replete with stainless-steel appliances. A manly kitchen. As they walked down a short hall to the main part of the building, the scent of newness—fresh paint, new wood, furniture that smelled like it came straight out of a warehouse, as it probably had—assailed their nostrils. The carpet was top grade, lush and thick, and the windows were covered not by drapes but natural-wood-colored plantation shutters. A few ficus trees and lush green plants were strategically placed in the foyer and all the offices. Dennis, who said he had a green thumb, had agreed to take over their care, watering and feeding them plant food according to the instructions that came with all the greenery.

There were six rooms in all, then one large room that ran the entire length of the building. The sign on the door said it was the COMPUTER ROOM. That meant it was Abner Tookus's domain and off-limits to everyone but him unless invited in. He had designed it to duplicate the special computer room he had at his own home. Jack had literally choked when Abner told him the equipment cost millions of dollars. Abner had personally bought, paid, and installed everything in the room at his own expense, which relieved Jack of all his anxiety. The guys, most of whom were seeing it for the first time, ooohed and aaahed, but it was Dennis West who said it looked like a room at NASA. And it was climate controlled, Abner said, because the machines were as delicate as the stuff NASA and the NSA had. He looked around at the group, and announced, "If the door is closed, do not open until you knock and I say you can come in." Heads bobbed up and down. In this room, Abner was king.

As they trekked through the building, they saw that each room had been furnished with a computer, a monitor, webcams, a fax, a color printer, and a landline. The building had seven different landline phone numbers. There were tablets, iPads, and a box of twenty-four different cell phones—all encrypted so as not to be traceable thanks to Avery Snowden—and each room had a seventy-six-inch television on one of the walls.

"What do you think, guys?" Jack asked anxiously. "Do you like the furnishings?"

Everyone started talking at once, with a lot of hand waving. The bottom line was, "You did a great job, Jack." Jack beamed his pleasure.

"What are we calling this . . . ah . . . enterprise? What does the plaque outside the door say this business is?" Ted asked.

Jack laughed. "BOLO Consultants. The plaque reads THE BOLO BUILDING, and underneath it says CONSULTANTS. We are whatever we want to be."

"What does that mean?" Dennis asked.

Sparrow raised his hand. "Let me guess. BE ON LOOK-OUT, right?" To the others, he explained. "It's a law-enforcement tag." Jack nodded, and, for the first time, noticed how dressed up Sparrow was. The rest of the group were in casual clothes, the same sort of clothing they had worn when they came to observe the renovations on the building.

He commented on Sparrow's attire, his gaze questioning. When Sparrow was not more forthcoming, Jack thought maybe he was going to attend a funeral or a wedding after the meeting. He led the group out to the main part of the building to a room off to the right, whose polished doorplate announced CONFERENCE ROOM.

The conference room was long and narrow, and featured a beautiful, antique, carved-mahogany table with twelve leather-covered chairs. There was a credenza of sorts against one wall, and two ficus trees stood sentinel in front of a shuttered bay window. The lighting was subdued and not offensive. The carpet was a dusty taupe and smelled new. Colorful Jackson Pollock paintings hung on the walls. All in all, a pleasant room but still a man's room.

Jack placed the shopping bag on the table and brought out the champagne and the jug of tea for Harry. Within minutes, the champagne was poured, and they were toasting their new BOLO venture. When the glasses were empty, Jack motioned to the chairs and told everyone it was time for an update so that they were all on the same page.

"First things first. Is everyone happy with the building and what we did with it?" He received a glowing response. "Okay then. Let's get to the financials, so we all understand where we stand. The building is paid for, so we have no mortgage to worry about. We prepaid our taxes and insurance for five years, so we don't have to worry about that, either. In case we hit a dry spell and money isn't rushing in. I like to be prepared. Utilities are paid monthly, and Abner said he would see to that. Just for the record, Bert, Ted, Espinosa, Harry, and I put in all the bonus money we received from Hank Jellicoe, which Lizzie Fox had invested for us. I must say, she was quite the financial guru because we more than doubled our initial investment. Sparrow put his share in from his winnings in Monte Carlo, and Abner sold off his beachfront property in Baywater, Maryland. With the exception of Dennis West, we are all equal owners.

"Dennis, with the help of Lizzie Fox, has turned most of his fortune over to BOLO. As you all know, Dennis recently came into a very large fortune. With the help of some excellent financial planners and Lizzie, money from that inheritance has been allocated by Dennis to many things. He now has trusts for any children he might have in the future. He's donated handsomely to many, many charities, concentrating on children's causes and animal-rights causes, and will continue to do so. He's made provisions for his parents and several cousins. He purchased a farm for himself in McLean, Virginia, which is not too far from Myra's and Annie's homesteads, but he has yet to move into his new digs. Dennis is set for life, thanks to his wealthy benefactors.

"And he has, with Lizzie's help, set us up so that BOLO is more than solvent. His contribution far outweighs what all of us put in the pot to buy this building, and that includes the equipment and the prepaid taxes and insurance. I want us to vote to give him a share just like ours in this building. Raise your hand to vote." Every hand shot in the air. Dennis's chest puffed out, his face pink with excitement at really belonging to this secret one-of-a-kind group.

"Now, to salaries. I'm the only one without a job at the moment. I plan to work out of this office full-time. I'm not looking for a salary—Nikki and I are financially set—but I would like an expense account. Actually, I think we should all have expense accounts, which are not to be abused. I think, and tell me if you agree, that we should all take a small salary of five thousand dollars a month. If we don't need it, we can pump it back into the business. I know I said I don't want a salary, but Lizzie is the one who suggested the salary in case of an audit and to keep things on the up-and-up. We've set up a special fund for Avery Snowden and his people. We all know how much that costs from the times that Charles showed us the financials back in the day. It goes without saying that Snowden and his group of retired spies are worth every penny. Are you all following me here? Raise your hands if you agree." Once again, all hands shot into the air.

"Okay, moving right along, the bottom line is that money will be no object thanks to Dennis West's generosity. In my office, I have a box of contracts for everything under the sun that were delivered yesterday from Lizzie. Before you leave, I'm going to need you all to sign each and every contract per Lizzie's instructions. Any questions?"

There were questions. The first was posed by Dennis, whose face was still pink from his compliments. "Are we a secret . . . you know, like a club that doesn't take on any new members? I understand what BOLO means, but are we going to be the male equivalent of the vigilantes and do the . . . ah . . . ladies know what we're doing? How secret is secret, and did Mr. Snowden sign on?"

"By my count, Dennis, that's four questions," Ted said. All eyes turned to Jack Emery.

"I guess you could say we are the male counterpart of the girls. I more or less . . . alluded to . . . certain things where the girls are concerned but I did . . ."

"In other words, the answer is no, the girls *don't* know," Espinosa said.

"Right!" Jack sighed.

"So are we secret or not?" Dennis demanded.

"How about this, kid? We're secret until we get found out. Then we'll figure out how to deal with it. Does that work for you?" Ted asked.

"Yeah, Ted, it works for me. I know how to keep a secret," Dennis shot back. "But my mother always said you need to be up front from the git-go, so nothing comes back to bite you. I don't like to lie."

"No shit!" Everyone turned to the voice coming from

the webcam. It was Bert Navarro. "Everyone lies at some point. Even that guy House on the television program says so. We aren't actually lying; we just aren't blasting out our business for the world to hear. If Lizzie Fox is okay with all this, then we're good to go. Speaking for myself here, I've put together a kick-ass security team that makes the Secret Service look like rent-a-cops. I can actually count on them, so my time is free to travel back and forth when you guys need me. You did say we all had the use of the WELMED corporate jet. Win-win!"

"Let's be clear on something," Abner said. "For the most part, we're just doing pro bono work, which means we aren't charging anyone for our services. I get the part about us stealing funds from the bad guys and using it for the good guys, but does that sum it up? Are you saying we're going to be modern-day Robin Hoods?"

"That's a nice way of putting it, Abner." Jack grinned.

Harry Wong took a slug from his green tea and looked around the table. "What about Charles Martin?"

Expectant gazes turned to Jack, who merely shrugged. "I don't know what to tell you. He's been gone for a whole year now. I asked Avery Snowden to look into it a month ago. Two days ago, he said he came up dry. Don't forget, Charles was the best of the best in the spook world. If he doesn't want to be found, for whatever reason, he is not going to be found. Other than that sighting in Vegas last year over Christmas, no one has seen or heard a thing. I don't even know for certain that it was Charles. Everyone has a double."

"Yes, but then there was Fergus Duffy right there with him at the second sighting. That's too much of a coincidence. And I, for one, have never believed in coincidences," Ted said.

The others agreed that they didn't believe in coincidences, either.

"We can't worry about Charles. It was his decision to

leave, so he has to deal with the fallout on his own. In case any of you are thinking that Avery Snowden is on Charles's side, get that idea out of your head. Snowden goes where the money is. He is not unethical. He is as good as Charles is when it comes to clandestine affairs. We got to him first, so that means that whatever Charles is up to or doing, he has not recruited Snowden."

"So, how is this going to work?" Espinosa asked. "Do we report in each morning, what? Where are our cases going to come from? That sign outside our door doesn't exactly imply we're open for business or let passersby know what kind of business we're in."

"Wait here, guys. Give me two minutes, and I'll tell you." Jack left the room and returned with a banker's box full of files. "I . . . ah . . . *borrowed* these from the D.A.'s office before I left. They're copies." Jack removed the cover and pulled out twelve files. "These cases were all tried, two of them by me. I won both, but both are on appeal, and the scum will get off. I know it as sure as I know that I'm standing here. Ditto for the other ten. But for our first case, there is no file. I came by it via Harry, who got it from some of the FBI agents who train with him. *It* meaning a *case* if we want to take it on. If not, it will get swept under the rug because the guy is big-time. These other twelve are cases we need to check out to see if we think we can make it right for the good guys. Questions?"

"I think Sparrow needs to tell you guys something," Bert said from the webcam. "Go for it, buddy, and don't be shy."

All eyes turned to Sparrow, who promptly stood and looked around the table. Then he laughed, a great booming laugh that was a surprise to everyone in the room. "Okay, here goes. Jack, I know you wondered why I'm dressed in my only good suit with a shirt and tie that actually match. Just for the record, they're all new. Because . . . when I leave here"—he looked at his watch—"thirty minutes from now,

I am meeting up with Lizzie, who will accompany me to . . . the *White House*!"

"Whoa! Whoa!" Ted exploded. "I thought Lizzie wrapped that all up and got you *beaucoup* bucks when she sued on your behalf and won. For being wrongly imprisoned when those skunks you worked with at the FBI framed you. I wrote the damn article, telling about how the president herself personally apologized to you in front of the whole world, pardoned you, and made that big splash and asked you to go back to the Bureau. You turned her down. Are you saying that this president is going to rescind all of that?"

"Nah, this president wants me to head up the FBI." Sparrow laughed. Bert joined in the laughter from the webcam.

"Oh, jeez, holy cow, and we just spilled our guts here! So now you're going to arrest us all or blow the whistle on us?" Dennis exploded.

Sparrow walked over to Dennis's chair and patted him on the back. "On the contrary, young man. Think of me as your inside source. Think of me as a friend in a high place. Think of me as your ace in the hole. Think of me as the guy who will save your ass if you ever get arrested. But, I didn't say I was going to take the job if it is offered to me. The president went through Bert to pave the way because, as he put it, he knew how I felt about the FBI after I put in twenty-five years of loyal service to have them turn on me, frame me, and send me to prison. Bert then went through Lizzie, and they arranged this meeting. So, what I want to know from all of you is this. Do you want me to take the job, so you'll have someone on the inside, or do you want me to pass on it? Makes no never mind to me one way or the other. A lot of the old regime is still there, so it's not going to be a day at the beach for me, but I'm willing to do it for *the cause*. Your call, guys. In the interest of full disclosure, I feel I should tell you that back in September, I had a personal visit in Vegas from a VIP, and Bert can back me up because he sat in on the meeting. Scotland Yard sent an emissary to ask me if I would be interested in heading up the Yard. Both Bert and I were dumbfounded, so I told them I would give them my answer by the first of the year. I'm thinking the president got downwind of that offer, so he made his offer.

"Before you can ask, I am Scottish. My mother was from Glasgow. My father was from Edinburgh, and my grandparents lived in Dundee. We moved to the States when I was ten years old. Other than that, I have no clue why they would pick me of all people. I was up front and told them about being framed and being in a federal prison. They said they already knew that."

Jack felt like he should look to see if his jaw was on the floor and needed to be picked up. "Man, that's about the last thing I was expecting to hear."

Harry asked, "How do we know we can trust you?"

"Because I said so. I also said it's your call. I can step outside if you all want to talk about this. Or I can just leave now and promise you that whatever was discussed here in this room will never pass my lips." Sparrow waited, his gaze expectant.

Jack looked around at the others. "I'm okay with everything he said. Raise your hands if you agree."

All hands shot upward.

"There's your answer, Sparrow. As you said, in the interest of full disclosure, check this out," Jack said, pointing to a minicam on top of the window treatment.

Sparrow laughed. "I spotted that the moment I walked into this room. Why else do you think I picked this chair. It sure wasn't because I'm photogenic. I wanted you all to know you have nothing to fear from me. Hell, I gave you a bundle of money. You have me dead to rights."

Harry leaned forward. "Or we could just kill you right now."

"That won't be necessary. I'm on your side. Look, I have to leave. As you all know, Lizzie does not like to be kept waiting. So, we're good?"

To everyone's surprise, Harry spoke first. "We're good. I think I speak for all of us." The others nodded.

The webcam came to life. "Good decision, guys. Gotta go; some high rollers just blew in. Have to get the red carpet ready to roll out. Time is money. See ya!"

A round of hand-shaking followed, and then Sparrow was gone. The conference room stayed quiet for a few minutes. Dennis broke the silence. "I like that guy."

Jack pushed his chair over to the window, reached up, and removed the disk in the camera. "This goes in the safe. I'm sure we'll never have to use it, but, like they say, never say never."

"Then how about we secure it in the safe at the *Post*?" Ted said. "Under seal."

Jack looked to the others, who were nodding. "That works," Jack said. He handed the disk to Ted, who secured it in his backpack.

"Okay, boys, let's get down to business," Jack said.

Chapter 3

After meeting with the president, Sparrow didn't say a word until he was behind the wheel of his rental car. Lizzie Fox, his lawyer, sitting next to him, was humming under her breath. "Say something, Lizzie," he said as he cleared a dark sedan to pull out of the lot where the Secret Service had told him to park.

Lizzie waved her index finger around and smiled. She commented on the snow flurries and the ominous dark clouds overhead. Sparrow got the message instantly. Damn, he should have gotten the message before she did. Of course the Secret Service might have bugged the car. Safe conversation only. Like he didn't know that. Crap, what was wrong with him this morning?

An adrenaline rush was all he could come up with by way of explanation. It wasn't every day a lowly civilian got to sit in the Oval Office with the president of the United States. Hell's bells, never mind every day. Try like never, Sparrow thought to himself, his eyes on the road to see if any of the dark sedans favored by the Secret Service had pulled in behind him.

Sparrow forced his thoughts in another direction. "I think we have time for me to take you for a quick lunch before we head to the airport. It's the least I can do. There's a great chili dive not far from here. When I lived here years ago, I hit it at least twice a week. Gotta tell you, though, you're going to need a pile of antacid tablets after you eat it. They keep the antacid bottles by the cash register. I think they make as much money selling them as they do from selling their chili. You game, Counselor?"

Lizzie nodded as she busily tapped away on her cell. "Flight's on time. My husband Cosmo said he'll be waiting at the airport. He misses me. Said Little Jack has a sore throat. I need to get home. Kids need their mothers when they get sick."

The conversation for the rest of the fifteen-minute ride to Red Hot Chili's consisted of tales of Little Jack that made Sparrow laugh out loud. He was relieved when he swung into the parking lot and brought the rental to a stop. Always the gentleman, he hopped out and ran around to open the door for Lizzie.

God, she was beautiful. Lizzie looked like a winter ice princess, with her long silver hair and long white coat. There was nothing lustful in his thoughts. Looking at Lizzie Fox was like looking at a rare, beautiful painting. The word *perfection* came to mind. He was glad he could count her as his friend as well as his attorney, all thanks to his boss, Bert Navarro. Sparrow gave her a quick hug, and said, "You were great. I don't think I could have handled it on my own. I hate to admit it, but for the first time in my life, I was intimidated."

Lizzie laughed. "You would have done just fine, Jack. Was it the White House or the man himself? You know, President Quintera puts his pants on the same way you do. He brushes and flosses just the way you do. And I happen to know he orders takeout from the very same restaurant we are going to dine in. Martine used to order here, too. She told me she left a note for President Quintera telling him which restaurants were the best in the area for takeout when she left office. As for the building itself, well, you have as much right, possibly more, to roam those halls as he does. You pay his salary the same way I do. Martine Connor, by the way, gave me the very same speech when I first went there to work for her."

Sparrow held the door for Lizzie. A warm blast of air from a vent over the door shot downward. He looked around and realized he had his choice of tables. He ushered Lizzie toward the back, so that he would have a clear view of the door, just in case anyone was tracking them. It was a ritual he still practiced from his years of being a Special Agent for the FBI. Lizzie nodded her approval as she allowed Sparrow to help her off with her stunning white cashmere coat.

Seated across from her at a round table covered in a pristine white tablecloth, Sparrow said, "You don't order here. All they serve is chili, ginger ale, and crusty bread with homemade butter. Dessert is a special homemade blackberry cobbler served with vanilla ice cream, also homemade. You can get as many refills for free on everything as you want."

"My kind of place." Lizzie giggled. "Cosmo would love this. Okay, down to business. The prez wants you, Jack. The job is yours. He's already smoothed the path and rounded up the votes, so you are a shoo-in. I know you said you wanted some think time, but do you really want to wait two whole weeks before you say yes?" She held up her hand to have him wait until she was finished with her little speech. "I know that, for forever and a day, you will remember those three years you served in a federal prison for something you didn't do. You can't hold the president responsible for what a few rogue agents did to you. He's trying to make it right, just the way Martine Connor did.

"All the good guys are on your side, Jack. You can make a difference. But in order to do that, you have to let the past go. Really let it go. Start fresh. Clean house. Right now, the Bureau is tainted; even the president said so. You can turn it around, I know you can. And that offer to head up Scotland Yard has everyone's knickers in a knot. That alone has to tell you what you're worth. So, why'd you tell President Quintera you wanted two weeks to think it over?"

"Just being ornery, I guess. I like to start new projects at the beginning. January second will work for me. Besides, I didn't want to appear too eager. I called the Yard early this morning and thanked them for their offer but said that I was passing on it."

Sparrow felt the special phone Jack had given him when he left the BOLO Building vibrate inside his pocket. He decided to ignore it since he didn't know how much Lizzie was privy to.

"Does that mean you want me to tell them you accept and will be ready to walk through the doors at 935 Pennsylvania Avenue, Northwest, on January second, or that's when you want me to tell them you'll take the job? POTUS does have some protocols he has to observe, but you heard him say they won't pose a problem."

Sparrow looked down at the fiery bowl of chili a waitress had put in front of him. "I'll report for duty on January second. God help us all," he said, dipping an oversized spoon into a bowl that was as big as a Frisbee. He smacked his lips as his eyes started to water. Looking across at Lizzie, he couldn't believe she had no reaction to the red-hot concoction.

"I grew up eating chili like this. But this is nothing like what my dad used to make. His chili would singe your eyebrows off, that's how hot it was. This is good, though. Anything else you want to get off your chest, Jack?"

Sparrow looked across the table with watery eyes. *Shit, she knows about BOLO.* What to say, what not to say. He shrugged as he dabbed at his eyes with the cloth napkin in his lap. "Like what?" He ripped off a chunk of bread from the miniloaf and dipped it into his chili. "Do you mean am I going to stay here or head back to Vegas to wait out the time? I haven't decided yet. Do I need to make a decision right now?"

"No. I was just making conversation. But, Jack, can I give you some unsolicited advice?"

Sparrow dabbed at his tearing eyes again. "Sure."

"Don't go near the BOLO Building again. If you absolutely need to talk to the guys, use that special phone in your pocket after you are officially the director of the FBI. Until then, you need to stay clean. Do you understand what I'm saying? Until you are the new head honcho, go through Bert, Cosmo, or me if you want to talk to Jack Emery or any of the others. You have to be as pure as the driven snow until January second."

Sparrow was so stunned at her words, all he could think of to say was, "You know?"

"Of course I know. Who do you think handled the sale of the BOLO Building? I'm your attorney, I'm Jack Emery's attorney. Actually, I am the attorney of record for all of you, even young Dennis West. How could I not know? You know all about attorney-client privilege. My lips are sealed."

"I guess I'm slipping, Lizzie. I just didn't . . ."

Lizzie looked down into her empty bowl and sighed. "It's okay, you're on overload right now. Come January second, things will all fall into place. You can spend the time until then deciding what you're going to do once you take up office in the J. Edgar Hoover Building."

"Hey, look at the time. We need to head for the airport. My son is waiting for his mom."

Sparrow pulled some bills from his pocket, helped Lizzie with her coat, then headed to the cash register. He grabbed a bottle of Tums and waved off his change.

"Oooh, it's snowing a little harder, but it doesn't look

like it's sticking. I'm glad you have this flight. If you had a later one, you might run into some problems. Straight through, right?" Sparrow asked.

"Yep. You okay, Jack? You realize I was never going to call you Jay, right? You're a Jack just the way Emery is Jack."

Sparrow grinned. "I'm good, Lizzie. I hated being called Jay even if it was for just a little while. You?"

"I'm good, Mr. Sparrow."

Chapter 4

Sparrow parked his car in the Embassy Suites oversized parking lot and made his way across the huge black expanse of the lot. He had some thinking to do and some decisions to make. And a lot of phone calls to attend to— the first one being to Jack Emery on his brand-new, state-of-the-art, outer-space, weird-looking cell phone. Even though Lizzie had said not to use it, he had to make at least this one call. He couldn't help but wonder if he'd ever figure out how to work it. He also wondered if the red button at the bottom would make the phone self-destruct, like some James Bond gizmo or the kind Tom Cruise used in one of his *Mission Impossible* movies. He was itching to press the damn thing.

As he walked to the building, the snow was coming down sideways and seemed to be slapping him in the face. He tilted his face upward and was immediately rewarded with a thousand needle spits to his face. The first thing he was going to do was check the weather, then the airlines. He entered the lobby and headed to the right until he was out of sight. He stood quietly behind a huge green plant to watch to see if anyone entered the building behind him. He wasn't being paranoid, just diligent, a trait that had served him well all his life. He fiddled with his cell, pretending to make one call after another, his gaze ever watchful. Twenty minutes later, with no activity in the lobby, Sparrow made his way to the elevator, confident there were no eyes or tails on him.

Sparrow hated hotels, motels, rooming houses, and fleabags. He'd had years of living out of suitcases and sleeping in a different place every night. These temporary digs were okay. He had a small sitting room done in manly brown plaid, a small kitchenette, and a king-sized bed. The bathroom was big and roomy and had an endless supply of towels. He'd been here over two weeks, so in a way it felt a little like he was settling in. He'd even stocked the regulation-sized refrigerator with fruit, beer, and milk. What he liked most, though, was the coffee shop, which served great coffee and decent lunches; the spectacular, complimentary full breakfast buffet, with a chef who cooked whatever kind of hot egg dish you wanted; and the decent restaurant on the ground floor that only served dinner.

Sparrow hung up his outerwear, popped a beer, and flopped down on the small love seat under the window overlooking the parking lot. He fished out his super-duper phone and pressed the number two, just as Jack had told him to. The moment he was connected, he said, "Does this little number come with a manual? What the hell is the red button for, Jack?"

"I thought you were an FBI agent. Oops, Special Agent. No manual, buddy. All you have to do is press one of the buttons through six, and you'll get one of us. The red button will make the phone sizzle and fry. If you plan on pressing it, do it quick and drop it, or you'll burn your hand off. Any other questions?"

"Yeah, where'd you get it?"

"Need to know, buddy, need to know. So, how'd it go over there at the big old White House on Pennsylvania Avenue? You in or out?"

"I'm in as of January second. Lizzie gave me my marching orders, which are that I cannot be seen with any of you guys, and I can't talk to you either except on this super-duper phone, and that only after January second. If I need to get in touch with you between now and then, I need to go through her, Cosmo, or Bert."

Jack laughed. "So, you hanging around or heading back to Vegas?"

"When I hang up from you, I'm going to call the airline to see if I can get on a red-eye. I just dropped Lizzie off at the airport. Nothing keeping me here. I feel like I'm deserting you guys."

"You need to get over that feeling real quick. We'll be calling you and counting on you from time to time. You sure you're okay with playing both sides? I sure as hell would hate to be blindsided down the road."

"You guys have those special gold shields, right?"

"Well, yeah."

"I'm going to call a special meeting as soon as possible after I take office, and the status of persons with those gold shields will be the first topic of conversation. I'll send out directives in a blizzard to every field office and police station in the country as well as the CIA, MI6, Scotland Yard, the Sûreté. Flash those babies, and you are home free, pal."

"You going to clean house, Sparrow? You got some deadwood in there."

"I am. There are a few guys left over from Zander. I'll do it slowly. There are two left who I have a personal beef with from my kangaroo trial. They are one of the first things I need to work on."

"Well, while you're at it, there's one guy that gave me so much grief back in the day, I wanted to kill him. He dogged me twenty-four/seven and slept outside my house. His name is Al Bertoli. Send the bastard to Fargo, South Dakota."

"Al's already on my list, Jack. If there's nothing else, I'm going to see about getting out of here. What's the weather? Have you heard?"

"Light dusting of snow through tomorrow. You need me for anything, just press two on your phone."

"You sure this doesn't come with a manual?" Sparrow said as he squinted at the phone in his hand.

Jack laughed. "Yeah, I'm sure. See ya, Sparrow, and congratulations."

Jack Emery, with Cyrus right behind him, looked into the retina scanner and waited until he heard the hydraulic hiss that would unlock the back door of the BOLO Building. He immediately turned up the thermostat, then went into the kitchen to make coffee. He knew the entire building would warm up within minutes due to the newness of the heating unit. He listened to the dripping water in the coffeepot as he stared out at the whiteness that surrounded the building. Three inches of snow. Not too bad. After last year's record snowfall, he'd had enough and promised himself a warm climate for the coming winter. Even then, when he made the wish, he knew it wouldn't happen. He did worry a little that Harry might not make it on his Ducati even though the roads were clear. No sooner had the thought whipped through his mind than he heard the distinct sound of the special cycle that Harry so loved. Right on time. In the blink of an eye, Jack had a pot of water on the stove for Harry's tea.

Cyrus ran to the door and let loose with an earsplitting bark. Harry tussled with the shepherd for a few minutes until he fished out a chew from one of his many pockets. Chew devoured, Cyrus trotted off happily until it would be time to greet the next person to come through the door. Cyrus loved all the same people Jack loved and hated the same people Jack hated.

"Your tea is in the second cabinet on the left. I bought

two whole pounds, so you won't run out. Tell me that you appreciate it."

"I do."

While they waited for the others, Harry, never one to talk if it wasn't necessary, watched his water boil while Jack watched the water dripping into the pot as he babbled about Jack Sparrow and Lizzie.

"Yeah, I got a text from him as I was leaving the dojo. He said he arrived safe and sound and wanted to know if I had a manual for the stupid phone."

Jack grinned just as Ted, Espinosa, and Dennis barreled into the kitchen. Cyrus did his thing and was trotting off when Abner blew through the door, along with a gust of swirling snowflakes. Confusion reigned because none of them had treats for Cyrus. The big dog showed his teeth and his disapproval as he nudged Harry, who was always good for an extra one.

"Get your coffee and tea, and let's hit the conference room. We have a case to discuss. Everyone good today?" Jack asked cheerfully. They all said they were good.

Jack took a few minutes to bring the guys up to date on Jack Sparrow and Lizzie. He shared with them Sparrow's intentions in regard to the gold shields. Dennis West's hand shot in the air. "I don't have one of those, Jack."

"Yeah, I know. And there's no chance in hell you're going to get one either no matter how much money you have. Maybe if you save the president's life or something, he might give you one, but even that's doubtful. You'll have to piggyback on Ted and Espinosa."

Dennis didn't know if he should protest or not, so he just shrugged. He had a new mission in life, to somehow, someway, get one of those gold shields.

"Okay. If there are no other questions, let's get down to business."

Cyrus was on his feet and racing out of the room just as a

buzzer sounded from the front of the building. "Company," Jack said tightly. "That's not a dire bark, it's a friendly bark. That means Cyrus knows who it is," Jack explained, racing behind the big dog, the others on his heels. "It's Tony from the Bagel Emporium. Oh, oh, there's a florist right behind him. Easy, Cyrus."

Jack pressed a code that allowed him to open the massive front door. "Tony!"

"Saw all the activity over here and wanted to welcome you to the street." He held up a large bag. "Bagels!"

"Thanks, Tony. How much, or should I start up a tab?"

"On the house. Good luck." He turned to go but bumped into two heavyset men carrying a huge banana tree.

"Where do you want this, bud?" one of the guys asked.

"I didn't order that," Jack said, trying to close the door behind Tony.

"It says here on the card it is a gift. So where do you want it?"

"Gift? Anywhere. Just put it down."

"Find a place so you don't have to move it yourself. This damn thing weighs a ton. Why do you think it's on wheels?"

"Okay, okay, stick it in the corner over there. Who sent it?"

"Like I know? Enjoy your banana tree, mister."

Jack peeled off two five-dollar bills and handed one to each of the two men. Ted practically shoved them out the door, then quickly locked it.

The boys stared at the tree, their eyes wide with suspicion.

"Do you think it's bugged?" Abner asked.

"Who sent it? Who knows we're here besides Sparrow and Lizzie?" Ted asked.

"Why don't we open the card that's stapled to the container?" Dennis said helpfully.

"Now why didn't I think of that?" Jack wondered aloud as he whipped at the envelope. "Oh, shit!"

"What? What?" the others clamored.

"Let me read you the card. It says, 'If you need us, just call.' It's signed by Nikki, Alexis, Kathryn, Isabelle, Yoko, Myra, Annie, and Maggie. I don't think they signed it personally, probably some worker at the shop, and it was probably a call-in. The bottom line is, *they know*."

"Oh, crap, Maggie knows," Ted groaned.

"They *all* know. How'd this happen?" Jack demanded. "Who gave it up?"

No one said a word.

"I know Sparrow didn't talk, and for damn sure I know Lizzie didn't spill her guts. So how did the girls find out?" Jack snarled.

No one said a word, but all eyes turned to Ted. Almost in unison, they said, "Maggie got hold of your phone, didn't she?"

Ted was so outraged his face turned purple. "No way!"

"Prove it," Harry said, menace ringing in his voice.

Ted cringed. "Since this all started, Maggie has not had a single opportunity to sneak a look at my phone. If you're insinuating that she got hold of it while I was sleeping or something like that, you're wrong. And everything on this phone is password protected anyway. I'm not stupid, you know. No, no, no. There's no way. That's the truth."

"I can vouch for Ted," Espinosa said. "There haven't been any sleepovers. Dennis?"

"I agree with Ted and Espinosa. No way."

"Then who is the snitch?" Jack demanded again.

"You sure Maggie didn't follow you guys a time or two?" Harry asked lazily, flexing his fingers.

"I can't guarantee that didn't happen," Ted said angrily. "I know she's sneaky, but I can't believe she'd let us get this far without saying something. She wants to be in on everything. She lives for crap like this and would die to one-up me."

"She wouldn't say anything if the girls told her not to. She's one of *them*," Jack observed.

"So where does this leave us?" Espinosa blustered.

"It leaves us with a damn banana tree that has to be watered, probably every day. And you have to shine the leaves with some kind of spray. Plus the girls know what we're doing. That's where we are," Jack said, peering at a tiny bunch of bananas growing on the big, ugly tree.

"Maybe it was that guy Snowden," Dennis said hesitantly.

The guys looked at one another. Ted looked hopeful that they were considering someone other than himself.

"Never," Harry said.

And that was the end of that.

"We'll figure it out eventually," Jack said as he led the parade back to the conference room, carrying the bagel bag. He plopped it in the middle of the table and took his seat. He looked around at his friends. "Obviously, the girls are okay with what we're doing. I did get the dig about us possibly needing them. That's not going to happen, right? Hands up if you agree." Every hand shot into the air.

Jack took a deep breath. He slid yellow folders across the table. "The name of the persons we're targeting are Tyler Sandford and his wife, Fiona. Tyler Sandford is the lieutenant governor of the Commonwealth of Virginia. He and his wife are slum landlords. This guy came onto our radar by way of Harry, who just happened to overhear two agents talking about the guy and how they couldn't do anything because an order came down as hands off. Too high-profile. There's a very good chance this guy is going to enter the gubernatorial race when Governor Rossiter retires next year."

"Every city and state has slum landlords, so what's the big deal about these two?" Ted asked.

"The big deal is that three children died in one of his

buildings. One from rat bites and the other two from lack of heat last year. That was all swept under the rug. Friends in high places. I think we should roll up that rug with Mr. and Mrs. Sandford in it. I'm open for some suggestions here."

The guys all started to yammer at once, their tones angry and filled with malice. Cyrus howled at the top of his lungs.

"Okay, glad that got your attention. We have a target, and now we have to get background from the day those two were born. One at a time now."

Chapter 5

"I have a question," Dennis said.

"Spit it out, so we can get down to business," Jack demanded, impatience ringing in his voice.

"It's about those gold shields. I get the part about my not having one and not ever getting one, but I'd like the story on it. I don't like not knowing all the details on something. I am, after all, a reporter. An investigative reporter," he clarified.

Jack sighed. "Okay, okay, then we're putting it to rest. This is the story as I know it. Now, if anyone else knows something I don't know, feel free to jump in and elaborate. Before Martine Connor left office, she arranged a telephone conference with the heads of MI6, Interpol, Scotland Yard, and the Sûreté, and they all agreed to what she called the Gold Shield Plan. It's another way of saying whoever has one of those priceless babies has a kind of diplomatic immunity, for want of a better explanation. All those agencies agreed to honor the holders of the shields. A global interagency thing, I guess, is what you can call it. Think of it as a get-out-of-jail-free card. It is my understanding that each agency agreed to issue no more than twenty shields. They were specially made and cannot be duplicated. I got that from Lizzie. I also understand that Lizzie has some kind of paperwork signed by the head of each agency. Martine

Connor insisted on that, and the others agreed. So there would be no blowback down the road for any of the recipients. I suppose it's a presidential order, but who the keeper of that order is is a mystery to me."

"So who did she give the shields to?" Dennis asked, his eyes round and inquisitive. "Does law enforcement know about this, or is it a secret?"

"One question at a time, Dennis. As far as I know, the holders of the shields are Charles, Myra, Annie, Pearl, Nellie, Nikki, Kathryn, Yoko, Alexis, Isabelle, Maggie, me, Ted, Espinosa, Bert, and Abner."

"That's only sixteen. Who has the other four?"

"I don't know. I don't even know if Lizzie knows, and if she does, I'm sure that comes under the heading of attorney-client privilege. In case you don't know this, Lizzie Fox and Martine Connor were, and still are, best buds from way back when. As to the second part of your question, the answer is I do not know. Sparrow said he is going to be sending a directive out to all the field offices and police departments across the country when he takes office, so that would lead me to believe the answer to your question is probably no, no one knows. But that's just my opinion."

Dennis wasn't satisfied. "How do you know the shields can't be duplicated?"

Cyrus, who was under the table, let loose with a bark to let the others know he was very much in the room, and it was time to get on with things.

"Because, Dennis, the president of the United States said so. Her word is good enough for me," Jack answered through clenched teeth. He wanted, needed, to move on.

"I think I want to know who has the other four. Think about this, *Jack*. What if the other four people turn out to be our archenemies? Well, Jack, are you thinking about it?" Dennis persisted.

"I wasn't until you just brought it up. Look, Dennis,

that's outside our purview. There is no way we can find out. In addition, it's not our business. For all we know the president could have kept them for herself. Sometimes, kid, what you don't know is more important than what you do know. Anyone have any other information they want to share in regard to the special shields?" When no one volunteered any information, Jack asked, "Can we move on?"

"Sure," Dennis said, slumping back in his chair. He wanted one of those shields, and, one way or another, he was going to get one.

Jack opened the thick folder on his desk. "I did some research, but it is by no means complete. I just wanted to get a feel for what we're dealing with. Here's the thing, I couldn't find any property listed in Sandford's name or his wife's name. I even checked the wife's maiden name, which is Peters. I'm sure those slum buildings he owns are hidden under shell companies, holding companies, what have you. My quick search only gave me a federal-style house in Georgetown and a horse farm in Middleburg, Virginia. Sandford was born and raised in Middleburg. His wife, Fiona, was born and raised in Arlington, Virginia. Unlike him, she did not come from money. If you're okay with it, Ted, you, Dennis, and Espinosa are assigned to the property search. Harry wasn't able to get details, just casual talk when the agents at the dojo were grumbling. You guys up for it?"

When the reporters said that they were, Jack made some scratch marks on his legal pad.

"Abner, it goes without saying that you're in charge of the financials. We need everything you can get, so we know what we're dealing with.

"Dennis, I'd like you, if you agree, of course, to search out Sandford's background, all the way back to the day he was born. Ditto on his wife. I understand there are two kids, one still in college. And the younger one is some kind of genius, from what I've heard. She, and I think her name is"—Jack referred to some scribbles on his pad—"ah here it is, Faylan Sandford. She has a PhD in biology and neuroscience, and she's only eighteen. Go figure that one! The lieutenant governor makes mention of that every chance he gets. The boy, whose name is Addison, is a senior at MIT, majoring in nuclear engineering. You up for this, kid?"

"Yup."

"Harry stays where he is at the dojo as our ears from the agents who come in for training. He's going to insist that his little FBI group aren't *quite* ready and that they need more classes. Disgruntled agents tend to mouth off, and they all trust Harry. It's a long shot, but Harry can't be away from the dojo, as we all know."

"What's your job, Jack?" Dennis asked.

"I'm going to be researching some of the families that live in those slums and going to talk to them firsthand. As soon as we come up with names." He looked around to see what the others thought of that just as his cell phone vibrated in his pocket. He yanked it out, looked at the caller ID, and saw that it was Nikki. "Hey, guys, I gotta take this. Kick it all around, and I'll be right back."

His wife was finally returning his call . . . what . . . thirty-six hours later. He walked to the kitchen and closed the door. "Hey," he said.

"Hey yourself. Sorry to be so late returning your call. The office is swamped, Jack."

"Yeah, yeah, I figured that." What he wanted to say but didn't was, "Don't tell me you couldn't find three minutes somehow, someway, to say hi, drop dead, go to hell, I love you, Jack."

"You said in your message you wanted to take me to dinner last night. I meant to call. I just got so sidetracked. I'm really sorry, Jack."

"Yeah, yeah, I figured that." He really needed some new

lines here. He wanted to shout at the top of his lungs, "What's happening to us, Nik? You don't get home till midnight, and you're gone before I get up in the morning. We haven't spoken to each other face-to-face in over a week, and when we spoke last time, all you did was scream at me, saying I didn't have an understanding bone in my body." But he didn't say that either. He also didn't say that Cyrus wasn't exactly his idea of an ideal bed partner. He was about to say he really did notice that she was sleeping in the guest room, but she interrupted him.

"You know what, Jack, let's make a date for Sunday morning. We'll sleep in, read the funnies together, have coffee in bed and . . . you know . . . if we want to do other things, we can. How does that sound?"

Sounds like a bunch of crap, he thought. Four more days till Sunday. Come Sunday, he knew in his gut that something would come up and that would be that. He tried to remember the last time they'd made love and couldn't come up with a time. That had to mean over a month. He took a deep breath and said, "Yeah, sure, that sounds great. See ya on Sunday." Under his breath, he muttered, "Don't bet the rent on it."

"Gotta run, I'm being paged. You okay, Jack?"

"Right as rain, Nik. Couldn't be better."

"Good. That's good. I mean that's really good. Love you."

Jack didn't respond because right that second he didn't know if he still loved his wife or not. He turned to the door, where Cyrus was scratching to get in. He opened it, and the big dog put his paws on his shoulder and nuzzled Jack's neck. He whispered in Cyrus's ear, "That's Nik's job, but you know that, don't you, big guy. It's okay, pal. Like everything else, this, too, will play out just the way it's supposed to. Let's go. We really have to nail this guy so you can bite his ass."

Cyrus liked the way that sounded and gave a joyous woof. Jack pasted a sickly smile on his face and walked down the hall to the conference room. It looked like he hadn't been missed. The boys were at it, squabbling over . . . what else, Dennis and the gold shields.

There was a huskiness in Jack's voice that did not go unnoticed when he said, "Let's put a cork in it and get on with why we're here. Now listen up. I want to give you what little background I have on Mr. Sandford. For starters, he's a nonstarter. As a rule, lieutenant governors attend funerals and do all the things the governor doesn't want to or can't do. Sandford is no exception. What he has going for him right now in the public eye is that he has charisma—he's a good-looking guy, dresses well and expensively, drives a flashy car, does more than his share of kissing babies. He supposedly helps to coach a Little League team whose games he rarely gets to because of government business. Of course, he's always on hand for the photo ops. He's big on photo ops.

"He has a killer smile and more teeth than all the Osmonds put together. He boasts about his daughter, Faylan, in every interview. He mentions the boy, but not with as much gusto.

"Sandford grew up with a silver spoon in his mouth. Never had a nine-to-five job. Went straight into politics and is considered as a possibility for a presidential run at some point. Right now, his sights are on running for governor when Governor Rossiter steps down. The smart money is saying he'll nail it if he runs. We need to make sure that doesn't come to pass—that he never gets his party's nomination for the post."

"Espinosa and I can dig in the archives for you," Ted volunteered.

Jack made some more scribbles on his legal pad.

"The wife's name, as I said, is Fiona. She's the classic

politician's wife minus any kind of public service. She does nothing, doesn't volunteer for anything, doesn't lend her name to charitable causes, and will never be named mother of the year. She spends a lot of time at spas, country clubs, and going shopping. She's had lots of surgery, all cosmetic. As one tabloid put it, she's been nipped and tucked, sliced and diced within an inch of her life. That same reporter went on to say she has bee-stung lips. I have no clue what that means since I'm a guy, but it isn't conjuring up any beautiful thoughts.

"Fiona comes from a middle-class background. Mother was a nurse, father was a math teacher. She never wanted for anything. She met Sandford in college. She never graduated—got married instead. I am sure that there is a ton more information out there to be gathered and that we'll be able to put it to use.

"Sandford comes from a long line of politicians. None of his family, it appears, has ever held a job. At least not that I saw in my sketchy research. We need to look into the monies that are paid for his personal security. His and the governor's bill for security totaled over a million bucks this past year. The state troopers who guard the two of them are on call twenty-four/seven. I read some op-ed pieces about how the fine citizens of the Commonwealth of Virginia are complaining long and loud over this. Over-the-top travel expenses are also part of the problem, though Lieutenant Governor Sandford, unlike his almost namesake, has yet to hike the Appalachian Trail. So far, neither the governor nor the lieutenant governor has commented other than to say that it is necessary. There is no transparency that I can see.

"During the day, the lieutenant governor hangs his hat in the Finance Building on Capitol Square. That's worth knowing should we need to find him in a hurry. In case you don't know this, and I didn't, which doesn't say much for me, the lieutenant governor is the president of the Senate of Virginia. Or maybe I did know it and just forgot. He is also, obviously, first in the line of succession should something happen to the governor. Unlike the governor, however, the lieutenant governor of Virginia can run for reelection."

Harry Wong shuffled his feet and looked around for a clock. "I need to get going, guys. I have a class in forty minutes. If you need me, you know where to find me."

Cyrus was on his feet a second later. It was his job to escort Harry to the door in the hopes he'd get another treat. Harry didn't disappoint, and Cyrus got a belly rub at the same time.

Chapter 6

After Harry left, the big shepherd headed back to the conference room. His tail swished importantly. His work here was done. He nudged his master's leg and woofed softly. "Good boy. We're almost done. Then we'll go for a long walk."

"We're heading back to the paper, Jack. When do you need us here again?" Ted asked.

"You make your own hours, guys, unless I call a meeting. I realize you have jobs. I'm sure we're going to overlap on our research, but that's just fine. More is better than less. E-mail, text, or call, but stay in touch. I'm going to call Bert and bring him up to date and have him call Sparrow to report in. Anything else, guys?"

Abner Tookus got up and flexed his fingers. He grinned at the others as he offered up an air wave. He needed to get to a computer, his lifeline to everything other than Isabelle that mattered in the world.

And then it was just Jack and Cyrus in the conference room. Jack felt his shoulders slump. Cyrus, seeing the slump, bellied over to the door and nudged it shut. He bellied back to where Jack was sitting and propped his big head in his master's lap as much as to say, *I'm here for you.* Jack swallowed hard. He rubbed the big dog's head as he mumbled and muttered under his breath. "I don't know what to do, Cyrus. I'm trying to be understanding, but enough is enough already. I've become an afterthought. I'm asleep when Nik gets home, she's gone before I get up in the morning. If I stay up and wait for her, she gets pissed. I can't win. No offense, pal, but I'd rather sleep with Nik than you. I hate that she's sleeping in the guest room, and, yeah, she did say she didn't want to wake me with her crazy hours. But that's bullshit, and she knows it!"

Cyrus threw his head back and howled. "Yeah, that's how I feel. You know what else, Cyrus, class-action lawsuits go on for *years*. That's just one. Nik's firm has three class-action suits going on. Nik's firm has become the go-to guys for that kind of stuff. Spouses are just . . . in the way. At least that's how I'm seeing it. I feel like a lovesick teenager right now." Cyrus joined his master in whining.

Jack continued to fondle the big dog's ears. Then he squared his shoulders, sat up straighter, and all but bellowed, "Okay, enough of this pity party. Come on, Cyrus, let's go for a walk and get some lunch." The words, *walk* and *lunch* were Cyrus's two favorite words.

Cyrus raced off and returned with his leash, swinging his tail back and forth at the speed of light. He danced around as he waited for Jack to pack up his briefcase and turn off the light. He was the first through the door and waited in the kitchen, while Jack put on his jacket.

There was a bite to Maggie Spritzer's voice when she said, "How nice that you decided to come to work." She pointed to the wall clock. The time was 11:50.

"Oh, lunchtime. Thanks for pointing that out, Maggie," Ted said airily as he swung around and headed for the door, and the elevator that would take him to the lobby of the *Post* building, Espinosa and Dennis West hot on his heels.

"Hold it right there! You just got here! *Four hours late.* And now you're going to lunch! I. Don't. Think. So."

Ted punched the elevator button before he swung around, knowing that Maggie had followed the threesome into the hall. "We're entitled to a lunch hour. Is this where you threaten to fire me or all three of us? Go for it," Ted snapped. "I'm sick and tired of your holding that power over my head. So is Espinosa. Dennis doesn't care, he's so rich he doesn't have to worry about paying the rent. What? Cat got your tongue? Well?" Ted snarled.

Maggie backed up a step. "All I said was you were four hours late and, no, you weren't going to lunch. What I meant was I wanted to know what you were doing and where you were that made you four hours late before you went to lunch. Are you planning on filing a grievance with the union? I am the EIC. That means I'm in charge. I have the right to ask you anything I want." But it was all said defensively, and Ted picked up on the tone immediately.

"If you keep bugging me, then the answer is yes." He knew in his gut that it was Maggie who somehow, someway, was responsible for the banana tree that had been delivered to the BOLO Building. His gut told him she'd been following him, and she was good enough that he didn't pick up on her doing so. But he knew, and that made him feel guilty. And the guys knew it, too.

The elevator arrived. Espinosa stepped in and put it on hold. Dennis stepped around him, leaving Ted and Maggie hissing at one another.

Maggie, former reporter and current editor in chief, and Ted, her former fiancé and current star reporter, eyeballed one another. Ted was livid and trying not to show it. Maggie looked like she regretted her outburst but wasn't about to back down.

Stalemate.

"Don't ever follow me again, or I'll quit, and don't

bother to deny it. You broke the rule, Maggie, and none of us is going to forget it. What that means is you can no longer be trusted. You want to know something, ask me. If it's something I think you need to know, I'll tell you. If it's my personal business, then I won't tell you. I'm speaking for Espinosa and Dennis, too. I'm working on a story, an exposé. That's all you need to know right now. If you have something you need us to do, tell me now.

"You don't, do you? That means I am free to continue what I'm doing. Ditto for Espinosa and Dennis. I would be remiss if I didn't tell you that you are now on the guys' shit list. Not a good place to be, Maggie. The banana tree was over the top. I'll take that a step further and bet a week's pay that the girls know *nothing* about that stupid banana tree and the BOLO Building. *Back off.*"

Maggie flushed, turned on her heel, and marched into her office, her eyes burning with humiliation. She had never backed off a story in her life, and she wasn't about to start. She swiped at her burning eyes.

Ted was right, though. She knew in her gut when she sent the stupid tree that she was making a mistake, but she'd done it anyway. She hadn't told the girls, so that was one good thing, but if Ted and the others thought she had, well boo hoo.

Maggie chewed at a nail that was already chewed to the quick. They were supposed to be a team. Team members didn't sneak around keeping secrets from other team members. That was dirty pool. She totally ignored the fact that she would have done exactly what Ted had done if she thought she could get away with it. Trusting her gut instinct, she'd tailed Ted for weeks and couldn't believe what she'd come up with. She'd let enough time go by to see if Ted would confide in her. When it was obvious that wasn't going to happen, she'd taken matters into her own hands.

Now she was on the outside looking in. Today, she'd

heard something in Ted's voice she'd never heard before—
he absolutely meant business. He'd walk away in a skinny
minute if she closed in on him, and the *Post* would lose its
Pulitzer Prize–winning star reporter. And it would all be her
fault. Now what did she need to do?

Maggie plopped down in the special chair John Cassidy
had left behind. He'd broken it in, and it was comfortable
enough to sleep in. Her insides were in a turmoil. It wasn't
just the confrontation with Ted; that was business. What
bothered her was he had moved on in the emotion department. She could sense it, feel it. What that meant was he
wouldn't be cutting her any special favors anytime soon.
Locked out emotionally. Not a nice place to be.

Maggie looked up to see her secretary, Emily Davis, rap-
ping softly on the door. Emily was everything Maggie
wished she was, drop-dead gorgeous without even trying.
She was tall, as tall as Ted. She had an athletic body that
still remained incredibly feminine. She dressed well, had a
glorious head of rich, natural blond hair and Bambi brown
eyes. In other words, a stunner. Plus, she was the most ef-
ficient secretary Maggie had ever come across. Somehow,
she could anticipate Maggie's every need. If there was such
a thing as perfection, then perfection's name was Emily
Davis. Except for one *little* thing. Emily Davis had the hots
for Ted Robinson.

"What?" Maggie barked. "Don't you have anything better
to do than stand in my doorway?" God, how hateful that
sounded. Well, she was feeling hateful.

Emily didn't take offense. "Actually, that's why I'm
standing here. Is there anything else you want me to do? If
not, I'm going to lunch. If I hurry, I can catch up to the
guys. It's my turn to buy anyway."

That threw Maggie for a loop. Her turn to buy. That had
to mean Emily had been going to lunch with the guys on a
regular basis. Well, crap!

"Go!" she barked again. Emily didn't need to be told twice. Maggie could see her texting as she waited for the elevator. Well, crap again.

Maggie's head started to ache. She'd just dug herself into a hole, and, right now, right this minute, she didn't know how to get out of it. *Think!*

"I'm thinking! I'm thinking!" she muttered over and over to herself.

She'd broken her own cardinal rule, and it was eating at her. She'd spied on her best friends. Friends as in plural but Ted in particular. Once they'd been lovers, engaged to be married, but that time was long gone. She'd married someone else and was now a widow. Her whole life had been turned upside down, especially during the last year, after her husband had left her to go back to war and been killed.

God, why was she thinking like this? Because she'd broken the cardinal rule and had to live with it. It wouldn't be so bad, she thought, but Ted knew what she'd done. Espinosa and Dennis knew, too. Probably the rest of those in her immediate circle knew, too. Ted's circle as well. She'd be a pariah. The guys would hate her, and the girls . . . God, what would the girls think? Especially Myra and Annie. Tears burned her eyes at the thought she'd be alone in the world, friendless, and all because she had to spy on her best friends.

If only she hadn't sent that stupid banana tree. If only. And what did she even hope to gain or to learn? That a building in Georgetown called the BOLO Building was a meeting place for the guys. So what? For all she knew, the guys were gambling away their free hours in the privacy of the building. She'd staked out the Bagel Emporium and eaten at least a thousand bagels as she watched the building. A total bust. Because . . . no one, as in ever, entered the building by the front door. The back entrance was used for some reason, and there was no way she could stake out the back without being spotted. The owner of the bagel shop, Ding something or other, said he didn't know anything about the building, just that it had new tenants.

Well, she knew a thing or two about pricey real estate, and the BOLO Building was as pricey as it gets. Why did the boys need such a building to gamble if indeed that's what they were doing? And there was no record that she could find for the ownership of that particular building. She'd need someone like Abner Tookus to find that out, but that was definitely out of the question.

She'd called around to the girls and tried to ask sneaky questions, but she'd come up dry. Then the brilliant idea of sending the banana tree came to her. She'd sat at a small table at the bagel place and watched as it was being delivered. Then she'd almost exploded off her seat when she saw Ding deliver a bag of bagels. To the front door!

Something was going on. Something no one wanted her or the girls to know about.

"What?" she thundered to her empty office.

Chapter 7

Maggie leaned back and squeezed her eyes shut. Just because she was the editor in chief didn't mean that her reporter instincts were dead. Once a reporter, always a reporter. Tack the word *investigative* onto that thought, and for sure she wasn't dead in the water. All it meant to her was that she had to be a little more careful and not make any more dumb moves like sending banana trees to the opposition. The word *sneaky* came to mind, but she quickly rejected it. When it came to scooping the opposition, everything was fair, and Ted, Espinosa, and Dennis had suddenly become the opposition. At the moment, she couldn't care less whether her assumption was true or false. The trio had broken the cardinal rule of being part of a team, so let the chips fall right on their feet for all she cared. If she was no longer a part of their team, then they were the opposition, whatever it was they were doing.

Eyes wide open now, Maggie bounced upright in her chair as she peered through the glass wall that allowed her to see Emily Davis's desk. She felt like she should rush out and put a nameplate on her secretary's desk that said TRAITOR.

Maggie took a moment or two to wonder if she was jealous. No. Yes. Well, maybe a tad, but not really. She had no strings on Ted. They'd talked their relationship to death so many times that she'd lost count. Finally, they had agreed to be friends and partners but not romantic partners, which in turn meant they could each see other people if they chose to do so. Nothing was said one way or the other about a booty call if the opportunity presented itself at some point along the way. Obviously, Ted had chosen to see Emily Davis. Or, at least, he was on the verge of taking that particular new friendship to another level.

It was amazing how she hadn't noticed anything during this past year. And a hell of a year it had been. In her mind, things started going south after Myra's Thanksgiving dinner last year, when Charles left for parts unknown. There wasn't any one thing in particular that she could put her finger on or point to, but things hadn't been the same since his departure.

Maggie knew it wasn't her imagination that no one seemed to have time for anyone else. Isabelle was in England and hadn't crossed the pond since she'd left. Abner had made the journey back and forth a few times, but if what Ted said was true, Abner hadn't been to England since July, five months ago. Since Abner was a very wealthy man, money was not an issue. So she couldn't help but wonder if there was trouble brewing in their marriage.

Then there were Espinosa and Alexis, who had chosen her career over a relationship with the man who was now her ex-fiancé. He'd been in such a funk over her rejection that Ted had hauled him off to a shrink to talk it out. He was better now but not whole, in Maggie's opinion. As far as she knew, Espinosa wasn't seeing anyone and sat around hoping that Alexis would call him.

Then there were Jack and Nikki. She knew there was trouble there because she only lived a few doors away and couldn't help but notice the crazy hours each of them kept. That, plus Jack's sudden neighborliness, stopping over almost every day just to talk and have coffee. Nikki's obscene hours were driving him nuts.

Tears sprang to Maggie's eyes at how, in just a single year, their tight-knit little group was disintegrating. Not only the group as a whole, but the individual relationships among the various partnerships were being turned upside down. She couldn't help but wonder if it all had something to do with Charles's abrupt departure last Thanksgiving. Was Charles the glue that held them all together? Actually, when she thought about it, she always considered that it was Myra, Annie, and Charles who kept them together. A trio. A trifecta. Take away one, and everything started to unravel.

Maybe she was the one who could get them all back on the same page.

Without stopping to think, Maggie pulled out her phone and hit the number that would reach Yoko. "Hey, I want to put my order in for my Christmas tree and ask if you're free for lunch tomorrow."

Yoko laughed and asked if she could bring a friend. That wasn't exactly what Maggie had in mind, so she said, "What friend?"

"Kathryn. She's delivering my bales of balsam and my Christmas trees. You get the first pick. I'm sure she'll be free for lunch, but she's heading up to Delaware to drop off another load of Christmas trees, all fresh from Oregon, before she heads back to Vegas. Does that work for you, Maggie? You sound . . . strange. Is anything wrong?"

"I don't know, Yoko. We can talk tomorrow. How about if I call the girls to see if they can join us. It's been so long since we all got together."

"Absolutely. I'll put Harry on alert, so he can pick up Lily from play school. Tomorrow is only half a day."

"Where shall we meet up?" Maggie asked.

"Well, you like the Squire's Pub, so let's go there, or that trendy little café right there on Dupont Circle. I think it's called Betty Lou's. Betty Lou's would be my choice since Squire's Pub is really a guy spot." Maggie agreed. "Twelve-thirty would be perfect for me. Do you want me to call anyone?" Yoko asked.

"That works for me. You call Nikki and Alexis, and I'll call Myra and Annie. We'll be short one because Isabelle is in England."

"No, she isn't! Didn't you hear? She came back over the weekend, and she and Abner had a huge fight, and she moved out. Harry didn't tell me this—I heard him talking to Abner on the phone—and, of course, I eavesdropped. You call her, Maggie."

"Well, damn! That doesn't sound good. I guess you don't know where she went, do you? I hope she still has the same cell-phone number. I'll give it my best shot."

"It would not surprise me in the least to find out that Isabelle went out to the farm. Isn't that where we all go when things go awry in our lives?"

"You're right about that," Maggie said when she remembered how she'd hightailed it to the farm after her husband died to fall into Myra's and Annie's waiting arms. "Thanks for reminding me. I'll call when I hang up. You okay?"

Yoko laughed. "It's the start of the Christmas season, so that means things will go nuclear real soon. I'm looking forward to seeing Kathryn. I haven't seen her since last Thanksgiving. Isabelle, too, now that I think of it. I don't suppose there has been any word on Charles, has there?"

"Not that I've heard. Okay, see you tomorrow. Give Lily a hug from her Aunt Maggie. By the way, what does she want for Christmas?"

Yoko laughed again. "Everything in the world, so you can't go wrong no matter what you choose. Don't go overboard. She loves storybooks. Hey, they're paging me for something. Gotta go, see you tomorrow. Thanks for calling, Maggie, I do need a break."

"Yeah, me too." Maggie sighed as she broke the connection.

She drummed her stubby fingers on her desk, her eyes on the bank of clocks on the wall that gave the time all over the world. She was going to stay right here until everyone got back from lunch. And she wanted to see how long the foursome would take. Her eyes narrowed into slits. *Everything* was her business now.

Maybe what she should do was drive out to Pinewood. Myra always said not to bother calling, her door was always open. Still, what if she wasn't home, and she made the trip for nothing. She finally talked herself into the trip as she recalled Yoko's words that Isabelle was probably there. And that's what she would do the moment the foursome returned from lunch.

For the next thirty minutes Maggie was a whirling dervish as she tidied up loose ends, delegated duties, and signed off on a dozen different papers shoved under her nose. Thank God it was a slow news day.

Maggie's eyes strayed to the clock again. Ninety-minute lunch hours were taboo unless approved. She knew in her gut that Ted was pushing her buttons. Lunch hours were one hour. Sixty minutes. Emily knew better, and this was the first time she had abused the rule. Let it go or make an issue of it? She opted to let it go, but she made sure the foursome saw her looking at the clock, then making a note on her desk pad when they returned.

With her afternoon cleared, Maggie gathered up her coat and purse. She made a production of locking her office door, something she rarely, if ever, did. She looked at the foursome again and left for the elevator. Let them all wonder where she was going. Two could play the secrecy game.

Emily Davis waited until her boss stepped into the elevator before she got up from her desk and walked into the newsroom. "What was *that* all about? Was it taking too long at lunch? In the two years since I've been here, this is the first time I've ever been late coming back from lunch. I've always prided myself on obeying the rules. Maggie looked . . . she looked . . ."

"Pissed to the teeth are the words you're looking for. She was that all right. But you did notice, she didn't make a *big* issue of it," Ted said airily. "Wonder where she was going."

"Why don't you call her and ask her," Espinosa said snidely. "You started this ball rolling, so see it through."

"I did not! She's the one who sent the damn banana tree."

"What banana tree?" Emily asked.

It was as though Ted and Espinosa forgot that Emily Davis was in the room as they ranted back and forth.

"Yeah, well, she's been following me. Us. That's as in you and me, Espinosa. Doesn't that damn well creep you out just a little? Oh, crap, I forgot, you're so wrapped up in Alexis's dumping you that you can't see the forest for the trees. You need to look alive here, *Joseph*!"

"Why would the boss follow you guys? Did you do something? What banana tree?" Emily asked for the second time.

Ted and Espinosa continued to ignore Emily and her words.

"Alexis didn't dump me. We came to a mutual understanding that wasn't, isn't, to my liking. And I am not in any damn forest. How do you explain, Ted, that you *didn't notice a tail*? You're the investigative reporter here. She's out for blood now. Yours!" Espinosa said ominously.

"Why would the boss be out for your blood? You're both talking in riddles, and I still don't understand about the banana tree. I do know they're hard to grow, though," Emily said.

"Don't you have somewhere else you're supposed to be and doing something to earn your paycheck?" Espinosa snarled at the beautiful young woman.

Emily Davis scurried back to her desk, her thoughts whirling and twirling in all directions. What was going on? She made a note in her day planner to pick up some flowers in the morning and a bag of Maggie's favorite pastries to make up for being late from lunch. She not only liked this job, she needed it. If there was one thing she didn't need, it was to have her boss upset with her. The bottom line was she shouldn't have listened to Ted when he said he was always late at lunchtime and Maggie didn't care. She made a mental note not to take Ted's advice on anything even though she was starting to have some strange, kind of nice feelings about the lanky reporter.

Emily tilted her head so she could see out the plate-glass half wall that separated her small office from the newsroom. Ted and Espinosa were still going at it. Whatever *it* was. Well, it was none of her business, so she might as well get down to the small mountain of work Maggie had left for her. She wasn't sure, but from the looks of things, it appeared to be a punishment. She sighed. She so hated game playing.

Chapter 8

Maggie turned on her turn signal, made a right turn, and drove down the long, winding road that led to Myra's private driveway. She pulled to the side and looked out the window. Was it a mistake to come out here? Was the decision to make the trip just a knee-jerk reaction to the situation? Guilt?

Whatever it was, she was here. But she could turn around now and head back to the city. She could do that. But did she want to do that? What would Myra and Annie think when she told them why she had made the trip? Whose side would they be on? Then there was Isabelle. How was that going to play out?

Maggie rolled the window halfway down and took in deep breaths of the cold, fresh air. She hated this time of year with a passion. It was always gray and gloomy, with snow flurries in the air. Then came the snow. It was bearable, she supposed, until the Christmas season was over. Right now, though, it sucked.

Go forward?

Turn around and go home?

Damn it, she was a reporter, and she lived by her instincts. It didn't matter if she was the editor in chief or not; at the end of the day, she was still a reporter, and she would be a reporter to her dying day.

Maggie clenched her teeth, moved the gearshift from PARK to DRIVE, and hit the gas pedal.

Arriving at the electronic gate, Maggie pressed in the code, gave a soft tap to the horn, and zipped through the opening. She parked next to a black Mustang, a car she didn't recognize. Probably Isabelle's.

As she ran across the courtyard, Maggie could hear the dogs barking. The kitchen door opened just as she hit the steps. In an instant, she was surrounded by Lady and her four pups. Suddenly, everyone was laughing, and then Isabelle was wrapping her arms around her and squeezing her so hard her eyes started to water.

"Oh, Maggie, I am sooooo glad to see you! You look great. It's been a year! Well, almost a year since we were together. What brings you all the way out here?" Isabelle gushed.

"A couple of things. I . . . I need to talk to someone. It's good to see you, Isabelle, really good. Yoko told me you were back. I didn't know."

"How did Yoko know?"

Maggie shrugged. "She heard Harry and Abner talking. She eavesdropped. You know how it goes, Isabelle, you gather your information however you can."

"Coffee?" Myra asked.

"Tea?" Annie offered.

"How about a cold Coke?"

Ten minutes later, the women were seated at the table, Isabelle with tea, Myra and Annie with coffee, and Maggie with her Coke.

"Give it up, dear," Myra said. "We need a diversion here."

Maggie gave it all up, even the part about signing their names to the gift card that accompanied the banana tree.

Isabelle frowned. "What do you think it all means?"

"The boys are up to something they don't want us to know about. The ritzy, shiny, brass sign says it is the BOLO

Building. I don't know if that's a true name or initials or what it stands for. I couldn't track down the ownership. I even asked some of the owners of the surrounding buildings. No one knows who the owner is. They all claim to have been aware of renovations over the past months but nothing that disrupted their own businesses. The building was sold off as part of an estate. Couldn't find out anything there. Pricey. This might be a stretch, but off the top of my head, I'd say it's worth around ten million. Like I said, pricey, because it's in Georgetown."

"I don't understand, dear," Annie said. "How did you find out about the building? What made you suspect the boys were . . . uh . . . up to something?"

"Come on, Annie! Are you going to sit there and tell me that you don't think this whole past year has been more than a little strange? Everything has gone to hell. You know it, and I know it. Just because we haven't been talking about it doesn't mean something isn't going on.

"Well, for one thing, Abner's out. No offense, Isabelle, but he's aligned himself with *them*, so I have to find a new computer guru who is as good as he is. You got any ideas?"

"No offense taken, Maggie. I've been kind of locked into my own personal problems here. Abner and I haven't exactly been warm and cozy these past five or six months. There is someone, but I don't know his name. Abner said in the past he'd like to strangle him because he is so good. I can't think of his name or even if I ever heard Abner mention it. I don't have a clue as to how you can get in touch with him. All I do remember is that he works for the CIA. Actually, he doesn't really *work*, as we normally define the word, for the CIA. He spies for them. He's not on their payroll. It's like Abner. He does the same thing for the FBI and a lot of those other alphabet agencies. Abner writes software. So does the other guy, but Abner says he's better at it than the other guy. That's all I know. What do you mean, he's with *them*? What's going on, Maggie?"

"I wish I knew, Isabelle. Maybe nothing, but I've learned to pay attention to my gut, and doing so has served me well all these years. The guys, the boys, whatever you want to call them, are up to something, and it does not include us women. Or if you like, us *girls*. Whatever it is, it's secret. In the past, actually from day one, I've always been able to get anything out of Ted. But this past year, I would liken him to a turtle. He pulled his head in and clammed up. So when my gut got the better of me, I started to follow him and Espinosa. As you all know, they're like Batman and Robin—one is always with the other. The boys have been meeting up regularly. On the face of that, it doesn't mean anything. Guys going out for lunch, out for a beer, going to a Redskins game. All normal. Then, when he started going to that BOLO Building, I hired a private detective to tail him." She looked at Annie and said, "On my own dime. I did not charge it to the paper." Annie simply nodded.

"What did you end up with, dear?" Myra asked.

Maggie shrugged. "Everything centers on the BOLO Building. For months now, they all go there almost every day. Not necessarily together. Sometimes, they stay an hour or so, sometimes longer. I know the kind of furnishings that have been moved in, the kind of floors they have, how many bathrooms, and the kind of equipment that's been delivered. The investigator was not successful in getting any of the delivery people or vendors to talk. All he had to go on was what he saw with his own eyes. He said he saw boxes with computers, the cost of which is not something any of us could or would pay. In other words, high-end industrial-spy stuff. Like that cave Abner has at his home. You know, the climate-controlled place with his millions and millions of dollars' worth of equipment.

"The front door is, according to the detective, impenetrable, and the back door, where the guys go in and out, has a retina scan and a state-of-the-art keypad as a backup. Then there's Jack's dog—Cyrus. He said it was impossible to gain entry. Why all the security? Then the guy quit on me, but only after he asked me what I was involved in. He said he ran an up-and-up legitimate investigative service, but something was going on there he didn't want to be involved in. So I paid him off and took up the surveillance again, but I didn't come up with anything more either."

"What does it mean?" Myra asked fretfully.

"Well, dear, all we have to do is call Avery Snowden and let him take over," Annie said.

"Wrong! I saw him going into the building a week ago. He's on their side or their payroll or whatever you want to call it. And are you ready for this? So is Jack Sparrow. I saw him with my very own eyes."

Isabelle leaned forward. "I think what you're saying is that the boys are going to pick up where the vigilantes left off. Is that what you're saying, Maggie?"

Maggie looked at Myra and Annie and nodded. "I can't be sure, but yes, that's what I think. And I think young Dennis is funding them. Oh, one other thing, all the guys are training under Harry, even Dennis. They meet every evening at seven o'clock and work out for two hours. On the nights when Harry has other classes, Jack teaches it. He, as you know full well, has a black belt, thanks to Harry. Ask yourself why all that is necessary.

"This is just a guess on my part, but I think the seed, the germ, whatever you want to call it, came about last year, right around Thanksgiving. The guys were huddling even back then. I think when Charles split, that was all they needed to make their move. I don't know how it's going to work with Bert in Vegas. They recruited Abner, Dennis is relatively new to the group, but he's in one hundred percent, and he has all that money for funding. Factor in Avery Snowden and his little group, then ask yourself if anything else comes to mind."

"What about Jack Sparrow? You mentioned him," Annie asked.

"Glad you asked that. I just heard a rumor a few days ago, and if *I* got downwind of it, then Ted for sure heard it. He has some of the best sources or snitches, whichever word you prefer, in the world. You pay for it, Annie, but those snitches always come through for him. Mine are only half as good as Ted's. The scuttlebutt is Sparrow was seen going into the White House. With guess who?"

"Who?" the women asked in unison, their eyes wide.

Maggie grimaced. "Lizzie, that's who. Our own Lizzie Fox!"

"But . . ." Annie sputtered.

"Mr. Jack Sparrow is going to be the next director of the Federal Bureau of Investigation. Mr. FBI himself. The boys' inside source, the way Bert Navarro was ours. What could be sweeter? That is my personal take on it. In other words, my gut. I'm never wrong, ladies."

"Oh, dear, that . . . that . . ." Myra reached for her pearls, her lifeline when things moved out of her comfort zone.

"Sucks, Myra. Go ahead, you can say it, it's not a bad word, but it sure sums up the way things are right now," Annie said.

"All right, all right, but what does all this mean?" Myra demanded.

"Well, look at it like this. Sparrow is probably going to be the new director of the FBI if the rumor is true. The boys all have the same gold shields we have. Carte blanche. Jack doesn't have a job—he quit Nikki's firm and left the D.A.'s office, so he's a free agent. There appears to be trouble in the marriage. Abner . . . I didn't know about . . . about your problem, Isabelle. He's always been a free agent, too. Alexis dropped Espinosa and chose her career over him. Ted and Espinosa, as well as Dennis, have hours and hours of downtime, so they're available for whatever is going on. Harry has the perfect job, what with all those agents he trains. They talk, the agents that is. Harry listens. Grist. Dennis has, we might as well say, virtually unlimited money, and he's probably funding whatever it is they're doing. The only thing Dennis West doesn't have going for him is one of the gold shields. What all that tells me is that the boys are ripe for *something*. I guess time will tell us what that something is. Now, I'd like to know what's going on with you, Isabelle. I need a break from all this heavy stuff. Talk to me, girl."

Isabelle drew a long, deep breath. "Abner and I hit a rough patch. I had hoped when I took that job in England we could weather a long-distance relationship. We did for about eight months. Abner would fly over once a month; and then he started getting sick with each flight. Upper respiratory infections, really bad sinus attacks, his ears acted up. He actually had tubes put in them. The specialists told him he couldn't fly anymore. He said his eardrums could explode. He would no sooner get better than another attack would hit him, always after a flight across the pond. At least until he was totally one hundred percent recovered from that flight episode. I couldn't make the trip over here because I had to be on-site seven days a week. At first it was okay—we had the webcams. We'd e-mail, talk, call, send texts. But on my time, not his. That didn't sit well. With either of us. Then there was the six-hour time difference. That just out and out played hell with everything. I asked him to move across the pond until the job was done. He refused. Then I made a big mistake and said it wasn't like he had a *real* job, and when he did work, it was doing illegal stuff. He retaliated by asking me if that wasn't the pot calling the kettle black. Referring, of course, to my vigilante days, for which I had no comeback. He was absolutely right. At that point, we both dug in, and that was four months ago. I came over last week. I have to be honest—we hit a big snag on the project, and things shut down. Otherwise, I wouldn't be here. Also, the weather turned awful in

England, so it was a good time to make the trip. I showed up and, at first, Abner wouldn't even let me in. He finally did, and we had a rip-roaring fight. He said we were married and belonged together, not on two separate continents. He said I could have all the work in the world right here on our home shores. I said I had to see the project through to completion, and he said he understood in the beginning. He totally ignored me when I told him he could do his spying anywhere. Then he said that was before he got sick, and why did he have to make all the sacrifices. It just got out of hand really, really quick, and I walked out. That's it. I'm leaving tomorrow to return to England."

Maggie nodded, trying to absorb all she was hearing. "How much longer is the project?"

"Two more years, maybe three. At this point, I can't be certain. For all I know, it could go to four. The Brits are sometimes difficult to deal with," Isabelle said, defiance ringing in her voice.

No one said a word because no one knew what to say.

Isabelle started to cry. "I'm damned if I do and damned if I don't. Talk about being between a rock and a hard place." She sobbed. Annie handed her a bunch of paper towels and patted her on the back, after which she put the kettle on for more tea.

"I don't want any more damn tea. I swim in tea when I'm there. That's all they drink. I hate scones, and I damn well hate kippers, and I sure as hell hate mutton."

Maggie threw her hands in the air. "Can't the two of you compromise somewhere along the way?"

"Abner does not know the meaning of the word *compromise*. I tried that."

"What and how were you willing to compromise, dear?" Myra asked.

"Well . . . I said I would do my best to come over for a long weekend whenever I could. I reminded him of the webcams, the texting, and the e-mails. He in turn said he wanted a flesh-and-blood person next to him. He refuses to understand that this is my career, something I've worked toward all my life. I finally got the brass ring. And let's not forget all those years when I lost everything and had to fight my way back. I just can't give that up. I can't. I *won't*."

"Well, then, I guess that pretty much sums it all up," Annie said cheerfully. "Why don't we all go out to dinner to celebrate Isabelle's decision? My treat. So, who is going to file for divorce, you or Abner?"

Maggie almost choked on the last swig of cola.

"Who said anything about a divorce?" Isabelle asked in a shaky voice.

"Well . . . I just . . . you know . . . assumed that that's where you were going with all this. You won't give up your career, and Abner can't cross the Atlantic for health reasons, unless he is one hundred percent recovered from his last flight episode. It's inevitable that you would each want to get on with your lives."

Isabelle burst into fresh tears and fled the room.

Myra grimaced. Maggie looked pained, but neither said a word.

"The word *divorce* might give her pause for thought. It was worth a try. Personally, I don't see it working. How can it when both of them are so stubborn. If they're meant for one another, they'll find a way. Actually, you two might not agree with me, but I'm on Abner's side in all of this," Annie said.

"I am, too," Myra said.

"Believe it or not, I'm on his side, too," Maggie said. "I hate it that I feel so disloyal, but it's how I feel. They have to work it out. So, are we on for dinner, or should I leave? I'm sure you two have a lot to think and talk about, so I think maybe I should get back to town. Are you up for lunch tomorrow with the girls? Betty Lou's. Dupont Circle. Kathryn is in town but only for a few hours."

"We'll be there," Myra said. "It will be great to get together again."

"What time is Isabelle's flight?" Maggie asked.

"I think she said it was eleven-ten, so unless she has some kind of an epiphany, she will not be joining us," Annie said.

Maggie grinned as she pulled on her jacket. "Annie, how many times have you said to me, if you snooze, you lose?"

Annie laughed. "Too many to count. Be careful driving back, dear. We'll see you at lunch."

Maggie hugged the women, looked toward the family room, and winced. "Tell Isabelle I said good-bye."

Maggie's cell phone pinged just as she was ready to make a left turn onto the highway. She listened to Annie's voice telling her to hire a new investigative firm with twenty-four/seven surveillance of the boys and to bill it to the paper.

Maggie's fist shot high in the air. "Yesssss," she almost screamed as she careened out onto the highway.

Chapter 9

Abner Tookus sat in a traffic jam in the middle of Dupont Circle. He drummed his fingers in frustration on the steering wheel as he stared at the long line of cars ahead of him. He was just ten minutes away from the White House and five minutes away from prestigious Embassy Row. Too bad neither place was his destination. Behind him, cars blasted their horns. Ahead of him, cars blasted their horns. He felt like doing the same thing but resisted the impulse because he knew it wouldn't get him anywhere. He could just imagine the curses being bellowed behind the closed windows of the cars. He looked into his rearview and side mirrors and saw dozens of raised middle fingers.

He'd just come from the area in the District called Foggy Bottom, where he had a midmorning meeting at the crown prince of the U.S. government—the Department of State—where he'd turned down a job that wasn't to his liking. He was absolutely certain that his contact person would be back in touch and offer to sweeten the offer by the end of the day. It always happened that way. Today, he knew, would be no exception. He loved it when he could make big government sweat.

Ah, traffic was finally moving. Abner inched forward, then came to another stop as the light changed from green to yellow, then red. "Crap!" He slumped in the seat of his Hummer and stared out the side window. Nine miserable days of weather just like today: gray, ugly, and depressing. He could hardly wait to get to BOLO and the bright, fluorescent lighting.

Abner blinked, then squeezed his eyes shut and quickly opened them. Did he just see what he thought he just saw? What a stupid question. Of course he had. Nikki and Alexis were literally running toward Betty Lou's Café. Right behind the running duo were Yoko and Kathryn, both of whom were sprinting to catch up. He frowned. "Hmmnn." He eyed the traffic in front of him, which still wasn't moving. Aha, Maggie, running solo, her flaming red hair billowing out behind her in the strong wind. He blinked again when he saw Annie de Silva holding the entrance door to Betty Lou's Café for Maggie, which had to mean Myra was already in the building. "Hmmnn." All present and accounted for except for Isabelle, who was probably already in the air heading across the ocean to her beloved job. *Don't go there, Abner.* Thinking about Isabelle required complete solitude in his personal comfort zone. Translation: home. *Concentrate. Think. What would cause all those women to be out and about at the same time on a day like today?* Particularly since today was a workday. You didn't need to be a rocket scientist to know that whatever it was, it had to do with him and the guys. He could feel it in his gut.

The light, probably the longest light in the District, finally changed, and he moved forward two car lengths, after which he had clear sailing. He stepped on the gas and, within minutes, was tearing down the alley that would take him to the back entrance of the BOLO Building. The moment he stopped, he sprinted from the Hummer to the door, then lowered his six-feet-four-inch frame to let the retina scanner search his eyeball. He heard Cyrus barking just as the pneumatic hiss of the door kicked in. A second later, he was inside, handing a treat to Cyrus, rubbing the dog's belly, and shouting at the top of his lungs. The guys all came running.

"They were all there except Isabelle," he said, winding down in his excitement.

"So they were going to lunch, so what? Women do that all the time," Dennis said.

"No, Dennis, they don't," Jack said, a frown building on his face. "At least not our women. They take brief lunches or eat at their desks. They only meet up as a group when something is important or one of them has news that needs to be shared in person."

"I agree with Jack," Espinosa said. "Alexis told me time and again she only has time to gobble down a hard-boiled egg at her desk. I asked her hundreds of times to go to lunch, even volunteered to bring lunch to eat in the kitchen at the firm. She said she couldn't take the time."

"Espinosa's right. Nikki said she doesn't even take a lunch and sometimes inhales a yogurt if she has time. She's lost seventeen pounds. She looks anorexic, and the last time I saw Alexis, she didn't look any better," Jack growled.

"Alexis has lost thirteen pounds," Espinosa volunteered unhappily.

"Listen, guys," Harry said, "I have to go. Yoko asked me to pick up Lily today. She said she had something to do. Guess we know what that was now, don't we. By the way, guys, I think I had a tail coming here. I also think I lost him but can't be sure. I'll let you know if he or she picks me up when I leave here. See you at seven. Don't be late because if you are late, you're going to work an extra hour."

Cyrus let loose with a howl that made everyone in the room shiver. He calmed down and walked Harry to the door, got his treat, and waited until the door closed behind Harry to trot back to the conference room, where he nudged Jack's leg to let him know everything was okay before he dropped down to chew on his treat.

"Guess we need to be a little more alert," Ted said. "If Maggie, and I'm sure it's Maggie, has a tail on us, she's doing it with Annie's approval. And that, gentlemen, is the reason for this lunch meeting today. I'd bet my Pulitzer on it. Any takers?"

There were none.

"To what end?" Dennis asked. "I don't like the idea of someone shadowing me. Why?"

"To find out what we're doing. What else? Use your head, kid," Ted barked. "Women need to know *everything*. I know this because Mr. Jack Emery, who is an authority on all things woman, told me so a long time ago. When women don't know everything, they become very unhappy. So they then take steps to find out what it is they think they need to know. That's why they hire private detectives. I bet we all have tails and none of us has picked up on it."

"Cyrus would have picked up on it, don't you think?" Jack said, the frown still in place.

At the mention of his name, Cyrus rose to his magnificent height and looked around the room as much as to say, *I did not detect anything. So there.* His point made, at least to Jack, he flopped back down and resumed chewing on his treat.

"I have to assume this just took place in the last day or so. Maybe all the operatives aren't in place yet. If that's the case, stay alert and stay in touch," Jack said. "Private dicks, at least the good ones, charge outrageous fees. To tail all of us has to cost a bundle, and the only persons I know who could afford something like that are Myra and Annie."

Jack's cell phone pinged. He looked down, and said, "It's Bert."

"Hey, buddy, how's it going out there in fantasy land? The guys are here except for Harry. What's up? I'm going to put you on speaker, okay?"

"Yeah, sure. Sparrow is here, too. Look, I don't know if

this means anything or not, but Kathryn just called about fifteen minutes ago and said she's going to stay on in DC for a few days after she drops off a load of Christmas trees in Delaware. She's going to be staying at her house there in the District. For whatever this is worth, she sounded . . . I don't know . . . *off* somehow. We had plans for when she got back for the weekend. Now that's been scuttled. As a rule, Kathryn never does anything at the last minute. She's a planner, and the good thing is that she sticks to the plan. Is anything going on there Sparrow and I need to know about?"

"Oh, yeah," Jack drawled. He quickly filled Bert and Sparrow in on what had just transpired.

"You're right, those girls are up to something. Looks like my employer is up to her eyeballs in this. Okay, keep us in the loop. Gotta go, time is money."

Jack returned the cell phone to his pocket and looked around at the guys. "Any thoughts here?"

"Just one. Why didn't Isabelle stay and attend the luncheon? Those women are tight. She might shove me under the bus, but not her sisters," Abner observed unhappily.

"How do you know she didn't? You said Annie was holding the door for Maggie, which means Myra was already inside. If Isabelle went to the farm, like we think she did, then it's a good chance she was inside with Myra. At least, we can't rule it out," Ted observed.

"She said she was leaving this morning to return to England."

"And you believed her!" Ted glared in disbelief at the computer hacker like he'd sprouted a second head. "Haven't you learned anything hanging around us? Those women stick together, no matter what."

Abner hung his head the way Cyrus did when Jack chastised him for something or other. "She is my wife. Husbands tend to believe their wives, at least this husband does. I'll make sure I don't make that mistake again, *Ted.*"

"Now what?" Dennis demanded.

Jack shrugged. "What do you mean, now what?"

"I had an idea, and I wanted to run it by everyone."

"Spit it out, kid. We can always call Harry and tell him your idea. And Bert, too. Why waste time?"

"I was thinking last night because I couldn't sleep. This case with the lieutenant governor is important. Children died, and he has to be held accountable, but where does it say we can't work on two cases? Nowhere, right? So, Jack, why don't we take on those people your wife's law firm is going after in the class-action suits? You did say one suit was about a drug given to children for leukemia that ended up killing hundreds of little kids. Hundreds. That is just not acceptable to me. And the case Alexis is heading up, the one you said was the biggest dog-food-processing plant, where all those poor animals died. If we went after them, then Nikki and Alexis would have more free time and could just be normal lawyers again, and you and Espinosa will get them back in your arms. To me, that makes sense."

When no one said anything, Dennis flushed. "Stop looking at me like I'm an idiot. It makes sense. Call Bert and Harry and ask them what they think. I'm not backing down, either," the young reporter said, defiance ringing in his voice.

Ted banged his fist on the shiny conference table before he leaped across it to land in Dennis's lap. "Kid, you make me proud to know you! I mean that. You are so on the money, you scare me."

"Yeah, me, too," Jack said, his expression filled with awe.

"And if we play our cards right, no one has to know it's us making life easy for Nikki and Alexis and taking care of the greedy badass guys at the same time. You have my vote, Dennis. Now, get that agile brain of yours working on Isabelle for me, will you?" Abner begged.

"Oh, you bet I will. I really will. So are we going to . . . you know . . . plot this out? I can't wait for my assignment. Boy, this is a great day, guys," Dennis shouted exuberantly as he smacked his hands together.

"Then let's get to it, boys. Once we make some inroads, I'll call Harry." Jack looked at his watch. "He's probably on his way back home after picking up Lily as we speak. By the way, kid, I like that you think outside the box." Cyrus wiggled under the table and nipped at Dennis's ankle, his show of approval, too. Dennis laughed out loud, a sound of pure joy. His reporter's gut instinct told him he really did belong to this group. He really did.

Chapter 10

Harry watched the cars behind him as he listened to his daughter, Lily, babble nonstop about her exciting morning at play school. He grunted from time to time to show that he was listening to her delicious, little-girl chatter. He was right: he had a tail, and it didn't have four legs. This tail was the same black Honda Civic that had followed him to the BOLO Building and again when he'd driven home to switch vehicles to pick up Lily. The guy was good, he had to give him that. He wound in and out of traffic, pulled ahead, then pulled back, all the while following Harry, no easy feat when Harry had been riding the Ducati. Even now, he was showing his expertise, which surprised Harry. A pro, that was for sure. He realized there was nothing he could do while he had Lily in the car with him. But the moment he dropped her off at home with the nanny, it was going to be a whole new ball game.

"Sing it, Daddy. I have to know all the words by tomorrow. It's my homework," Lily squealed from the backseat. "Sing it, Daddy! Sing loud!"

Harry racked his brain, but all he could come up with was, *The itsy bitsy spider . . .*

Lily sighed. "Does Mommy know the words?"

"Yeah, yeah, Mommy knows the words," Harry said, believing he was off the hook.

"Okay, Daddy, I'll tell Miss Charles you didn't know the words. Miss Charles said that all mommies and daddies know the words. How come you don't know the words? You have to write me a note saying you don't know the words."

"Because I'm Chinese, that's why," Harry barked, and was instantly sorry at his tone. "Mommy will write the note, okay?"

One eye on the road in front of him, the other eye on his side mirror, Harry mumbled something under his breath that sounded like, "Oh, shit!"

"Oh goodie, we're home. I can hear Cooper," Lily said, unbuckling her safety harness and hopping down out of her seat. "Are you coming in, Daddy?"

"For a minute. I have to switch up and go back to work. Maybe Cassie knows the words to the song. Did your teacher give you a paper?"

"Two papers. You have to sign one."

"Okay, let's go! First one in wins a marshmallow!" Harry lagged behind, so his daughter could win. Flushed from the cold air, her cheeks rosy pink, Lily screamed her victory just as the nanny opened the door. Cooper barreled out, all but knocking Lily to the ground, where he proceeded to try to lick her to death. He loved the sound of his daughter's infectious laughter and Cooper's excitement at being reunited with his playmate. He knew in that instant that he wouldn't trade one second of his wonderful life for anything in the world. He made a mental note to learn the words to the spider song. If there was one thing he never wanted to do, it was to disappoint his beloved little daughter.

Ten minutes later, assured that Cassie did indeed know the words to the itsy bitsy spider song, Harry started up his Ducati. He knew that the black Honda would pick him up once he rounded the corner to the next street. The jerk probably thought he was going back to the dojo, but instead he was going to head for the park where Lily and Cooper romped in nice weather. There wouldn't be anyone there today, he was almost sure of it. He would set a trap, and the spider would fall right into it. Harry shook his head to clear his thoughts. He must have spiders on the brain. But if it worked, it worked. He knew he had the advantage with his two-wheeled vehicle.

Sure enough, the black Honda picked him up just as he hit the long, narrow street. Harry goosed the Ducati and roared his way to the park, where he had open road all around him. He lucked out when he didn't see any other vehicles, with the exception of the black Honda, anywhere near the park. And it was far enough back that the tail didn't pose an immediate threat. He knew he had the advantage since he visited the park on a regular basis and knew every road and footpath. He checked his side mirror to see what his tail was doing, which was nothing but following him. "Fool!"

Harry rounded a dogleg and came up on a side road that was little more than a path but still wide enough for one car. In the blink of an eye, he went off road, whizzed past a lush grouping of thick, hedgelike boxwood, and disappeared from the road's view. He waited until he saw the black Honda slow, then speed up. From his position behind the boxwood, Harry waited, counting slowly under his breath until he got to the number ten. He roared out of his cover, raced alongside the Honda, then skidded to a stop with inches to spare. The Honda's brakes screeched, and Harry sniffed at the scent of burning rubber. He was off the Ducati, his hand on the door in a nanosecond. He reached in and literally pulled the driver out of the door and onto the ground, where he stomped on his neck. "Move, and I'll break your neck. You know I will. Do we understand each other?"

The driver tried to nod but thought better of the idea. "Yeah," he mumbled.

"Here's the deal. I'm going to remove my foot from your neck, and you are going to get up nice and slow. Then you are going to lean against the car and spread your legs and arms. We good so far?"

"Yeah."

Harry sized up the driver. Six feet, looked to be in good shape, probably in his midthirties.

"You married?"

"What the hell! Who are you? What business is it of yours if I'm married or not? I'm calling the police! I don't have much money on me, sixty bucks or so. Take it, and I'll forget about this."

Harry laughed. It was an evil sound. "My name is Harry. The reason I asked if you were married is because I'll need to notify your next of kin after I kill you. Let's cut to the chase here right now. You've been following me all day. And you followed me when I had my child in the car. That's something you never do, put my child in jeopardy. So we're clear on that point. I know you're some kind of private dick, so spit it out right now. Who hired you? Who do you report to? You go all shy on me, then I'm going to have to get creative and shove your dick up your ass; and then I'm going to pull your ears off your head and stuff them down your throat. You'll probably choke to death, but if you don't, then I'm going to shove your tongue up your nose to cut off your air supply. Talk to me."

"You need to get a life, mister. You watch too many kung fu movies. I don't know what the hell you're talking about."

"Well, I did ask nicely," Harry singsonged as he advanced on the driver, reached out with both hands, lifted the giant off the ground, and heaved him over the top of the black

Honda, and he landed on the ground with a thump. Harry ran around the car and stepped on the driver's chest.

The driver groaned in pain, knowing he had cracked ribs. He wished now he hadn't been so verbal, not to mention stupid, especially since Spritzer had warned him about his subject. He also wished he had believed Maggie Spritzer when she extolled the martial virtues of one Harry Wong.

"If you move, you could push those broken ribs up into your lungs. Where's your ID?"

"In the car," the driver groaned. "Aren't you going to call an ambulance?"

"Why would I do a stupid thing like that?" Harry called over his shoulder as he rifled through the Honda. He helped himself to all the equipment, including the man's cell phone, which was ringing as he picked it up. He carried it over to the driver and smiled the same evil smile. "Answer this, and if I hear one word I don't like, you will be eating your ears."

"Suliman here," the driver said. He listened, and said, "I'm following Wong. He just dropped off his kid. I don't know where he's going, maybe back to his dojo. He was at the BOLO Building but didn't stay long. Yeah, yeah, they were all there." He listened again, thought about choking on his ears, and said, "I said I'd call if there was something to report. There is nothing to report, Miss Spritzer. Listen, I have to pay attention to the road." He broke the connection but held on to the phone.

Harry reached down and snatched it. "I like a man who follows orders. Who hired you?"

Mike Suliman thought about his dick, his ears, and his tongue. He wanted to keep them all intact on his body. "I think, and I say I think, some woman at the *Post* but not the Spritzer chick. You think my boss tells me? This is a job, a tail job. I get paid by the hour to tail and surveil you. That's the beginning and end of it."

"How many of you are assigned to my little group of friends?"

"Hey, man, I'm dying here. It's cold as hell. Call an ambulance, okay?"

"I never ask a question twice," Harry said.

Mike Suliman bit down on his lip. "All you guys have a tail, and they're twenty-four/seven. That translates to big bucks for my boss. That's all I know. He warned us not to screw up and said this was an important case. And he promised bonuses. Now, are you going to call an ambulance for me or not? I could die out here, it's freezing."

"Yeah, I know," Harry said thoughtfully. "So Maggie Spritzer is your contact?"

"Yeah, the one with that wild bush of red hair. Damn, she's almost as scary as you are. She warned us not to mess up. She said you guys are slick. Especially you and Jack Emery."

"Guess you'll be getting into another line of work, huh?" Harry said, pleased that his and Jack's expertise did not go unrecognized.

"If I don't die first." Suliman groaned. "C'mon, man, help me out here. You don't want me on your conscience, do you?"

Harry shrugged as he looked around to make sure they were still alone in the park. Seeing nothing to alarm him, he dropped to his haunches and stared into the private investigator's eyes. Then he smiled. Mike Suliman wanted to cry.

"I'm going to ask you a few questions, and depending on your answers, I will know whether or not I should call nine-one-one for you. Okay?"

"I told you everything I know. You can peel off my skin, and I can't tell you anything else."

"So you say. How well do you know the other dicks assigned to this case?"

Suliman tried to rear up, but the pain in his side was so intense, he fell back to the ground. He clenched his teeth. "I'm a licensed private investigator, not a dick. It's a job. An honest job. So do whatever the hell you're going to do or leave me here to die."

Harry was not moved. "I didn't ask you for a dissertation. I also told you I wouldn't ask you twice. Talk."

"I know them, that's it. They do their job, I do mine. 'Hey, how are you?' That kind of thing. Will you call nine-one-one already?"

"You want to make a deal?"

"I'll do whatever you want if you call nine-one-one. *Anything.*"

"Stay right here. I have to make a phone call."

Harry moved off, called Jack, and explained what was going on. "I'm thinking, Jack, we can turn this guy. How much money can I offer him to spy for us while in the employ of the *Post?*"

"You're the man, Harry. As much as it takes. Can you trust him?"

"Oh, yeah," Harry drawled. "Listen, I really do have to call nine-one-one before this guy freezes. I'll call you when I get back to the dojo. Hey, do you know the words to the itsy bitsy spider?"

"Well, yeah, everyone knows that little ditty. Why?"

"Sing it for me," Harry said. Jack hung up on Harry Wong.

Harry helped Suliman to his feet and settled him in his car. He turned the key and hit the HEAT button. "You can call nine-one-one yourself. After they patch you up, come by the dojo. You breathe one word of this to Spritzer or your people, and I *will* find you and finish the job. You understand that, right?" Suliman nodded weakly. "I'm thinking that four o'clock should see you standing in my doorway. For sure, you don't want me to come looking for you. Four o'clock, not one minute later. It's okay to be early. I'm leaving you with all your junk to show you what a nice guy I am."

Suliman nodded as he struggled to take a deep breath. He was punching in 911 when Harry roared off on his Ducati, laughing like a lunatic.

Chapter 11

As always, when the sisters got together after a long absence, it was bedlam, chaos, laughter, hugs, and kisses, then more laughter as they jostled one another, each of them talking and gesturing, the language of true friendship that only they understood.

Finally, the hostess managed to get all the women seated and placed menus in front of them. Each menu was a single sheet of heavy parchment paper that was printed fresh each day and covered in designs that Betty Lou, the owner, created herself. Today's menu carried an evergreen design with tiny Christmas trees loaded on the back of a Santa sleigh that raced across the top of the menu. Trailing down both sides of the menu were miniature gift-wrapped presents. All in all, a cheerful introduction to a festive luncheon. It didn't hurt that Betty Lou gave Christmas names to each of her one-of-a-kind specials for that day.

Betty Lou's was a small mother-daughter restaurant in Georgetown that was absolutely unique. It was small and always full, with a waiting line outside the door during the two-hour lunch period. Inside, it was warm and cheerful, and the owners changed the decor to fit the seasons. In the spring, Betty Lou and her daughter decorated it with spring flowers, watering cans, and a fake waterfall to represent

April showers. In the summer, they strung hammocks and painted all manner of seashells on the walls. September brought bales of hay and pumpkins. This being the Christmas season, Betty Lou and her daughter had already put up a real evergreen tree in the window, and it smelled as delicious as the aromas coming from the kitchen. Garlands of fresh evergreens draped the windows, and outside, a monster-sized fresh balsam wreath, custom made by Yoko, hung on the front door. But it was the fireplace burning white birch logs that drew the patrons to the restaurant. On the mantel sat a sleigh with eight prancing reindeer. More than one person had curled up on the chairs by the fire and fallen asleep.

Because of the limited time that Nikki and Alexis had for anything other than working on the firm's class-action lawsuits, Maggie took charge and ordered for all of them. "Whatever is the special is what we'll all have. Your house white wine and just bring the salad dressing whirligig and leave it." Maggie looked around to see if everyone agreed, but the girls were so busy talking to one another that she just shrugged.

The door opened at the front, and cold air rushed through the opening as a lone woman, attired in a long, white, leather coat and an ermine hat stood for a moment, looked around, then skirted the tables as she ran across the restaurant.

"Isabelle!" the women cried as one. Bedlam once again took over as the girls all rose and tried to crush Isabelle to them. "This is soooo great. Now we're all here," Kathryn said. "One more!" she shouted to the startled waitress, who was looking for another chair and worrying about the already crowded table.

The girls all talked at once, but Isabelle's voice was the loudest. "They were boarding, I was halfway to the plane when I realized I had to come back. I can take a later flight at four. I did it all on my phone on the taxi ride here. Damn, girls, it's good to see you all again. I missed you. You have no idea how much."

"Yes, we do know how much because we all missed you just as much," Yoko said as she pulled out pictures of Lily and Cooper to show Isabelle, who understandably ooohed and aaahed over the tot and her guardian, Cooper.

Annie nudged Myra. "Just like old times, eh, Myra." She lowered her voice, and whispered, "I had a gut feeling Isabelle might switch flights. She's a sister through and through, and right now I'm thinking she needs them to rally round her. You agree, Myra?"

Myra nodded as she watched the sheer joy on the faces of her little family. It warmed her heart at how close the girls were and how they'd drop everything if one of them needed the others at her side.

Myra and Annie were like two sponges as they sat back to allow the girls to play catch-up. They didn't miss a word, and later, when they were back at the farm, they would dissect each and every one of them to make sure they hadn't missed a single nuance.

Kathryn tore off a chunk of dark, warm pumpernickel bread and popped it into her mouth. Even before she was done chewing, she fixed her gaze on Nikki and Alexis, and blurted out, "My God, you two look horrible. Not only do you look anorexic, but you look as if you're miserable. What is up with the two of you? Don't look at me like that, I'm just saying what we're all thinking. C'mon now, what's the story here?"

"Work, three class-action lawsuits at the same time," Nikki muttered, her eyes on her watch.

"We're working eighteen hours a day, eating on the fly, and living on black coffee and hard-boiled eggs. Nikki eats yogurt every other day," Alexis said as she shredded a slice of the warm bread in front of her.

Annie and Myra wisely refrained from commenting and just listened as the others weighed in on Nikki's and Alexis's physical appearance. Both women knew that if Nikki and Alexis would listen to anyone, it would be their sisters.

Always the brashest and the most outspoken, Kathryn wasn't finished. She zeroed in on Isabelle, and said, "And what's up with *you*? Is it true you and Abner are splitting up? Big mistake, girl!"

Annie kicked Myra under the table, a silent plea that perhaps they should step in. Myra gave an imperceptible shake of her head, which meant, no, not yet.

Ten minutes later, Maggie had had enough and offered up a shrill whistle. "Enough, already. If you two"—she pointed to Nikki and Alexis—"want to drive yourself into an early grave for the sake of money, go for it. I, however, thought you were both smarter than that. Jack and Joseph deserve better than they're getting. As for you, Isabelle, Abner is the best thing that ever happened to you, and you're driving him away. Right now, you should be with him, trying to make things right, not here with us. There, I said it, and I'm not taking back one word. Oh, wait, I think the three of you are just plain stupid! Okay, there, now I'm done."

The silence at the table had suddenly become so ominous that the two waitresses backed up a few steps, their eyes wide at what was going on at table six.

Nikki, tears glistening in her eyes stood up. Because she was so tall, she now looked skeletal, her suit hanging on her slender frame. "I thought I came here for a pleasant lunch, not to be raked over the coals. And I'll thank you, Maggie, to stay the hell out of my business." She grabbed her coat and raced out of the café, Alexis hot on her heels.

Not to be outdone, Isabelle also stood up, and said, "Well, I certainly know where you're coming from, Maggie. Weren't you and Abner a thing at one time? More than a thing if what I heard is correct. Guess you know what you're talking about since I can see a guilty look on your face. I'll thank you to stay out of my business unless I ask for your help. And you, Kathryn, you're a fine one to talk. Who's been leading Bert around like a dog on a leash? Don't try to tell me what to do and not to do. I'm sorry I canceled my flight to come here and see you all. Have a nice lunch, girls." And then she was standing and struggling into her coat, the other diners in the restaurant wondering what was going on at table six.

"You are so off the mark, Isabelle. That was below the belt and unworthy of you. Abner and I were nothing more than friends, like brother and sister. There was never anything between us, and you know it damn well. How can you say something like that unless you're guilt ridden? I feel really sorry for you because you're screwing up your life and are too damn dumb to know it. Go ahead, be a quitter, get on your plane, and go back to Merry Old England and eat your crumpets and drink your tea. Who cares? Not I, anymore," Maggie sniped in return.

Isabelle sprinted from the restaurant, tears streaming down her cheeks.

"Well, that didn't go exactly as I planned it," Maggie mumbled as she motioned to the two hovering waitresses to set the food on the table.

"How did you think it was going to go, dear?" Myra asked softly.

Maggie bit down on her lower lip. "Not like that, that's for sure. All three of them are feeling guilty because they know that I'm absolutely right. Guilt, as we have all learned the hard way, is a terrible thing. And pride is still worse. I'm sorry if the rest of you are upset, but it all needed to be said. We're talking about three wonderful, loving relationships going down the tubes if they don't come to their senses. I also know it's not all about the money, but money does play a part in their lives right now." Maggie looked around, not sure what she was seeing on the faces of her friends. "What? Now you're all going to judge *me*?"

"Absolutely not, dear. What we're going to do is eat this delicious-looking chicken parmesan. That's what it is, right?" Myra asked in an innocent-sounding voice.

"We have to do something. We can't just let it all fade away," Kathryn said fiercely. "I started it by saying how awful Nikki and Alexis looked. I was so shocked at their appearance, it just came out. As for Isabelle . . . I understand where she's coming from, what all she had to overcome to get where she is, but to lose the man who made her whole again . . . I cannot comprehend that. I just can't."

"What can we do?" Yoko asked as she played with her food. "Does anyone have any ideas? Why exactly are we here, and what is it we're supposed to do?"

"I hope you all decide quickly because I have a bunch of Christmas trees I have to deliver to Delaware. I'll come back and stay on for a few days, so if you need my help, I'm all yours. Three days is the longest I can stay because I have signed contracts I have to honor," Kathryn said.

"I'm available; I hired a bunch of college kids to help at the nursery. I'm assuming this is all about not letting the guys know anything, so that means I will have to have the nanny pick up Lily from play school. It's all doable for me. Just tell me what you need me to do," Yoko said.

"Annie and I are free, too," Myra said.

"My time is our time," Maggie said. "I have to tell you, this is the first time in my career, and a first since I met Ted and Espinosa way back when, that I cannot figure out, much less predict, what they're up to. Ted called my bluff when he told me to back off or he would resign. If he goes, so does Espinosa, and, for sure, young Dennis will follow his idol. I have to be careful. That's why I wanted to hire the detective agency to keep tabs on all of the guys.

I can't be visible. I hired the best agency in the area. They are superprofessional."

"So you're saying we're in good hands?" Annie queried.

"If you believe their PR, then yes, Annie, I think we are in good hands. All we can do now is sit back and wait for something to happen. I hate that part of it. I want to be in there with both feet and arms swinging."

Kathryn looked at her watch. "I gotta go. I came with Yoko, so she has to drop me off at my truck out at her nursery. Call me on my cell if something comes up. I'll be back by noon tomorrow. I'll be at my house, so that's where you can find me. It was nice seeing you all again. I'm sorry it didn't work out with Nikki, Alexis, and Isabelle. Let's all hope that, when they take a minute to think seriously, they'll come to their senses. If not, at least we tried."

And then it was just Maggie, Myra, and Annie, and a table of uneaten food.

Her eyes misty, Maggie looked across at the two women she most admired in the whole world. "Was I wrong? Tell me the truth."

"No, dear, you weren't wrong," said Myra. In fact, you were so right that the girls themselves knew it, and that's why they scurried out of here. Right now, I do not know what the answer is. I do have to say I was stunned to see Isabelle, which alone tells me how committed she is to all the sisters."

Maggie sniffed. "Did you come to that opinion before or after she pushed us under the bus and left like a scalded cat?"

"Boxes to go?" the waitress chirped, coming up behind Maggie.

"One big one. I'll take it all. Something tells me I am not going to have time to go food shopping. Unless either you or Myra want it?" Maggie said as an afterthought.

"That's fine, dear, you can take it all," Annie said.

"I feel so shitty. Like I betrayed you all—Nikki, Alexis,

and Isabelle in particular. I love those girls. I'd do anything in the world for them, and now it's come to this."

As she struggled into her heavy winter jacket, she turned, looked around, then said, "I hate not being in control. The thing is, I'm not exactly sure when I lost that control. That bothers me more than anything. It's like I lost my edge, and now I have to rely on private detectives for information when I should be able to gather it myself. It's what I do, for God's sake!" A lone tear rolled out of the corner of Maggie's eye as Myra and Annie gathered her close.

"Everything happens for a reason, dear," Myra said. Maggie looked up at her out of bleary eyes as much as to say, *and you really believe that?*

And then they were outside, shivering in the gusty wind. "We do understand, Maggie. It's like Myra and I getting older with each passing day. It would seem that as you age, no one takes you seriously anymore. When you try something, and it doesn't work, regardless of the circumstances, you chalk it up to senior moments. We were so used to being in the thick of things, taking charge, it's hard to tell when our own control slipped."

"What's the answer then?" Maggie hiccuped.

Myra surprised both women when she said, "Then, my dear, you take the bull by the horns and wrestle it to the ground even if your joints creak and groan in the process."

"Good Lord, Myra," Annie said, "that was a profound statement if I ever heard one! Doubly so since it came from you. If we were men, this is where we'd say one of two things: grow a set or balls to the wall, fellas. But since we're women, ladies, if you will, let's just go with in the end we'll be the ones standing in our rhinestone cowgirl boots. You two need to dust yours off. Like today. It's a subtle message, but sooner or later one of those duds will recognize our message. Sometimes, I am just so smart I can hardly stand myself."

The women burst out laughing as they bucked the wind and headed to their cars.

Chapter 12

The clock on the wall of the dojo said it was 3:55.

Harry Wong stood, hands on hips, staring at his new class of recruits straight out of Annapolis. "Listen up, midshipmen! I have been in business for more years than I care to remember, and I can truthfully say you are the sorriest bunch I've ever had the misfortune to have enter my hallowed doors. I expected . . . hell, I don't even know what the word is to describe you miserable human beings. You're a bunch of *wusses*. The only thing I can say for you is you sweat like a bunch of girls. Smelly sweat at that. I train women who, in the blink of an eye, could nail your sorry asses to the wall and not break a sweat. You don't even have the grace to look ashamed or embarrassed. And to think you are going to be the ones possibly running our military someday in the future somehow makes me want to puke.

"I'm stuck with you because I signed a contract with the powers that be, the ones who control your lives, at least for now. By the time you get back to Annapolis in that fancy bus you arrived in, my report will be in the hands of your superiors. You need to think about that on the ride back." A hand shot in the air. Harry ignored it. Another hand went up.

"Here is my number-one rule: you never speak to me

unless I give you permission. Here is rule number two: you never, ever question me. Rule three is you never offer up an excuse. One last thing. When you return here tomorrow, bring a check with you. I'm changing your workout clothes to pink. You have to pay for the privilege of wearing *pink*. You want to act like girls, then you are going to dress like them. You also get to pay for the photo op that will follow you back to your superiors."

Harry looked at the clock on the wall. He had one minute left. "I am giving permission now for one question if anyone wishes to pose one." No one did. Harry smiled his special evil smile when he heard someone in the back row say, "I hate your fucking guts, Master whatever the hell your name is. And I'd like to see you deck me out in one of your shitty pink outfits."

The door opened at the front of the dojo. Ah, private investigator Mike Suliman. Right on time. Harry smiled again. He did so love punctuality, especially punctuality brought on by fear.

"You're dismissed, midshipmen." It was all Harry could do to keep a straight face as the midshipmen scrambled to form straight lines and bow to Master Wong. At least they'd gotten that part right.

Harry walked out of the training room and up to the front of the dojo, where a nervous-looking Mike Suliman was viewing, with some trepidation, the plaques and pictures on Harry's four walls. His insides started to curdle when Harry motioned him to take a seat. "Tea?"

Suliman hated tea. Cold tea, hot tea, herbal tea, he hated it all. He was a coffee drinker. He was an eight-cups-of-coffee-a-day man. "I'd love a cup of tea, Mr. Wong."

Harry putzed and puttered with the little pot of tea behind a bamboo partition. His object was to have Suliman nervous and twitchy to the point he would do whatever Harry wanted. Fear was such a strong motivator. He leaned up against the wall as he contemplated his next move, which was to call Jack to see if he had any ideas on how he wanted Suliman handled. But he'd have to go somewhere else to make the call. More stall time for Suliman.

Harry handed over the small cup with no handles to the detective. "Enjoy your tea, Mr. Suliman. I have something I have to attend to. I'll be back in a few moments. As you know, tea is to be savored, to be enjoyed."

"Uh-huh," Suliman grunted. He took a cautious sip when Harry left the room. The tea tasted like tree bark, wet dog, and moldy leaves.

While Mike Suliman was gagging over his tea, Harry was hissing and snarling at Jack on the phone. "What? What? Spell it out, Jack. I already scared the shit out of him. You want me to coddle him? How the hell do I know if he's reliable? You want me to make sure he's on our side as a double agent when he leaves here, is that what you're saying?" Harry listened. "How much of a bonus? Yeah, yeah, how many times have I heard you say money talks and bullshit walks? Too many to count. And what did Abner find out about him when he ran his profile?" Harry listened again. "Okay, I got it. I'll call you back when he leaves." Just as he was about to break the connection, he heard Jack ask about the midshipmen. Harry laughed and then filled Jack in with all the details from his class with the midshipmen.

"That bad, huh? Well, you'll whip them into shape. Pink, huh? Oooh, I like that, Harry. Tell them West Point is sending its graduating class to you for a full month of training in January, then say there will be a dust-off when both sides compete, and Navy has to wear pink unless they perform to your standards. It's that old Army-Navy thing. See ya, Harry."

Harry was grinning from ear to ear when he finally signed off. Now, why didn't he think of that? Guess that's why Jack earned the big bucks.

Back in the waiting room, Harry eyed the private detective and the empty teacup. "More?"

"Ah . . . no thanks. Can we just get to it, Wong."

"I like that, a man who likes to get to the point, as long as it's my point." Harry straddled a straight-backed chair and focused on the detective. "Okay, Mr. Suliman, this is what I *know*. You're thirty-two years old, never married. You have women falling all over you because you like to wine and dine and party with them. That takes a lot of money. You live in a crappy garden apartment and make the rent, which is quite reasonable, by the skin of your teeth. You drive a muscle car, payments up to date. You work out at Gold's Gym, which is a high-dollar place to get fit. You wear Brooks Brothers suits, but you do have one Armani that you haul out for special occasions. You have monogrammed cuffs on your shirts. You take a Caribbean vacation twice a year that you can't afford, and your credit cards are about maxed out. How'm I doing so far?"

Suliman grunted.

"Okay, you wear boxers and like bold . . . um . . . patterns. You save the tidy whities for your dates to show off your muscular legs. You have a six-pack of designer beer in your refrigerator, twenty-seven bags of Ramen noodles, and your brown eggs expired last month. You need to throw them out, Mr. Suliman. You whiten your teeth, use Crest for cavities, and have a variety of manly colognes."

"You son of a bitch; you invaded my space!" the detective exploded.

"How does it feel, you piece of shit? Okay, now that we have leveled the playing field, we're starting from square one. You on board or not?"

"Yeah, I'm on board. Spell it out, Wong."

"Okay, I want to know everything your fellow dicks find out about my colleagues. Daily. You screw up, and you will regret it. I will tell you what you report to Miss Spritzer, so we will have a standing six o'clock appointment daily. How you ferret out the reports from your colleagues is up to you, but I want detailed information. As a reward, you will be paid one thousand dollars a week. In cash. Under the table. No paper trail. You following me here?"

All Suliman heard was $1,000 a week in cash. Man, this weirdo was truly saving his ass. He nodded because he felt too giddy to speak.

"Do we have a deal, Suliman?"

The detective finally got his tongue to work. "We have a deal."

Harry nodded. "I have a class coming to the dojo in fifteen minutes. I want you to sit here and compile your first report. Be as creative as you wish. I'll be grading you. I'm going to help you out here, so that you can talk to your fellow workers. My colleagues will be filtering in here one by one, starting at six o'clock, at which point you will be outside in the cold watching this dojo. You can all convene outside the dojo, talk it to death, but lead them to believe this dojo is where all the action takes place. Secret meetings, telephone calls, strange goings-on. Like I said, be creative. I want you to fax me a copy of your daily report by nine this evening. Before you report to Spritzer. In case I need to make any changes."

"You're trying to screw this Spritzer babe, is that it?"

"That's a rather crude way of putting it, Mr. Suliman, but yes, we want to come out on top. With your help. By the way, when this is all over, and you've complied with all I asked you to do, I'm authorized to tell you there is a bonus of ten thousand dollars on the table."

Suliman barely heard the words; his mind was already on possibly relocating to one of the high-rises in Crystal City and turning his life around. Maybe this psycho kung fu artist was his savior. Well, damn.

Harry favored Suliman with his evil smile, narrowed his eyes, then turned and padded away.

When his heartbeat returned to normal, Mike Suliman took a deep breath and closed his eyes. Well, damn!

Chapter 13

Nikki Quinn shoved her shoulder against the door and held it for Alexis to barrel through. Both women were gasping, breathless from the run across the parking lot to the warmth of the lobby.

Panting, Nikki yanked at the scarf around her throat as she steered Alexis down the hall and around a corner to the building's coffee shop. "We need to talk."

"That we do," Alexis said, following Nikki into the steamy warmth of the little coffee shop, which had four small tables and one secluded booth in the rear. Nikki headed for the booth. Lunch hour was over, so the place was virtually empty.

The women ordered the restaurant's specialty, tuna on rye and black coffee.

"That was a fiasco if ever there was one," Alexis said, referring to the sisters' luncheon as she squirmed out of her down jacket. "But that's not why you want to talk, is it, Nikki?"

Nikki looked down at the watch on her wrist, a birthday gift from Jack several years ago. She let loose with a long, drawn-out sigh. It seemed as if her entire life was scheduled in minutes. Six minutes to do this, nine minutes to do that, fifteen minutes to do something else. At the end of the day, every day, to her own chagrin, she simply ran out of minutes.

"No, it isn't. I just want to give you a heads-up. You're my friend, my employee, an associate at the firm."

Alexis held up her hand to stop Nikki's flow of words. "Nik, you don't owe me an explanation of anything. I work for you. I have no intention, ever—that's as in ever—of asking you to make me a partner. I'm happy as a clam with the salary you pay me, which is more than I deserve. I don't want or need any extra responsibility. I don't want for anything, I'm content with what I have. I just hope you are satisfied with my work performance."

"Alexis, we're soul sisters. When I started the firm years and years ago—and they were lean years, believe me—I had a goal. I reached that goal. Now, my back is to the wall, and my employees are making demands I will not tolerate. The meeting at two-thirty, with Allison, Irene, and Pamela, is not going to go well. I'm going to cut them loose. I've already alerted security to be on standby, and HR knows what is going down."

"If you're asking me if I approve, the answer is yes. We'll manage without them. I know three lawyers who would jump at the chance to work for you. They're young, fresh out of law school, but that's what you need, Nik, young blood, gung ho, and ready to set the legal world on fire. Georgetown Law will give you a steady flow of young lawyers. You and Jack are both alumni, and they'll bend over backward to help you. You hire more paralegals. We can wind these class-action suits down if we have enough eager bodies willing to work late and weekends. Every young lawyer knows you have to pay your dues before you make the big bucks."

"You make it sound so easy, Alexis. It isn't. I think I'm a hair away from Jack's asking for a divorce. It's my fault, too. I took on too much. I didn't think it all the way through, then Jack up and left the firm. I was counting on him. I couldn't stand in his way when he said he wanted out. We're a hot mess is what we are at the moment."

"Kind of like me and Joseph. I hear you, friend."

Their food arrived, and both women gobbled it down and asked for refills on the coffee.

"Beats that hard-boiled egg I eat every day at my desk," Alexis said, laughing in a way that indicated a total lack of amusement. "What do you need me to do, Nik?"

"Sit in on the meeting with me. Then, or before if you have time, call around, find me some good lawyers who are willing to come on board. The firm has a healthy bank account, so offer double what the other firms are paying, with a robust bonus when we wrap up these three class-action suits. And, of course, a generous expense account. I want them ready to go to work Monday morning. Make sure they understand we will be working through the holidays, with Christmas Day and New Year's Day our only days off, and make sure you tell them there will be travel involved. Lots of travel."

Nikki whipped out her company credit card and handed it to the waiter.

Ten minutes later, the two women were in the elevator, heading toward the offices of the Quinn Law Firm, which took up the eighth and ninth floors of the huge office building in Georgetown. Nikki looked down at her watch. She had forty-five minutes to get her ducks in a row. She stopped at reception to ask if HR was on standby and if security was ready to go. Betsy, the grandmotherly receptionist, assured Nikki that everything needed for the aftermath of the upcoming meeting was in place.

"I'll start on my calls. Meet you in the conference room at two-thirty." Alexis was a whirlwind as she moved down the hall to her office.

Nikki walked down the opposite hall to her own office. She stood in the open doorway, staring at what she called her space. She'd decorated it herself. It had comfortable furniture that stopped just short of being called cozy. She'd picked this particular room when she started her firm because of the real wood-burning fireplace. She did love curling up next to it in the winter, while she wrote briefs and studied depositions. There was greenery, not a lot, but what she had filling the corners was lush and healthy-looking. She tended the plants herself. She looked at her Christmas cactus, which was full of cherry-red blooms. She smiled. Isabelle had given her the plant years ago.

The walls were covered in bookshelves, holding books that she referred to on an almost daily basis. Her walnut desk was covered with files and folders. Her chair was a gift from Myra, who said it had once been her father's. She loved it, and the old cushions on it, which were almost flat from years of use.

The plank floor was covered with colorful hooked rugs she'd picked up at a long-ago flea market. The small fish tank, with beautiful tropical fish, was a gift from Jack five years ago on Christmas. All the fish had names: Teddy, Freddy, and Lettie. She had no idea, and neither did Jack, if the fish were boys or girls. All in all, a very pleasant workplace.

Nikki hung up her coat, stashed her handbag in one of the desk drawers, and walked over to the fireplace to poke at the dying fire. She added another log. Her favorite wing chair, covered in nubby chocolate-brown fabric, beckoned her. This was where she sat to take deep breaths and focus on troubling issues. Staring at the flames somehow seemed to calm her, gave her perspective, and managed to rejuvenate her. She hoped the magic worked today.

At twenty after two, Nikki stood up, smoothed down her jacket, and was nearly overcome by the realization that she'd screwed up her marriage, had overextended herself with the three class-action suits, and was indeed a mess. She took a deep breath, fought the tears burning her eyes, and made a vow to ask Jack for help.

Would he help her?

Countdown

Chapter 14

Jack Emery could hardly believe that he was actually having a real face-to-face conversation with his wife and that she had cooked breakfast for the two of them. He pinched himself to see if he was alive and really sitting here. Cyrus seemed to be of the same mind because the big dog was pacing the kitchen.

The pinch hurt. Yep, this was real time, so that had to mean the wild, unbelievable night of sex had been real, too. Well, he could feed off that for a whole week if he had to, but right now he needed to pay attention to what Nikki was saying. God, how he loved this woman. He knew right then, right that very minute, that if she had asked him to run through fire for her, he wouldn't hesitate to do so. If she asked him to climb to the moon, he'd start to fashion a ladder that would take him there. Nikki was his life, his love, the reason he got up in the morning.

"Tell me, Jack. Was I wrong to fire them? I snapped when they tried to push the blame onto you, that you left everyone in the lurch with double the work. That was just a side issue on their part. The three of them want a partnership. I told them early on that was never going to happen. For crying out loud, Jack, you're my husband, and

I never made you a partner. Nor did I make Alexis one, and she's like a sister to me. Say something, Jack."

"I didn't leave the firm in the lurch, Nik. You and I talked about my leaving, and you were okay with it. You're the boss. Those three women were just associates. I read their contracts. What they did was unprofessional, and none of them have any grounds to bring a suit against the firm. I'd go to the wall defending your firm on that one. They just wanted to put you over a barrel, so you'd cave and make them an offer because you were under the gun. You called their bluff. As Myra is so fond of saying, everything happens for a reason. And you know if you need me for anything, I'm here for you. Having said that, it sounds to me like you have the situation well in hand."

Nikki leaned across the table and reached for Jack's hand. Her eyes were misty with tears. "You know I love you more than life itself. I am so sorry, Jack, so very sorry that I . . ."

"Shhh," Jack said, placing his index finger against her lips. "You'd better get going, or you're going to be late. I'll clean up here, and let me say right now, those pancakes you made were better than any Charles made for us over the years. And before you can ask, no, there's nothing on Charles."

"I didn't think there was. Thanks, Jack, for being so understanding. I promise I will work overtime to make it up to you. With all the new people coming on board, I can actually see daylight ahead."

Jack walked his wife to the front door. He held her coat for her to slip into. Then he wrapped a warm scarf the color of a ripe melon around her neck.

Nikki turned and wrapped her husband in her arms. "Don't ever for one nanosecond doubt my love for you." Her tone was so serious, so fierce, Jack felt his insides start to shake.

Cyrus bounded into the room with such gusto the floor

shook. He started to bark, the sound high and shrill. "I get it, Cyrus." Nikki laughed. "We share him, okay?"

Cyrus let out a joyous woof and circled Nikki's legs until she bent over to give him what Cyrus considered his daily dose of loving.

And then she was gone.

Cyrus sat on his haunches, panting, as he looked at his master to see what was coming next. "I think we're back on track, buddy. If not, we're on the way. It won't be the end of the world if you have to sleep on the floor. You take up half the bed, you know that, right?"

Cyrus ignored him as he ran to the kitchen. If he pouted, he knew that Jack would let him lick the breakfast plates. And he'd spotted the half slice of bacon Nikki had left on her plate. For him. She always left a half slice just for him.

The minute he licked the breakfast plates clean, Cyrus ran into the family room to rummage through his basket of treasures for one to take to work. He heard Jack shouting from the kitchen, "Just one, Cyrus, not the whole damn basket."

Jack looked around to make sure the kitchen was tidy before he turned off the lights. He checked the back door to be sure that the storm door was locked and the dead bolt in place. All he had to do was put on his jacket, set the alarm, and he and Cyrus were good to go. Oops, he'd forgotten to turn down the thermostat. He did that and, as an added precaution, checked to make sure the glass doors on the fireplace were closed, too, so that no dying embers would spark outward. Now, they were ready to leave.

Jack stood on the front stoop as he looked up and down the street for his tail. He didn't see anything that looked suspicious, but he knew he or she was out there just waiting for him to get into his car.

A light dusting of snow had fallen during the night, and the day was overcast, typical December weather. As he let his gaze travel up and down the street, he noticed Christmas lights, garlands, and Christmas wreaths on several doors—a reminder that he needed to do some decorating himself. He made a mental note to call Yoko to order his tree and wreath. He hoped the Christmas spirit would invade his being sometime soon.

Twenty minutes later, given the heavy traffic, Jack waited for a break in the flow of cars, so he could make a left turn into the alley that would take him to the back door of the BOLO Building. He stopped short when he saw a gaggle of Asian men jabbering and pointing to him as they waved their arms every which way.

Jack lowered the window, and before he could ask what was going on, a little man with a snow-white beard said, "Harry sent us. Back up, park someplace else today. You pay half now. Okay?"

"Huh?" was all Jack could think of to say. Cyrus weighed in, howling his displeasure. The little man raised one finger and stared at Cyrus, who suddenly went silent. Jack thought the wise thing to do would be to follow instructions. As he did so he was texting Harry, who texted back: PAY HIM HALF NOW.

Jack parked at the Bagel Emporium, then crossed the street. His tail was going to be hard-pressed to find a parking spot. The thought pleased Jack as he walked along with Cyrus, who was clutching his tattered duck, which had only one leg and half a beak.

Back in the alley, Jack motioned for the little man to follow him. Inside, he asked him what he was doing for Harry.

"Iron gate. With electricity. Secret stuff. Pay half now."

"Yeah, yeah, I get the pay now, but what about the other end of the alley?"

"We do that, too. Shop owner know you pay. They okay with iron gate."

Cyrus looked like he was about to protest until the little man stared him down and pointed his finger at him.

Jack wrote out the check and winced at the amount but kept his cool. He escorted the man to the door, Cyrus beside him, the tattered duck clutched between his teeth. The little man bent low and whispered something in Cyrus's ear. The duck fell to the floor, and, a second later, Cyrus had his two front legs wrapped around the little man in a dog-human hug. The man smiled, patted him on the head, and left.

"What the hell, Cyrus! I don't even know that guy, and you're hugging him! For all we know, he could be a terrorist. You should be ashamed," Jack ranted.

Cyrus looked up at Jack as much as to say, *do you really think Harry would send a terrorist to ask for a check?* Realizing the absurdity of his statement, Jack bellowed, "All right, all right, I'm going to give you that one," as he stomped his way into the kitchen, his cell phone in hand.

While the coffee dripped into the oversized pot, Jack listened to Harry explain that he thought it was imperative to secure the back end of the premises. He went on to say he'd spoken to the two shop owners who shared the alley space, and they, too, liked the idea of the electronic gate as long as they didn't have to pay for it. He went on to say the work would be completed by the end of the day. Jack huffed and puffed, muttering something or other about how advance warning would have been nice. Harry hung up on him in midsentence. Harry was such a card.

Jack carried his coffee back to his office. He passed Abner's room and saw that the red light was shining over the door, which meant Abner was hard at work. He walked right on by without missing a step. In all likelihood, Abner had spent the night here, probably the last few nights if he was any judge of his work ethic. When Abner had a mission, he had a mission, and he worked around the clock.

It was all Jack could do not to burst out laughing when he saw Cyrus's battered duck on the seat of his chair— Cyrus's apology for making friends with the little man. Jack set his coffee down on his desk, dropped to his haunches, and tussled with Cyrus to show there were no hard feelings. A treat was all it took for Cyrus, who snatched it and his duck, to race to the door to greet whoever it was that was entering the building. Jack grinned when he heard Dennis West greeting Cyrus with a routine he had established that made Cyrus go nuts barking.

Dennis, in one long burst of monologue, announced, "Ted and Espinosa are coming separately because Maggie had them chasing something down, and wow, what a neat idea to put those gates up, and the price isn't all that bad— not that I know anything about wrought iron, but still . . . And the other owners are in agreement, and I have some news to report. Do ya want to hear it verbally, or do you want a written report? And you know what else, I didn't have a tail coming here. I checked, so I guess we threw them for a loop when I split off from Ted and Espinosa. What time did Abner get here?" Then Dennis wound down like a pricked balloon.

Jack blinked. "And you know all of this . . . how?"

"I asked. The rest is observation. Plus I saw your car parked at the Bagel Emporium. Remember that I'm an investigative reporter. You know what else—I lost seven pounds on that diet Harry put me on. You're lookin' good this morning, Jack. Guess you got a good night's sleep. You were really looking peaked last week. That's what my mother used to say to me when I was getting ready to get sick," he mumbled as he started pulling papers and scraps of paper out of his backpack. "If you're not too awfully busy, do you think you could talk to me about something on a personal level?"

This kid was going to drive him nuts. "Yeah, I did get a good night's sleep. Sorry you thought I was looking . . . peaked. I have a few extra minutes. What do you want to do first, explain all those papers or the personal stuff?"

"Let's get the personal stuff out of the way so we can

really concentrate on what I'm going to share and show you. Okay, here's my problem," Dennis said, taking a deep breath. Jack steeled himself for what was to come. Cyrus appeared out of nowhere and took up a position next to Jack. He, too, was all ears.

"With this new weight loss and working out every night with Harry, I was thinking maybe I should finally make a move on this girl at the office because . . ."

Jack held up his hand for Dennis to stop. "Stop right there. You said girl. A girl to my mind is a sixteen- or seventeen-year-old. Girls giggle, chase boys, flirt, play tennis, tattle and wear ribbons in their hair and spritz way too much perfume on their persons. A young lady or a young woman is something totally different from a *girl*. Now, which is it?"

"Wow, Jack! I never thought of it like that. The guys are right; you do know everything there is to know about women. Okay, okay, she's a young woman, and she dresses like a lady. I have a thing for her, but I get tongue-tied when I'm around her and I . . . I *blush*. I hate that I blush, and sometimes I stammer. She makes me hot all over.

"But the worst part of it is I think she has the hots for Ted. I'm not sure about that, though. I have myself halfway convinced that she flirts with him to make me jealous. I'm probably delusional. We always eat lunch together, and she manages to stop by my desk a few times each day. Sometimes she brings me a Nehi orange soda. But that could be wishful thinking on my part, and she's just doing it because Ted sits next to me.

"I'm thinking when I take off the other fifteen pounds Harry said I had to lose, I'd make my move. Or maybe I should wait till I get a brown belt, which will probably be when I'm seventy, by which time I won't even care. Women like that a man knows all those wild moves, Harry said. What do you think, Jack, what should I do?"

Oh shit was what Jack thought. Jack cleared his throat. "Um, Dennis, have you had . . . you know, any relationships?"

"Are you asking me if I've ever had sex? Well, yeah, but it was pretty much a disaster, and we both went running in opposite directions. You know, too quick, too fast, not enough . . . oh, hell, you know what I'm talking about. And I wasn't drinking either. Neither was she. It was . . . it was . . . *experimental.*"

I do not need this right now. I absolutely do not need this right now. I will not need this tomorrow or the day after tomorrow either, Jack thought. He grappled with something to say that would come out sounding halfway right or what Dennis wanted to hear.

"Okay, listen up. Let's go with the assumption that the young lady is indeed flirting with you and hopes to perhaps take it to the next level. As it stands now, she sees that you have some weight to lose so obviously that is not an issue for her. If I were you, I'd play it cool, lose the weight, prevail with Harry, *then* make your move. You'll buy yourself some cool duds, maybe pierce your ear, get a kick-ass haircut, spring for one of those muscle cars, and see what happens. It's a goal, Dennis, shoot for it. That's another way of your knowing if she likes you as a person or the new improved version. By the way, does she know how rich you are?"

A look of awe spread across Dennis's face. "My God, they were all so right; you do know everything there is to know about women. This is the proof. You should write a book on all that you know. I bet it would be a best-seller. Okay, I'll do what you say. No, she doesn't know I'm rich. At least, I don't think so. I don't talk about it and told the guys not to mention anything. I don't think Maggie would blab it, but you never know about Maggie. Jeez, Jack, thanks. How can I repay you?"

"No thanks necessary, kid. Glad to help. Now, show me what you've got."

Chapter 15

Dennis heaved a mighty sigh as he struggled to put all the papers he'd taken from his backpack into some kind of order. "Over the weekend, I went out to SE Washington, and that's not a place I want to go again; but I will, of course. The gangs are . . . everywhere. One of the leaders accosted me, and I told him why I was there. That I was an investigative reporter, and I was trying to get the goods on the landlord for the people living in the buildings he owned. The leader was no dummy. He asked to see my credentials and suggested I also look into the management company that is supposed to take care of the buildings. Once we had a rapport going, he gave the okay to talk to some of the tenants. The tenants that are within his *gangdom*, if there is such a word. He said he'd pass the word to the other leaders if they wanted to . . . ah . . . come on board. He said he'd let me know and said he'd pave the way for a sit-down meeting.

"Here's the thing, Jack. They told me they would help but only if I got the tenants some heat. It was the weekend, there was nothing I could do but wait for this morning. I was at the power company when they opened, and I laid down some serious money to pay for some heating. They assured me there would be heat by noon provided the units were in working order. They promised to send crews out there to work on the units. I laid down some more money to pay for new units if need be, parts, fuel, etc. Luther, the guy I talked to . . . ah . . . offered his gang's help. I said I'd call on him if I needed him.

"Here's the thing, Jack, yeah, these are punks, but they take care of their own the best way they can. There are quite a few old people living in those rat traps. These guys steal for them. Luther admitted it. Like he said, they tried the system, and it doesn't work for people like them, so they took matters into their own hands."

Jack looked at his watch. It was quarter of eleven. "Have you spoken to Luther this morning?"

"Before I came here. He said the neighborhood is buzzing with all kinds of contractors, electricians, and the management-company spokesperson, who he himself personally ran off. The guy's name is Lionel Marks, and he owns District Management. He was mouthing off about trespassing, illegal installations, and a bunch of other stuff. He said he was coming back with a lawyer and the police. I don't know whether or not that was bravado, but the guy ended up walking away because when he wasn't looking, the gang members jacked up his car, a fancy Mercedes, and stripped it down, leaving nothing but the shell. Short of a SWAT team, few police, I'm told, ever venture out there in what the gangs call Never Land. They'll sell the parts to some chop shop, take the money, and disburse it through the section they control. You know, warm clothes for the kids, food for the old people, and they pay for cell phones for them, too, in case of an emergency. At first glance, they, the gang members, look kind of fierce, but they're just kids underneath, and they're fighting the only way they know how. It's the slums, man. They don't see a way out from where they're standing. We can help, Jack."

"I think you made a hell of a start this morning, kid.

That's a good thing you did. Money talks, and I'm glad you have a boatload of it. So what's our next move here?"

Dennis glanced at the clock on Jack's wall. "I gave Luther my number and yours. Since he hasn't called either one of us, I'm thinking things are progressing. Do you want to take a ride out there? It wouldn't hurt for you to see it all for yourself."

"Sure, why not. Let me check with the guys, and I'll be ready in ten minutes. What are you driving?"

"The *Post* van. Espinosa took his car when he left with Ted. You can bring Cyrus if you want."

"I want," Jack said through clenched teeth. "So what do you think, young Dennis?"

"I think I have to admire their fight for survival. Yeah, the gangs are wrong, but they don't have a way out. You play the hand you're dealt. Who's to say you or I wouldn't do the same thing if we walked in their shoes. Oh, one other thing, they make sure the little kids get to school and that they have all the supplies they need. Luther told me there is one little boy who can play the piano so well it makes tears come to your eyes. They take him for lessons in the hope he'll be able to get out of there someday. I have no clue where they get the money for the lessons, but they get it. I was not about to ask, either. There's another little girl who needs some medical help, and they're working on that. Good and bad in everything, Jack."

"Well damn," was all Jack could think of to say. "Okay, I'm ready. You're driving, I assume."

"I am driving," Dennis said curtly.

Luther Jones was a tall, gangly young kid. If he was seventeen, he was old. He greeted Dennis like a long-lost brother, and said, "Your wheels are safe. Nice dog, mister. I love dogs. My granny has a cat so's to keep her warm.

We make sure he gets plenty to eat, so he don't go all skinny on us.

"Dennis, my brother, I don't know what kind of magic you worked, but lookie here at all these fine people out here to help us. We getting new furnaces and hot-water heaters, and they are telling us that by suppertime my street is going to be warm and cozy. Unless Mr. Lionel Marks shows up with the cops to strip everything outta here."

"That won't happen," Jack said. Cyrus barked his approval as he sniffed Luther's leg. He held up his paw to shake hands. Jack decided right then and there that Luther was A-okay.

"He smells my granny's cat on me. Fool animal likes to sit on my lap when he ain't sitting on Granny's lap. She calls him Loopy because he loves Fruit Loops."

"Luther, we need to speak with the family that lost their children last winter. Can you arrange a meeting?"

"I wish I could, but I can't. They moved in April, couldn't stay here any longer. A cousin drove up from Miami and took them away from here."

"Do you know how we can get in touch? We want to make things right for them. As well as the rest of your neighbors."

"I'll ask around. It's not like we have cell phones growing out our ears around here. In this neighborhood, there's but five of them. Four for the old folks, and they share among themselves, and I have one. I'll see what I can find out."

Dennis was hopping from one foot to the other to ward off the cold. "So, what else can we do for you before we leave?"

"Man, I have to wonder what planet you dropped from. Nobody has ever been this good to us. Why? What are you getting out of this?"

"Not a damn thing. We just want to help. Now, what else do you need?"

"Is the dude serious?" Luther asked Jack directly.

"He's serious," Jack said solemnly.

"Well, then okay. We could do with some real good food. You know, for suppertime, when we're all warm and cozy. There's a market over there on the avenue. I can have two of my guys go with you to shop if you're sure you want to do that."

"Round them up and let's go. We can pack a lot of stuff in the van."

Luther stood back and watched the van disappear from view. He scratched his head as he tried to figure out what had just happened. He pointed to three of his members and told them to spread the word: food was coming. Good food.

Two hours later, the van showed up just as Ted and Espinosa pulled to the curb. "Dennis sent us," Ted said as he exited Espinosa's SUV. We're here to help. We work at the *Post* with Dennis."

Luther scratched his head again. "Okay. Your car is safe."

"Glad to hear it since it isn't paid for yet," Espinosa muttered.

Ted looked at Luther, uncertain how he should say what he wanted to say. In the end, he just blurted it out. "How do you guys feel about being on the front page of the *Post* tomorrow morning?"

Luther pondered the question for several moments. "Who do you mean when you say, you guys?"

"You, your . . . ah club members, the tenants—anyone who wants to talk to us."

"I don't see a problem. You gonna talk to Mr. Lionel Marks?"

"We'll call him, and if he cares to comment, we'll print it. I'm thinking he won't want to do that because he'll be way too busy trying to salvage his cutthroat company."

Dennis blew the horn on the van. The back doors flew open as the call went up and down the street for everyone to assemble.

It only took an hour to disburse the food and another two hours for Ted and Espinosa to interview anyone who wanted to talk. He did a separate interview with the young pianist and the little girl in need of medical help. He knew within twenty-four hours both children's futures would be secure because if there was one thing the *Post* was good at, it was getting people to help other people. Not to mention that one of Espinosa's pictures was worth a thousand words.

Maggie Spritzer gaped and gawked as Ted fed her the story that would be the headline for the morning paper. She could smell a Pulitzer for Ted and Dennis. She was so jealous, she wanted to chew nails and spit rust.

Chapter 16

Lionel Marks, the owner of District Management LLC, glared at the morning edition of the *Post* as he watched e-mail after e-mail ping to life on his computer. Just minutes ago he'd slammed into his plush offices and bellowed to his secretary to hold all his calls and to lock the office doors. He'd made a stupid mistake coming into the office, one he now regretted.

The staff, which numbered nine altogether, looked at one another and knew instinctively to keep their heads down and do as instructed. The boss was in an uproar. Rightly so, they all thought smugly. Lionel Marks was not a beloved boss—he was a hated boss, but he paid well, and his benefits package was for the most part worth the aggravation.

Marks looked at the stack of pink message slips, his insides crunching into a tight knot. Landlords—the most hated people on earth next to the people who managed the landlords' properties—were right up there with used-car salesmen and insurance agents, and their agents, who were responsible for keeping their names out of the public eye. Today's edition of the *Post* stared up at him like a large, square, benevolent eye.

Marks let his thoughts go to his beloved Mercedes, which

was nothing but a shell sitting at the curb in SE Washington. Damn scavengers. Should he report it or suck up the loss? Well, he had another Mercedes, so it really didn't matter all that much in the scheme of things. Then again, it did matter. He looked down at the printed page of the newspaper, which had a full frontal shot of himself, his lips drawn back in a snarl. Christ! He looked like a rabid dog.

As Marks read the article under his picture, he had to marvel at how the reporters had gathered so much information in such a short period of time; unless, of course, they had this all planned and were just waiting to spring a trap on him. His gut told him that this was just the tip of the iceberg. He tore his eyes away and started to finger through the stack of pink message slips. Nine from Fiona Sandford. Who else. Like her politician husband could be bothered even to comment on ownership of all his properties in SE Washington. Keep the secret at all costs. It's all about the P&L sheets. "Bastard!" He wondered how long it would be before all the alphabet agencies in town started crawling up his ass. Days, he decided if those two reporters had anything to do with it. He could see this being front-page fodder for weeks to come. And right before Christmas, too, when news was usually slow here in the nation's capital. He'd get a full-court press for sure.

Marks turned on the TV and watched in horror as the local station showed its viewers all the activity going on in the SE. He saw his car and winced. He turned up the volume and listened to a shivering reporter as she tried to keep the hair out of her eyes. "All this," she said, waving her arms to indicate the power-company trucks, water-company trucks, civilian contractors, three different exterminating companies, and people clotting the streets, "is the result of an unknown benefactor who has pledged to give the people living here a decent home. The benefactor, who chooses to remain anonymous at this time, has vowed to go after the slum landlords and the management company that has allowed these deplorable conditions to exist. If you all remember, it was exactly a year ago when three children died here on this same street. Until today . . ."

Sick to his stomach, Marks turned off the TV and slumped back in his chair. No way in hell was this going to go away. He picked up the phone and dialed Fiona Sandford's private, unlisted number. She snarled a greeting after only one ring. "What do you have to say for yourself, Lionel?"

Marks bolted upright in his special ergonomic chair. There was plenty he wanted to say to the bitch talking to him and to her highfalutin lieutenant governor husband. He took a deep breath and marveled at how steady he felt, how much in control of himself. "I think you should be more worried about what you and your husband are going to say, not me. I'm just a hired gun following orders, so you and your husband can remain lily-white. I'm rather busy right now, so I'm sure you can understand if I cut this conversation short. So, if you have nothing else to say to me, I'm hanging up. Oh, wait just one minute. If I'm forced to, I *will* give you up. You do realize that, don't you?" Whatever retort was hanging off Fiona Sandford's collagen-enhanced lips went unsaid because Marks broke the connection. She'd call back—she always did—because she was relentless.

A knock sounded softly, hesitant. "What?" Marks bellowed.

His secretary, a dumb blonde if there ever was one, in his opinion, poked her head in the door and announced that three different reporters were in the lobby asking for comments, and no, none of the three were from the *Post*. "Tell them I have no comment at this time and do not bother me again. If you do, you're on the unemployment line." The door made no sound when it closed.

A monster headache was brewing behind Lionel Marks's eyes. He knew what he was experiencing was the beginning of the end. Time to pack up and head for the hills. In his case, Hong Kong, where he could get lost among the millions of people who lived there. He owned multiple properties in the New Territories, where he could hide out for the rest of his life if need be. He just wasn't sure he could live in that culture. Still, when he'd made his plans for a getaway years ago, he'd convinced himself it would work. If it didn't, then he'd go to Plan B, which was to relocate to Dubai. Now that the time was here, suddenly he wasn't so sure. Especially if reporters were going to start to dog him.

Marks thought about his wife then and his three children, who were grown and off on their own for the most part. He gave little thought to his four grandchildren. He wouldn't miss any of them. They, on the other hand, needed his money to keep up their lifestyles, especially his wife, who thought money grew on trees. If he left, he'd just simply walk away, no baggage, and head for the airport. He wouldn't look back, either. But he was going to need a foolproof disguise if any of it was to happen. He had long ago invested in an alias, complete with a full set of credentials in case a hasty departure was called for. His long, manicured fingers drummed the top of his shiny desk. Christmas. Maybe he could hold out, bluff it through till after the holidays to try to keep things as normal as possible. Then again, maybe he should start putting his exit plans into gear right now.

Marks still kept an old-fashioned Rolodex on his desk. He fingered the cards, mentally cataloging how much money he made a year off each client. If even one of them thought they could make him their scapegoat, he'd throw their sorry asses under the bus so fast, they wouldn't know what hit them.

Time, he thought, to bring out his Rosetta Stone to brush up on his Chinese.

While Lionel Marks was rummaging for his Rosetta Stone disks, Annie de Silva was showing that morning's edition of the *Post* to Myra. "The kids did a great job on the article, don't you think, Myra? I see Ted and Dennis playing this out for a Pulitzer, and that's a plus for the paper. I saw on the news this morning that the tenants in the article have an anonymous benefactor. I have to assume it's young Dennis, and that's a good thing from where I'm standing. I just love it when right wins out. Maggie is rather upset that Ted has moved on and is doing his own thing. She called me last night, I think in the hopes that I would reel him in so that she could control what he does. I hated to do it, Myra, but I had to tell her it was hands off where he is concerned because I know that if she baits him too much, he'll up and leave. And if he goes, so will Joseph and Dennis. I can't have that. Tell me what you think. Was I wrong?"

"Good heavens no, Annie. You are the boss. Sometimes, you seem to forget that. Ted is exemplary, and so is Dennis. I've yet to meet a photographer who can hold a candle to Joseph. The paper would falter without them. Maggie has to learn to put her personal feelings aside. Although I do understand what she is going through. You know what they say, business is business, and there is no room for personal vendettas."

Annie got up to pour more coffee in their cups. "She's also upset that the private detectives have come up with nothing, which is rather strange in itself."

Annie eyed the long, narrow length of yarn Myra was working on. "Isn't it time to give that up?" she said, pointing to the pile of messy yarn at Myra's feet.

"Are you serious, Annie? If I did that, how would my friend Claudeen out in Arizona—your friend, too, I might remind you—who spent hours on Skype teaching me how to knit, feel. I can't just quit. I'm getting better, and you know it. I would never want her to think I wasn't trying. I know I'll never be able to knit like she does for the terminally ill at hospice. She loves that yarn ministry we put together. My goal is to help out as soon as I get good enough.

"Hopefully, sooner or later, I'll improve. We need to recruit more knitters for the ministry. When I think about all those gorgeous afghans Claudeen makes for terminally ill patients, I get all choked up. She's a really good person, as you know. Swear to me, Annie, that you won't tell her what a messy knitter I am. It would break her heart."

"I'm not going to tell her. Why don't you tie it off or whatever you have to do to finish it and let the dogs lie on it by the fire?"

Myra sighed as she packed up her knitting. "I tried that, but they get their nails caught in the stitches because they're too loose or something. Let's not talk about this anymore, all right?"

"What do you want to talk about, Myra? Christmas?"

Myra let loose with another long sigh. "It is fast approaching. We could get in the car and drive to Yoko's nursery and pick up the Christmas wreaths that she's holding for us. I'm not sure anyone will be joining us this year, and I guess that's why I didn't really make any plans for a party or a get-together. It might be just you and me. How sad is that, my friend? And we have to help Nellie with Elias. We promised. It's just one Christmas, Annie. Elias has to come first."

"I haven't heard from anyone in quite a while; well, there was that disastrous luncheon, but no one has called to check in. It's like we're forgotten. I don't like the feeling, Myra. You're absolutely right about Nellie and Elias—they have to come first. Nellie didn't say it out loud, but I don't believe she thinks that Elias will be around for another Christmas."

Myra fingered her pearls, which adorned her neck, her lifeline to life. "I don't either, but there's not much we can do about that. I suppose we could go to Vegas, so you can stir up some trouble. But even that has lost its allure."

"Myra, look at me. What's your feeling on our going to the FBI and asking them to initiate a search for Charles? I'll even throw Fergus into the mix if we can make it work for us. The papers have been full lately about Jack Sparrow taking over the directorship of the Bureau. Of course, that would have to wait till January if he takes office, which I'm sure will come to pass. That would still mean from now to then, we are sitting here doing absolutely nothing."

"Okay, we'll think about it. Get dressed, and let's go to see Yoko. She might have some kind of news. We could even pop in at Nikki's firm to see how she and Alexis are doing. What do you say?"

"I say let's go. I'm driving because I want to get us there today, not tonight, the way you drive."

"You're such a critic, Annie, but I love you anyway."

Chapter 17

Jack Emery, his mood buoyant after his patch-up session with his wife, was staring off into space. They were out of the woods, he was sure of it. Nikki had been so contrite, so loving, so willing to make amends for the months of misery she'd caused him. Life was looking better than it had in months. And soon it would get even better once his little group embarked on young Dennis's plan. Win-win.

Cyrus heaved himself up and raced from the office. Jack looked at the clock on the wall. He'd called a meeting late last night, sending out texts to the guys to report in no later than ten. It sounded from where he was sitting that the guys had all arrived at the same time. He knew that Abner was already here since he'd noticed the red light over the computer door when he'd come in. Cyrus had verified it by sniffing the door and offering up a bark of agreement.

Dennis's exuberance was infectious as he slapped down six copies of the *Post*. Jack whistled when he scanned the article. Abner, who had exited his lair, grinned from ear to ear. "They are toast! By they I mean Sandford and Marks. I've been hacking for forty-eight hours, and it's mind-boggling what I came up with and downright scary the lengths those two have gone to attempting to hide their assets. But I found them!"

Cyrus barked shrilly, then threw his head back and howled. He loved it when his friends got excited; he would bark and they'd all give him a treat to show their appreciation. Today was no exception. One by one, the guys handed out the treats they now knew to carry with them. Cyrus was officially one of them and in excellent standing.

"Are we gonna love your findings?" Espinosa asked.

"Absolutely. Stealing it is another matter entirely," Abner said happily. "Here's the thing: Lionel Marks was accessing some of his accounts while I was in full hack mode, and the dumb schmuck didn't even know it. I'm thinking I need to do something to . . . ah . . . maybe freeze his monies. I'm also thinking he might be thinking about a hasty exit sometime soon."

Dennis's eyes grew round. "You can do that?"

"Oh, yeah," Abner drawled.

"But what if you get caught? That's illegal," Dennis said in a jittery voice.

"Rule Number 3, kid," Espinosa said.

"What's Rule Number 3?"

"Same as Rule Number 2," Ted said.

Dennis was getting more jittery by the moment. "What's Rule Number 2?"

"Same as Rule Number 1," Harry snapped.

"And what's that?" Dennis demanded, his face beet red.

"Rule Number 1 is the same as Rule Number 2 and Rule Number 3. We do whatever it takes. End. Fini. ¿Comprende?"

"Okay, got it. Whatever it takes. Okay. Okay."

"Can we move on here now?" Ted asked. "I want to know about Sandford."

"The guy is too cocky in my opinion even to think he could be tied to the real estate in SE. You want me to knock him down a peg or two?"

"Not yet, Abner. I think we should keep our eye on

Marks. Ted, you're going to continue this daily, right, make a series out of it?"

"You bet. I can feel a Pulitzer all the way down my spine. Dennis and I have our next installment about ready to go. We just need to tweak it. What's with this meeting anyway?"

"Some assignments. Ted, I want you and Espinosa to go to Middleburg and talk to Mrs. Sandford. I saw in the home style section yesterday that she left their government house to get her farmhouse ready for the holidays. She always wins some kind of prize for her decorations according to the local paper in Middleburg. I want you to take a lot of pictures and try to come up with our snatch and grab when the time is right. We need to get this set up, start a countdown so we wind it up by Christmas. We need to have a clear slate come January 2, so we can take on Nikki's class-action cases. You okay with that, Ted?"

"What about me?" Dennis howled.

"You, my friend, are going back to SE and make more friends. Convince Luther to get the other gang leaders to come into the fold. I want you to assure all those tenants that their lives are going to take on a whole new meaning starting right now. We need order, not chaos. Delegate but oversee. Talk to the pastor at the church where they worship. He's going to be your best ally. I know this is going to sound frivolous, but I want you to arrange for a bang-up Christmas, with toys for the kids, Christmas trees for everyone, those red Christmas flowers, whatever they're called, for the pastor's church, the whole ball of wax. Spare no expense. If Abner is right, we need to put some of Sandford and Marks's money to good use before we steal it. I'm sure the women will be more than happy to volunteer."

"Okay," Dennis said agreeably.

"Harry, you want to volunteer for anything, or do you need to get back to the dojo?"

Harry laughed. "My midshipmen are due at noon, so no, I really don't have any free time today. You need me tonight, I'm all yours. I stopped by the nursery just to throw Suliman for a loop, and guess who was there? Myra and Annie. We waved, but that was it."

"Is this your 'pink day' for the midshipmen?" Jack grinned.

"Uh-huh. Call me if you need me."

"What are you going to do, Jack?" Abner asked.

"Careful with your tails today, guys. Me, I'm going to Lionel Marks's office and pretend to be a property owner who wants to rent out a whole block of investment condominiums. I need to take this guy's measure."

Dennis looked at Jack, his eyes full of questions. "What about your tail? Do you want him to know where you're going? What about Ted and Espinosa? I understand they can follow me because it's already out there and in the paper. Do we want them to know what we're doing and where we're going? They might not figure it out, but when they report to Maggie, she will for sure."

"I'll lose him, no problem." Jack looked at Ted.

"We'll go back to the paper and sign out a vehicle from the motor pool. Dennis can take the van. It's doable."

"Well, now that we have it settled, let's hit the road," Jack said, packing up his briefcase. "Abner, are you staying?"

"I am. My tail must be bored out of his mind. I haven't left this building in seventy-two hours. Can't imagine what his report reads."

"Check in every couple of hours," Jack reminded everyone. The guys nodded and left until it was just Jack, Abner, and Cyrus. Abner moved off, Jack calling over his shoulder to remind him to water the stupid banana tree. Cyrus barked long and loud to show what he thought of the stupid banana tree that needed watering.

* * *

If Maggie had been anywhere else but behind her desk with the half glass wall that made her visible to the reporters seated at their desks and cubbies, she would have pitched a fit and stomped on the investigative reports she was reading. She might as well have been reading a child's textbook. There was nothing in any of the reports. Zip. Nada. Zilch. How was it possible that six grown men hadn't done anything out of the ordinary in three days? With the exception of the exposé in SE Washington. How?

Maggie scanned the reports again, hoping she'd find something she'd missed the other three times she'd read through them line by line, word by word. Jack Emery got a haircut. Big deal. Showed no signs he was aware of being followed. Harry Wong beats to his own drummer, is in another world. Picks up daughter, goes home, stops by nursery to see wife, goes back to dojo. Dennis, Ted, and Espinosa were all linked into one report. It was a detailed one about the tenants and what had gone down in SE Washington. Well, she already knew that. What she didn't know then but knew now was that Dennis had stopped at a Cole Haan store and bought a pricey pair of snow boots. She also now knew they had dined the previous night on Japanese hibachi in Crystal City. Another big deal.

Abner Tookus was a different story simply because there was no story. He'd entered the BOLO Building and never left. Maggie wrinkled her nose. Seventy-two hours inside one building. Knowing Abner, that had to mean he was working on something so red-hot he couldn't leave. Still, seventy-two hours was a lot of time not to at least stick your nose outside the door. No food deliveries were detected. The bottom line read: "Target possibly dead inside." Maggie whooped in disgust.

Maggie craned her neck to look around her desk to see if her office door was closed. It was. She picked up the phone and started calling the detectives one by one. She started with Allison Murdock, Ted, Espinosa, and Dennis's tail. She wanted to scream when she heard the detective say Ted and Espinosa were inside the *Post* building, and Dennis had left in the van. A second-tier newbie was following Dennis, and it appeared he was en route to SE Washington. Alone.

"So, what you're telling me is you lost Ted and Espinosa. I thought you were a professional," Maggie shrilled.

"No, ma'am, that's not what I'm saying. What I am telling you is that Mr. Robinson and Mr. Espinosa are inside the *Post* building. They did not leave is what I'm telling you. I am sitting in the garage, and neither one of their personal vehicles has moved. They are *inside* the building."

Maggie gritted her teeth. "No, they are not here. What they did was go to the motor pool, sign out another car, and leave. You allowed that to happen. Get your butt over to the motor pool and see what car they signed out. Not that it's going to do us any good now. When they bring it back, find out how many miles they traveled. That's all logged in when you sign out one of the *Post*'s vehicles. Are you getting it now, Miss Murdock? They made you! They know you've been following them, and they evaded you. Now do something!" she screamed.

Next, she called Mike Suliman, Harry's tail, and asked for an update.

"He's at the dojo, Miss Spritzer. A busload of midshipmen from Annapolis just arrived, so I guess he has a class. He is inside." Maggie's comment was to stay on him.

Her next call was to Jack Emery's tail, an older man named Clyde Evers. He sounded frazzled. "You lost him, didn't you?" Maggie said through clenched teeth.

"Yes, ma'am, I did. It was traffic. I don't think he knows he's being followed. In fact, I'm almost sure of it. I had to pull over for a fire engine, the light turned red for me, but he went through on the yellow and was gone. He was at the BOLO Building for about an hour, then left with a big old dog. For whatever this is worth, there is a group of Asian men installing a rather high-tech iron fence at the entrance and exit to the alley. Two other shopkeepers will be using it along with the tenants of the BOLO Building. The only thing I can do now is go back to the BOLO Building and stake it out."

Maggie was seething. She made no comment as she broke the connection. She tried to calm herself down by taking deep breaths before she called Neil Parsons, the tail assigned to Abner Tookus.

Parsons sounded bored when he clicked on his cell phone. "No sign of activity, Miss Spritzer. I think the man's dead inside. The building has been under surveillance for the last seventy-two hours, and he has not left the premises. Nor have there been any food deliveries, strangers visiting, nothing. It's quiet. Workmen are installing what looks like an iron gate at the entrance and at the exit to the alley. Five other males appeared and stayed for about an hour, then left separately. Check with the other operatives on their whereabouts."

Maggie bit down on her lower lip. "Stay on it and let me know when he leaves, and I can guarantee you that Mr. Tookus is not dead. There is a kitchen in the building as well as a shower. I'm sure there is a sofa or a cot also. Don't let him out of your sight if he leaves."

"Yes, ma'am."

They know. Sure as I'm sitting here in my office, those guys know they have tails on them. "I know it, I know it, I know it!" Maggie muttered over and over to herself. She banged on her desktop, but all that produced was a pain in her hand that made her bite her tongue to keep from crying out. "Now what do I do?"

Chapter 18

Ted Robinson looked at the beat-up car he would be driving to Middleburg. No GPS. Crank windows. He hoped the heater worked. He looked at Espinosa and shrugged. "Hey, it has wheels and will get us there. At least I hope so. It's only forty-five miles or so to Middleburg. With luck, we should make it in about an hour. Punch it in on that supersmart phone of yours and just read me the directions. Keep an eye out to make sure we really did shake our tail."

Ted sailed up the ramp and roared out of the garage, stunned at the power under the hood of the car he was driving. As far as he could tell, no one was following him. He paid attention to traffic while he listened to Espinosa fire off directions for fifteen minutes before he settled down for the stretch of highway that would take him to the Sandford family farm.

"What's our plan, Ted? Do we even have a plan?"

Ted grinned. "Sort of. More or less. Key in the local newspapers in Middleburg. I think it's the *Middleburg Life* that caters to the Sandfords and their Christmas decorations. Mrs. Sandford wins every year. I'm thinking we can bluff our way through something there. We might have to convince Maggie to let us run some fluff pieces to make it legit. We might need to be extra charming, so work on that, Espinosa."

Espinosa grunted something that sounded like *I'm always charming*, to which Ted muttered something that sounded like, in your dreams.

They rode in silence for a few moments, Ted's eyes on the road and on his rearview mirror, Espinosa's eyes on the screen of his smartphone.

"Two weeks till Christmas! Hard to believe. Are you planning on buying Alexis a Christmas present?"

Espinosa stopped what he was doing and looked over at Ted. "Is that a trick question? She dumped me. Why would I buy her a present? Are you buying Maggie one?" he asked snidely.

"As a matter of fact, I am. I'm buying her a banana tree. What do you think of *that*?"

"I think you're nuts is what I think. At this time last year, we were already invited out to Myra's for Christmas. I didn't get an invitation or a call, did you?"

"Nope. I'm thinking it's just going to be me, you, and Minnie and Mickey this year," Ted said, referring to his two cats. "I'll cook if you want to come over. I'm going to pick up my Christmas tree this weekend. Want to help me decorate it on Sunday?"

"Sure. Okay, here we go, five miles as the crow flies, you make a right on Stallion Road, you follow that for two miles, then that should take us to a private road called Sandford Farm Lane, which will take us to the front door. I sure as hell hope this works, but I doubt that it will. I have not read one pleasant thing about that woman."

"The woman hasn't been born yet who doesn't or won't react to flattery. I learned that from Maggie. We pour on the charm, tell her she'll be on the front page of the Lifestyle section. That's big time."

The duo had ridden in silence for another ten minutes

when Espinosa said, "Slow down. See that prancing stallion on the side? Make a right. We're almost there."

"Do you think they have any kind of security out here?" Ted asked.

Espinosa shrugged. "The lieutenant governor travels with a carful, but I think I heard a while back or read somewhere that out here in the boonies, he's just another farm owner, and there's no need. That might have changed since I heard that."

"The only time you need security is when you're doing something wrong. Don't go jumping down my throat, it's just my opinion," Ted said as he maneuvered the motor-pool car over the rough shale road. He could hear the rocks bouncing off his fenders, and the sound irritated him.

"So far so good," Espinosa said, peering out the side windows, then the back. "I don't see anyone. That's the house up ahead. I guess you just drive up to the front, and we walk to the front door and ring the bell. How cool is that?"

"Way too easy, especially after our headlines this morning. I was expecting everything to be battened down."

"You didn't mention the Sandford name in the piece you and Dennis wrote. They probably think that guy Marks is not going to give them up. Arrogant rich people think like that," Espinosa said knowingly.

Ted brought the battered car to a smooth halt. "Here goes nothing," he said as he settled his backpack firmly in place. "You got everything handy, all your creds? That's the first thing whoever opens the door is going to want to see. Paste that winning Espinosa smile in place. You ready?"

"I'm ready," Espinosa said, getting out of the car. He looked around. The place looked deserted to his eye. He also didn't see much in the way of holiday decorations. He said so under his breath.

"I think it's all about lights more than statues and stuff. Oooooh, look up at the roof and that wire sleigh and all those reindeer by the chimney, and look over there on the side; damn, there must be at least twenty wire things. Wonder what they are. It's hard to see them against all the snow piled up. How the hell did we miss all that crap lining the driveway? Bet it all lights up at night. That article did say it was a light show once it got dark. Check out the wreath on the door. It's not even real. The doodads look kind of worn and tattered to my eye, but what do I know! I'm just a reporter, but I want to say, right here and now, that this crap offends my eyes. You might have to digitally enhance it."

Ted slapped his head in frustration. "Joe, what was the name of the homeowner who came in second on the decorations? Quick, we might need the name."

"Ah . . . um . . . Cornelia something or other . . . Wait a minute. Lowden. Yeah, it's Lowden. Cornelia Lowden. She's the mayor's wife. She decorates the mayor's office, too. She won a prize for that."

Ted looked up at the ornate door knocker, which was a replica of the prancing stallion on the sign out on the road. He wondered if the Sandfords raised Thoroughbreds out here in Never Never Land. He lifted the ornate knocker and gave it a good bang. He could hear the sound reverberating all through the house. Loud enough to wake the dead or, at least, someone wearing two hearing aids.

The door opened suddenly. Fiona Sandford, dressed in a pink pantsuit with a Popsicle-colored blouse, blasted them before they could catch their breath. "How did you get in here and what do you want? This is private property, and you are trespassing."

"Ted Robinson, ma'am, and this is Joseph Espinosa. We're from the *Post* in D.C. We've been trying to contact you for the longest time. We heard about your exquisite Christmas decorations and how you've won first prize six years in a row. We want to do a feature story on you along with some other equally talented homeowners. We've already scheduled McLean and Leesburg, but we were told they can't hold a candle to yours. We did send two inquiries to the lieutenant governor's mansion but never heard back. So, as our deadline is drawing near, we thought we'd take a chance and just ride out here to see if you would be agreeable to letting us show you off a little."

Fiona Sandford's talonlike fingers flew to her bee-stung lips in stunned surprise. "Oh, dear, I'm so sorry for greeting you like that. It's just that no one comes out here unless they're invited. My manners are atrocious. Please, come in out of the cold. Can I offer you some coffee, tea?"

"No, ma'am, we're good. We would have called, but your number is unlisted, and rightly so, your husband being who he is and all," Ted said with a smile in his voice. "So, will you grant us the interview? If you say no, then we'll have to ask Mrs. Cornelia Lowden as our second choice."

"Of course! Of course! I can't let Cornelia one-up me now, can I? We've had this . . . little Christmas rivalry going on now for a good many years. All in good fun, of course. Just follow me into the great room, and you can see what I've done so far. I'm not finished yet. Actually, it's a work in progress and never seems to get finished until Christmas Eve, for some reason. I'm sorry my husband isn't here to speak with you. He loves to get into the season and usually he strings all the lights outside, with the help of our barn manager. We have thousands of lights, just thousands. It really is a light show at night," Fiona Sandford babbled.

Ted Robinson thought he had seen everything there was to see in the way of Christmas decorations, but his jaw dropped, as did Espinosa's, when they entered the great room. There was not one inch of space that wasn't adorned with some ricky-ticky, honky-tonk wall hanging, ornament, or statue. The Christmas tree went all the way to the ceiling and was white and silver, with a mishmash of ribbons, colored popcorn, bangles, and garish ornaments. A tarnished angel graced the top of the tree.

"What do you think? Am I or am I not first-prize material?"

"That you are, ma'am, that you are. Joe, make sure you get it from every angle."

"I've been at this for weeks now," Fiona said proudly.

Ted was so dumbfounded at all the junk he was seeing that all he could say was, "I can see that." He risked a glance at Espinosa, who seemed to be having trouble focusing his camera. Either from laughter or pure dismay that he was actually here doing what he was doing.

"A collage would be nice, you know, all entrances, exits, and windows so we get the whole picture," he said to Espinosa, so he would remember the real reason they were here.

"There's just so much," he mumbled.

"It's taken me all my life to collect everything. Every ornament, every statue, every card, every single decoration has a story behind it. I'm sure you don't want to hear them, but they mean so much to me."

"Do you have any decorations made by your children over the years?" Ted asked.

"I do, but I don't put them out. My children do not share my passion for Christmas, so I don't bother pretending. Now, if that makes me a horrible mother, then so be it. They aren't even coming home for Christmas this year. Can you believe that?"

Ted's ears perked up. "Really. That's too sad."

"My mother would kill me if I didn't show up for Christmas Eve. Christmas Day is different; we each do our own thing. It's Christmas Eve that is important to my mom," Espinosa said, clicking away.

"Well, I'm sure you'll have a houseful of guests if not family. You do want to show off your"—Ted waved his arms about to take in the cluttered, mind-boggling room—"Christmas decor."

"In years past, yes. Unfortunately, not this year. I'm just devastated, but maybe doing this interview with a high-quality, top-notch newspaper like the *Post,* and seeing you bringing to life all my treasures, well, it just might make up for it. The lieutenant governor has so much government business on his plate this year that he won't even be coming here until December twenty-third. I gave my household staff the time off. They all left yesterday and won't be back till January second of next year."

Empty house. Great. Jack is gonna love this.

"Well, that's it for this room," Espinosa said. "Do you have any other rooms you'd like us to feature?" *God, let her say no,* he thought to himself.

"Absolutely I do. I decorate the entire house, including all six bathrooms. Just follow me, and I'll show you. I so have this passion for reindeer. I wanted one when I was a little girl, but my daddy said no. I was brokenhearted. Now I have over a thousand of them. Isn't that marvelous?"

"It certainly is," Ted said as he tried to tear his eyes away from a giant, plastic snow globe in the middle of the dining-room table. Inside, fake snow rained down as a fat, miniature Santa tumbled over and over. Gold-plated reindeer were spread over every square inch of the table.

Ted couldn't help himself when he said, "Guess you're eating Christmas dinner in the kitchen, huh?"

Fiona Sandford thought that was the funniest thing she'd ever heard. "We'll eat off trays in the family room. It took me too long to set all this up, and I don't want to disturb the arrangement."

"I don't blame you," Espinosa mumbled.

"Do you get the *Post* way out here?" Ted asked, hoping to move things along.

"I read it online every morning. My husband insists I keep abreast of what's going on. I do like the paper."

"What did you think of today's article about what

went down in the SE section of the District?" Ted asked nonchalantly as he pretended to admire a fat Santa with a green sack of tiny, wilted-looking packages. He racked his brain to remember where he'd seen a duplicate of what he was looking at. And then it came to him—the Dollar Store.

"Why would you ask me something like that?" Fiona asked, suspicion ringing in her voice.

"Because I'm a newspaper reporter and that's what we do; we ask questions and hope for feedback. I guess you don't have an opinion. That's okay, a lot of people don't. I'll tell you who I really feel sorry for; it's that guy who runs the management company. He's going to go *down,* and he'll take all his slum-landlord clients with him. So, Mrs. Sandford, we'd like to take some pictures of you with all your treasures. We have another thirty minutes if you'd like to change into something . . . festive. Or we can just shoot you as you are. You look lovely, but pink isn't exactly a Christmas color. The decision is entirely up to you. This article is about you, so it won't matter if your husband is in any of the shots or not. I'm sure we can dig something out of the archives if we change our minds."

Fiona suddenly looked angry, frustrated, hopeful in quick succession, as if she couldn't make up her mind. "What? Did I say something to upset you? Was it that your husband won't be in the pictures?"

"No, no, not at all. Yes, I would like to change into something more formal. Would you like something to drink before I change? There's coffee in the kitchen. Help yourselves. What did you mean when you said that person was going to go down?"

"Oh, that!" Ted shrugged. "I'm just going by what that rich guy promised to do, which was go to the ends of the earth to dig up the owners of those slums. He meant business. He's one of those dog-with-a-bone kind of guys. You'd best hurry, Mrs. Sandford; we don't have much more time. Do you want us to send you the proofs, so that you can pick the ones you'd like us to put in the feature?"

"Well, of course. That would be lovely," she said, tottering away on her spike-heeled shoes.

The minute Fiona Sandford was out of earshot, Espinosa hissed, "Tell me this is some damn nightmare, and we're both going to wake up any second now."

"I wish I could. Did you get pictures of the locks on the door. I didn't see any kind of alarm panel anywhere. Did you?" Espinosa shook his head. "Take a picture of the lock on the back door. The locks look pretty ordinary to me. Jack is going to want to see everything."

"She got a little antsy when you brought up the property-management company."

"I saw that, but I also saw that the woman is incredibly vain, and this little photo shoot means more than what went down out in the SE. When we leave, and she has time to think about it, it might be a different story. I think we need to nail down where the two kids are going to be for Christmas and verify it. That's the first thing Jack is going to want to know."

"Yoo-hoo!" Fiona trilled as she whirled and twirled for their benefit. Ted longed for sunglasses. Espinosa gulped and almost choked. "The pictures will be in color, right? I've had this outfit since I was nineteen. It was the first thing I bought with my very own money. The material is called taffeta, in case anyone asks. It's metallic and is really festive. It more or less blends with the Christmas tree, if you know what I mean. Each year, I have my husband take a picture of me by the tree. The top is all hand-sewn, multicolored sequins. You couldn't touch this outfit today for under three thousand dollars and mind you it only cost me twenty back in the day. I so treasure it."

Espinosa had a fit of coughing. He brought up his camera and clicked and clicked. "Smile. Show me some pearly whites." The bee-stung lips parted in a garish smile. "Okay, now point to that glorious parade of reindeer by the fireplace. Walk over to them, bend down, adjust their collars. Ah, perfect! You're a wonderful subject to photograph."

"Thank you for saying that. What about the interview?"

"Tell me if this will work for you, Mrs. Sandford. I'll type up the questions and send them to you via e-mail. Write as much as you want, and if there's anything I don't ask, feel free to include whatever it is you want said. I'm willing to work with you one hundred percent. I just wish everyone was as nice and cooperative as you've been. Give me your e-mail address please."

Fiona rattled it off, and Ted wrote it down. Almost as an afterthought, he asked, "Where will your children be this Christmas if they aren't coming home?"

Fiona's face darkened. "Faylan, my daughter, is going to Texas to spend Christmas with her boyfriend's parents, and Addison is going skiing in Colorado. Sometimes, children are very thoughtless."

"Yes, that is true. Well, thank you very much, Mrs. Sandford. I'll be in touch later this afternoon with my interview questions. If I don't see you again, have a wonderful Christmas."

"You, too, Mr. Robinson. Thank you also, Mr. Espinosa."

Outside in the frigid air, Espinosa ran to the car, certain he was going to explode. Ted climbed into the car, turned on the engine, and burst out laughing. "That was a piece of cake. Soon as we get clear of this house, I'm going to text Jack. Start uploading those pictures to him."

"All of them?"

"Every single one."

"I hope he made out as well as we did with Mr. Marks," Espinosa said.

"I'm sure he did. Okay, now key in the location of the mayor's office. We need to scoot over there and take a few pictures to make this all look legitimate. Then head over to the Lowdens' home and shoot a few from outside. Then we're done here."

Chapter 19

Jack parked his car, looked over at Cyrus, and said, "You gotta stay in the car, buddy." He reached into his pocket for a chew. "Don't let anyone steal you. If anyone comes near the car, blow the horn. You know how to do that." Cyrus looked up at his master as if Jack was an idiot and growled. "Well, sometimes you forget, Cyrus." The shepherd growled again, which meant, *get real oh Mighty Master.* Jack grinned as he made his way out of the busy parking lot and headed toward the office building that housed Lionel Marks's management company. He really loved that dog.

One look at the ornate lobby of the building he'd just entered told Jack he was in a high-dollar building. Marks had to be paying top dollar for digs like these. He signed in at the information desk and received a pass. He walked over to the elevator and pressed the button. He looked around, surprised that no one else was in the lobby. He looked up at the large sign next to the elevator that listed the tenants and their floors. Inside the elevator, he pressed the number eight and waited for the door to close. The elevator shot upward so fast, Jack lost his balance. When the door opened, he gawked at what he was seeing. Green marble floor, a horseshoe-shaped desk with what looked, to his trained eye, like a blow-up doll. Bleached blond hair, heavy makeup, scarlet lips that matched the polish on her long nails. Chesty. Low-cut blouse. Eye-catching to say the least. Jack offered up what he called his killer smile and said he would like to see Mr. Marks to ask him to take over his account. "I don't have an appointment, I'm sorry to say. I'm just in town for a few hours, and it has to be now, or else I'll have to find another management company."

"You really need an appointment, sir. I can probably fit you in tomorrow late afternoon, but today is not going to work."

Jack leaned over the desk, and said, "How about this? You go in and tell your boss I have a block of twelve condos in Watergate and four properties in Georgetown and two on Wisconsin Avenue. I can sign a contract right now, but it has to be right now because I have a flight to catch that I can't miss." He let her see the hundred-dollar bill in his hand that was meant for her if she cut through the I'm-too-busy-to-talk-to-anyone crap. Before Jack could blink, the blonde snatched the bill, and said, "Wait right here, and I will see what I can do."

"Money talks and bullshit walks," Jack mumbled under his breath as he walked around the entryway and stared at the artwork on the walls. He was no art connoisseur, but what he was looking at looked like quality, pricey artwork. Jackson Pollock and Jasper Johns. Nice. Very nice.

While Jack was viewing the art on the walls and checking out the two doors that led away from the area he was standing in, Lionel Marks was berating his receptionist. "But, sir, he said he had a block of twelve condos, plus properties in Georgetown and others on Wisconsin Avenue. You can't turn that down! Besides," she said brazenly, "you will owe me a finder's fee because I could have sent him away, but I didn't. He has a plane to catch. What do you want me to tell him?"

Marks forced himself to calm down. What the hell, he'd snag the retainer, talk to the guy, and leave him in the dust. Since he wasn't going to claim the destruction of his car in

SE, someone had to pay for it. Why not this guy? "Okay, send him in, but tell him I only have ten minutes."

The buxom blonde tripped her way back to the foyer on her stilettos, and said, "Mr. Marks is making an exception and can give you ten minutes. Follow me, sir."

Once inside Marks's office, Jack extended his hand, and the term sleazeball came to mind. "Mitchell Tremaine. Call me Mitch," Jack said. "So, are you interested in representing me? I hate to put a rush on things, but I have a plane to catch. I want to warn you that the management company I just fired cooked my books. I will not tolerate malfeasance. I am prepared to deposit a hundred thousand dollars in an escrow account to cover maintenance. Whatever is left at the end of the year is yours. Plus a ten-thousand-dollar bonus paid out December thirty-first. If we sign a deal, it's win-win for you as there are only a few weeks left till December thirty-first. I will fax you a list of the properties. My lawyer will review your contract, at which time the money will be deposited in the escrow account. I assume your retainer is the same as every other management company's I've dealt with—fifty thousand dollars. It will be paid when the contracts are signed. I'll be back in town in ten days. Can we do business, Mr. Marks?"

Marks pretended to think. If Jack didn't know better, he would have thought Marks was a legitimate businessman. "What's the total of your rentals per month on all your properties, Mr. Tremaine?"

"Roughly sixty thousand dollars a month."

Marks's jaw dropped. "For all those properties! For those locations, you should be getting double that. If I take you on, after I inspect the properties, what's your feeling on rental increases?"

"I'm all for it if you can get it. What do you take off that?"

"Two percent."

"That works for me," Jack said happily as he gazed around the office, looking for exit doors. There was only one door to the side that either led to a bathroom or an outside hall. He saw no evidence of a safe, so he bluntly asked.

"Of course I have a safe, Mr. Tremaine, but I certainly don't advertise it to clients."

Jack nodded and stood up. "If we have a deal, I'll have my attorney get in touch with you, no later than this afternoon. She has my power of attorney, so she can sign for me, and the money will be deposited at the same time. We're good till the end of the month."

"Who's your attorney?"

"Lizzie Fox."

Marks swallowed hard as he stared at Jack. "I must say, you certainly go for the best."

"You know what they say, you get what you pay for. By the way, just between us, client and management, who are some of your clients? I heard that the lieutenant governor of Virginia is one of your clients; is that true? Actually, that fact alone is the reason why I'm even standing here. I figured if you're good enough for him, then you're good enough for me."

Jack loved the way the man's right eye started to twitch. His voice was gruff when he said, "I never discuss my clients with other clients, Mr. Tremaine."

Jack nodded. "I like that. I subscribe to that motto myself, Mr. Marks. My attorney will be in touch." He couldn't resist adding, "Merry Christmas, Mr. Marks."

The property manager merely nodded as he escorted Jack to the door. He didn't offer to shake hands, and neither did Jack.

Back in the car, Jack looked at Cyrus, and said, "The guy is a real sleazebag and I think I conned him. Greed always wins out with guys like him. He was a real jerk. How about we hit up Arby's and get us a really big roast beef sandwich?"

Cryus let loose with a loud bark to show he was in agreement.

"Arby's it is."

Chapter 20

While Jack and Cyrus were chowing down on thick roast beef sandwiches, Ted and Espinosa were taking the elevator to the newsroom. It was a little past noon, and the room was bustling with reporters yelling at other reporters as they pounded away on their keyboards. There was no sign of Dennis West.

Ted looked over to the half glass wall that separated Maggie from the newsroom. She was looking straight at him. "Okay, Joe, I'm going to beard the lioness."

"Good luck," Espinosa said as he sat down and turned on his computer so he could upload all the photos he'd taken in Middleburg.

Ted rapped on Maggie's door, opened it, and poked his head in. "You got a minute, Maggie?"

Well, that's civilized, Maggie thought. "Sure," she said warily. "What's up?"

"Not much. Christmas season and all. Espinosa and I just got back from Middleburg. I had this idea. I probably should have run it by you, but I wasn't sure if I could tie it in to what appears to be a breaking scandal. You know the governor of Virginia and his lieutenant governor and all that money they're wasting. I'm still not sure if it will work, but Espinosa sent you some pictures of Lieutenant Governor

Sandford's Christmas decorations, compliments of Mrs. Fiona Sandford. My thought was to run an article with pictures every day until Christmas. We also have some quality shots of the mayor's office, the outside of his home. The Sandfords, well, they pretty much speak for themselves. What I need for you to do, Maggie, is assign a couple of the guys to hit these homes. To make it look legitimate."

Maggie blinked. There was so much she wanted to say, and questions she wanted to ask but she felt tongue-tied for some reason, so she just nodded. Finally, just as Ted was turning to leave she found her voice. "Ted, hold on a minute. Close the door, okay?" Ted obliged. The moment he turned around, Maggie blurted, "Ted, what happened to us?"

"Us? As in you and me? There is no us, Maggie. You made that very clear.

"Yeah, we were once lovers and once engaged. You dumped me. You got married. Then you became a widow and came back into all of our lives. We welcomed you, at least I did. I was hoping for more at some point but accepted that it wasn't to be.

"Then you started sticking your nose into my personal, private life. That did not work for me. I told you so, but you didn't back off. Then you started spying on me and the guys. Friends don't spy on friends. Friends try to talk it out, resolve whatever the problem is. And on top of that, you tried to pull rank. I told you if you did it again, I'm outta here, and so is Espinosa and the kid.

"Now, Maggie, here's the kicker, you sicced private dicks on all of us. We picked up on that the minute you hired them. Either you hired some misfits, or we're better than they are. Because, like I said, we picked up on it. Why? Why would you do that to your friends? The guys are really pissed. I'm really pissed. Did I answer your question satisfactorily?"

Maggie felt her eyes start to burn. She cleared her throat twice before she could get the words out. "You're right, Ted. About everything. I know saying I'm sorry isn't enough but I am sorry. I . . . I wasn't thinking clearly. It was like all of a sudden everyone in my life had no time for me. I mean, I got it with the girls, but when you guys shunned me—and don't say you didn't—I started to lose it.

"At first I thought I had done something wrong, and you all hated me for that. Then I realized I hadn't done any such thing, and you all were just moving away from our old life, like the girls had. Then the reporter in me kicked in, and I realized you all were up to something and that that something was secret. You know me and secrets," she said ruefully.

Ted could feel the guilt starting to set in. He was putty in Maggie's hands. Her phone took that moment to ring. Maggie ignored it. Two young reporters banged on the door, and Maggie waved them off. Whoa. His old friend and lover was serious here. She could no more let a phone ring without answering than she could stop eating. As to the knock on the door, she couldn't resist wanting to know what the person wanted. That just wasn't who Maggie was. This was indeed serious.

Ted looked out into the newsroom to see Espinosa glaring at him. Ted felt his back stiffen and the guilt start to diminish. "You admit you hired private detectives to spy on me and the guys? You admit you've been having us followed?"

It wasn't a statement; it was a question. "What is it you want from me, Maggie? Spell it out because I'm just not getting it."

Maggie shrugged. She hoped the burning in her eyes wouldn't produce tears that would roll down her cheeks. She tried to square her shoulders, but she failed. She'd never been so miserable in her whole life.

"What? The cat caught your tongue all of a sudden? I repeat, what do you want from me, Maggie?"

Maggie flopped down in her predecessor's chair because she didn't think her legs would hold her up much longer. "Yesterday, Ted. I want yesterday back," she whispered.

"Yesterday's gone, Maggie, tomorrow isn't here yet, and all we have is today. I can't give you yesterday. I wish I could, for you and for me as well, but I can't. I loved you, Maggie, so much that my hair hurt."

Ted looked out through the half glass to see Espinosa still glaring at him. A good thing, too, or he would have buckled when he saw the first tear roll down Maggie's cheek. He turned and called over his shoulder to Maggie, "Let me know what you think of the pictures."

Instead of heading for his desk, Ted bolted for the hall and the elevator, Espinosa right behind him. The door slid open, and Dennis stepped out. Ted grabbed him, swung him around, and all three descended to the lobby.

"What's up? You guys look . . . I don't know . . . kind of shitful. Anyone hear from Jack? Where are we going? By the way, it's snowing out, in case anyone is interested."

No one was.

"I say we hit the Squire's Pub since it's the closest," Espinosa said.

"That works for me," Dennis said happily.

Ted just hunkered into his jacket, his head down as they walked into the wind.

Maggie sank down into the chair she was sitting on and turned so that she was facing the wall behind her. She wanted to cry, to stomp her feet, to pitch a hissy fit. She bit down so hard on her lower lip that she could taste her own blood. She swung back around and grabbed a tissue from her desk to dab at her lip. Her eyes were wild when she looked around her neat-as-a-pin office. She had to get out of there. Immediately. That instant. She bellowed for her assistant before she could change her mind. As she was struggling into her jacket and looking for her scarf and backpack, she rattled off a list of things that needed to be done. "You'll see me when you see me. While I'm gone, you're in charge." As she whizzed by her secretary's desk, she bellowed, "Emily, call James and tell him to pick me up in front of the building right now."

"And another drama-filled day is under way at the *Post*," Emily Davis muttered under her breath as she sent a text to Maggie's driver. She sent a second one with the initials *ASAP*.

Maggie pushed through the revolving door and was surprised to see that it was snowing. The cold air felt good on her flaming cheeks. She couldn't remember a time in her life when she had felt as stupid as she felt at that moment. Stupid, embarrassed, humiliated, guilty, sad, and angry. She needed to go home so she could lick her wounds in private and cry. She'd never been a crier, not ever. Crying was a sign of weakness. She was just beginning to wonder if she was having a nervous breakdown when her driver pulled to the curb. Maybe her husband's death was finally catching up to her. Maybe a whole lot of things were catching up to her. Inside the warm car, Maggie buckled up, and said, "James, take me home, please. And you can have the rest of the week off. I won't be needing you."

"Thank you, ma'am. My wife and kids are going to appreciate having me home. I've yet to set up the tree and hang the lights outside. But if you change your mind, call me at home."

"I will." Maggie leaned against the window and closed her eyes. All she wanted to do was cry. Cry till her eyes fell out of their sockets. *And what will that do for you, Maggie?* she asked herself.

Fifteen minutes later, Maggie's driver pulled smoothly to the curb. "Don't get out, James, I'm fine. Go home now to your family." A second later, she was rummaging in her pack for the house keys. That's when she saw a mangy, bedraggled cat pawing at her door. She frowned but bent down to see if the animal was injured. She couldn't see any marks or blood. She dropped to her knees and stroked the cat's wet head. The cat purred.

Maggie didn't stop to wonder if the cat would bite or scratch her. She picked it up and opened the door. With the cat still in her arms, she quickly turned up the heat and rushed to make a fire. From there she ran to the laundry room and got a towel to wrap the shivering cat in. He or she purred louder. She carried the cat into the kitchen, took off her jacket, and tossed it into a corner, along with her backpack. She made coffee, then opened a can of tuna fish and set it down by the cat, along with a small bowl of water. She watched as the cat ate daintily. No collar. Stray? Did it belong to someone? Why did he pick her door to scratch at? Everything in life happened for a reason. Was she meant to find this poor animal? Was that why she left the office in such a hurry? Or was this going to be one of those mysteries in life that was never solved? Her voice was fierce, protective when she announced to the cat and her empty kitchen, "You're mine now!" She wasn't alone anymore. She had a friend. Her mood lightened.

Maggie waited until the cat finished eating before she picked it up and carried it into the family room and set it down by the fire. She ran upstairs to change her clothes and ran back down. The cat hadn't moved an inch. She hoped it wasn't sick. In the blink of an eye, she had a mission. She put on her jacket and ran out of the house and up to the small corner market, where she bought kitty litter, cat food, some catnip, and a few toys she saw hanging on a notions rack. She asked for a cardboard box to use for the kitty litter until she could get a real litter box.

Fifteen minutes later, she was back in the house. Her new roommate was sound asleep by the fire. She smiled. She took a moment to wonder when she'd smiled or been happy lately and couldn't come up with a time or a place. Well that was then, and this was now.

A cup of coffee in her hand, Maggie squatted by the cat and stroked his head. The way the cat was lying she could see it was a boy cat. A name, she needed to name him. Names were important. A name defined a person. Maybe something symbolic. The cat purred in his sleep. Maggie smiled again as she set her cup on the hearth and made herself comfortable in a nest of pillows. She had some heavy thinking to do. Apologies first and foremost. She'd go to Harry's dojo tonight at seven o'clock, when all the guys would be there for training, and apologize. Then tomorrow or possibly later tonight, she'd tender her resignation and start sending out her résumé. The decisions made, Maggie closed her eyes, and, within seconds, she was sound asleep.

Chapter 21

Shortly before six, Maggie woke with a start when she felt something nuzzling her neck. In her foggy, sleep-filled state she thought it was Ted and almost said his name aloud when she opened her eyes to see a pair of emerald green eyes staring at her. Not Ted. She laughed out loud and sat up, the unnamed cat sitting on her chest. "You're making yourself right at home, I see. The cat purred and rubbed against her arm and chest. Maggie thought it was the most beautiful animal she'd ever seen, and he was all hers. She had a friend now to talk to. She could tell him about her worries, her fears, share her victories and her failures and he wouldn't judge her. He'd listen, purr, and let her know he was there for her. A true friend. Something she'd forgotten how to be.

As Maggie stroked the cat in her arms, she stared into the fire and thought about her conversation with Ted and what she had to do to try to make things right. She stretched her neck to see up at the clock on the mantel. A little after six. If she didn't get to Harry's dojo before the training class, she could go later and wait till it was over, which would probably be the better idea.

Maggie fed the cat again, showed him where she'd placed his litter box in the downstairs powder room, then made up a special bed for him by the fireplace. She got a perverse sense of pleasure by using Ted's pillow for the cat.

In the blink of an eye, she whipped up an omelet for herself, ate it, cleaned up, then added some more logs to the fire. She closed the glass doors to make sure no sparks flew out that could set the carpet on fire. She smiled as the cat settled itself on Ted's pillow and went to sleep. She really had to come up with a suitable name for her new roommate.

Satisfied that her house was in order, Maggie called for a cab to take her to Harry's dojo. She could have taken her own car, but she didn't want to walk six blocks to the parking garage where she kept it. Besides, she didn't like driving in snow. Or rain, for that matter.

When she climbed into the cab, Maggie was stunned at how calm and peaceful she felt. When she'd come home earlier in the day, she'd been tied in knots. To think that a little two-pound ball of yellow fur could have such an effect on her was mind-boggling.

Normally, the ride to Harry's dojo would have taken sixteen minutes. She knew this because she'd once timed it. Not tonight, though, not with the snow, and the plows working to sand the roads. The driver dropped her off fifty-two minutes from the time she'd stepped into his cab.

Maggie was crossing the street when a horrible idea hit her. What if Harry had canceled his class because of bad weather, and she'd made the trip for nothing? She strained to see through the falling snow, and could see a dim yellow light in the front windows. It was impossible to see who was parked where. She forged ahead and trudged her way around to the back so she could use the rear entrance. Only the boys and friends entered the dojo from the back. Not sure if she was friend or foe, she took the high road and tapped on the back door. When there was no response she opened the door, poked her head in, and called out. When there was still no response to her verbal greeting, she shut the door and advanced into the room. She froze in place when she heard a bloodcurdling bark, then a deep growl. Cyrus. Maggie sucked in her breath and didn't move until she saw Jack and the others outlined in the doorway.

"I came to apologize to all of you," Maggie said in a jittery voice. "And to tell you that I'm tendering my resignation and will be going back to Maryland." She started to shake then, not sure if it was from the cold or because of the men standing in front of her.

"Easy, Cyrus. It's okay, boy. It's Maggie. You know Maggie."

"It's cold out here. Come into the waiting room," Abner said.

"It's okay, I'm not staying, but thanks for thinking of my comfort. I'm sorry that . . . that I spied on all of you. You're my friends, and I guess I forgot that for a little while. But having said that, in my own defense, you all closed me out. Everyone is always so damn busy that it's a major problem to send a text or call just to say hi. I don't even know you guys anymore. And you know what else, I'm not sure I want to. Why'd you all have to sneak around? It was like suddenly you all were guarding this planet's biggest secret. We were supposed to be . . . family, able to count on each other."

Maggie's voice broke on a sob, but she rushed on. "I've always been there for each and every one of you, time after time, and you damn well know it. Yeah, sometimes I'm bossy, yeah, sometimes I'm over the top with my ideas and plans, but in the end, it always worked. Until recently," she said, her tone fierce.

"I called off the detectives. You guys are unfettered now to do whatever it is you're doing. I'm sorry, too, about that banana tree. It was a stupid thing to do. I just wanted you all to know you weren't as smart as you thought you were, and if I could figure it out, so can certain other people. Well, that's all I have to say. Good luck with whatever it is you're doing."

To her dismay, tears started to roll down her cheeks. Cyrus started to whimper. Maggie gave her muffler a wide swing, wrapped it more securely around her neck, and turned to go.

She was almost to the door when she felt her feet leave the floor and she was suddenly airborne. And then she was falling and felt someone catch her. Jack! Harry had tossed her to Jack. Oh, God, they were going to kill her. Cyrus barked his head off, then started to howl.

Everyone started talking at once but whatever they were saying made no sense to Maggie. Either they were going to rip her apart or they weren't. "Okay, okay, how many times do I have to tell you I'm sorry? I'm sorry, okay? I'm going to get out of your hair; there's no need to kill me or . . . to . . . do whatever it is you're . . . ah . . . planning."

"No one is killing anyone," Harry said. "We accept your apology in the spirit it was given. We're going to welcome you into our little club, aren't we, guys?"

"Uh-huh," Jack said.

"You bet," Abner said.

Maggie looked at the Big Three: Ted, Espinosa, and Dennis. The three of them were smiling and nodding. She swooned. "You forgive me?"

"It's either that or kill you, and we have never been in the killing business," Harry snapped.

"Oh, God! I love you guys!" Maggie said, as more tears flowed down her cheeks.

Chapter 22

Maggie walked on air as she made her way upstairs to Harry and Yoko's spacious apartment on the second floor of the dojo. She would spend an hour with Yoko and Lily until Harry and the boys finished their seven P.M. class and Jack offered her a ride home. She felt light-headed with relief that the boys had welcomed her back into the fold. Even Ted, who had been stone-faced in the beginning, had hugged her and then given her the famous lopsided grin that she loved. For now her world was right-side up. Childishly, she crossed her fingers, so that it would stay that way.

Yoko hugged Maggie and ushered her into the kitchen, where she offered tea and rice cakes. Lily, she said, was in her room playing and would be ready for bed in a few minutes. "You look . . . I don't know, extra happy." Yoko smiled. "Do you have a new man in your life, or did you and Ted patch it up?"

Maggie debated a full moment. What to say, what not to say? She pointed to the floor, and said, "Let's just say I have a whole bunch of guys in my life." Before Yoko could ask any more questions, Maggie inquired about how the nursery was doing. The nursery was the love of Yoko's life. She loved planting seedlings in her greenhouse and watching them sprout and come to life. She loved the Christmas season and pretty much lived on-site, with Harry taking care of Lily because business was better than brisk.

"You aren't going to believe this, Maggie, but guess who came by to buy a Christmas tree today? I waited on him myself. The vice president, that's who. He said his secretary always buys her trees from me and recommended me. I had Secret Service all over the place. I wanted to whip out my gold shield, but I was very good and I didn't." She giggled, and Maggie giggled, and then they were hugging each other and laughing till their sides ached. *Oh, this feels so good,* Maggie thought.

The two women talked then about everything and nothing, just two old friends playing catch-up. They stopped once to put a sleepy Lily to bed. Cooper, Lily's protector, eyed Maggie warily until she left the room. At which point he hopped on the little girl's bed and dropped his head on his paws as he settled down to guard his small charge.

Maggie and Yoko returned to their tea in the kitchen and picked up where they had left off. They chatted until Jack whistled from the bottom of the steps that he was ready to leave.

Maggie grabbed her coat and pack, hugged Yoko, and promised to help out at the nursery on the weekend, the last weekend before Christmas, when things got so hairy Yoko's workers didn't know if they were coming or going, and any help at all was appreciated.

Maggie was stunned at the snow on the ground when she climbed into Jack's car. She shivered until the heater kicked in, then relaxed. For the most part, they made the trip to Georgetown in silence, Jack concentrating on the road conditions and Cyrus being uncommonly quiet. When they reached the street they both lived on, Maggie noticed that Jack and Nikki's house was dark, which meant Nikki wasn't home yet. "Want to come in for a beer or a sandwich, Jack? I don't know about you, but I didn't have much to eat today, and I know you guys never eat before a workout. Your house is dark, so Nikki isn't home yet. It's up to you."

"Sure," Jack said agreeably. "Just let me drop Cyrus off at home." Maggie's sigh of relief at not being rebuffed made Jack grin in the darkness.

When she and Jack got back to her house after settling Cyrus at Jack and Nikki's, it was not until she slid her key into the lock that Maggie remembered about her new roommate. She froze in place and slapped at her head. "Oh, my God, I forgot about . . . jeez, I hope he's okay. I just got him. Oh, Jack he was so bedraggled. I need a name. I couldn't come up with a name because I was so upset with all of you, and . . ." She pushed at the door and looked around frantically. Jack stood rooted to the floor as he looked around to see what Maggie was talking about. He smiled when he saw a skinny yellow cat with green eyes coming toward Maggie. The mangy cat circled her feet and purred so loud, Jack laughed out loud.

"This is your new roommate?"

"Yeah. Yeah, he is. He's not much to look at right now, but I'll fatten him up. He likes to sit on your lap. He's sweet. He came . . . at just the right time. I had pretty much hit bottom. I was ready to throw in the towel and hit the road." Maggie's tone turned defensive as she scooped up the yellow cat and nuzzled him under her chin. He purred even louder. "Everyone needs someone at some point in time, Jack. Today was my point in time."

Jack nodded. *That*, he understood. "What do you call him?"

Without missing a beat, Maggie blurted, "Hero. Because he is."

"Sounds good to me," Jack said as he tweaked the cat under his chin. Hero hissed his disapproval. Jack laughed. "Once he gets to know me, he'll love me. Animals love me. I bet Cyrus and he will get along. Maybe a play date. While you cuddle with him, do you want me to make my own sandwich and yours, too?"

"Sure. I have some pickles in the fridge. Put some on my plate. Coffee or beer?"

"Too late in the day for coffee. I'll go with the beer," Jack said, taking off his jacket and making himself at home in Maggie's kitchen. Something he'd done often in the past.

Maggie looked around, set the cat down, and removed her jacket. It was almost like old times. Almost. And almost wasn't going to cut it with her. She needed to hear words, wanted precise explanations. In short she wanted yesterday but was not foolish enough to think that's what she was going to get. But she was desperate enough to take whatever she could get and work from there. "So, talk to me, Jack."

Jack talked while he made the sandwiches and uncapped the two beers he set on the table, laid out napkins and paper plates. Even though it was bad manners, he talked while he was eating and was still explaining things as he opened the second set of beers. He finally wound down by saying, "That's pretty much it. I don't think I left anything out. You got questions, ask me now before I head on home."

Maggie's arms flapped in the air. "Why?"

Jack shrugged. "It just evolved, Maggie. Everyone seemed discontented, especially me, so I guess you could say I was the catalyst. You girls had moved on. Then there was that disastrous Thanksgiving last year with Charles. I guess you could say we were all ripe for doing *something*. Especially me since Nik and I hit a rough patch, Abner and Isabelle were snapping and snarling at each other, and you and Ted were . . . whatever you and Ted were doing, which, according to Ted, was that you left him swinging in the wind.

"We were actually starting to talk about it before dinner

that Thanksgiving, and Charles was on board. The truth is that of all of us, Charles was the most gung ho. He said he was sick of writing his memoirs that no one would ever read. That's one of the reasons I think we decided to forge ahead once he was gone. We couldn't have gotten it off the ground without Dennis and his money.

"Yeah, we were trying to keep it secret, at least for a little while. Stand on our own laurels, so to speak. We're on a case right now. There's no doubt in my mind or the others' that if we somehow managed to run aground, we'd call on you girls. If you need more than that, you're out of luck, I'm afraid. It's the best I can give you right now."

Maggie nodded. "I'm good for now with what you've told me. Does the case you're on have anything to do with that slew of pictures Ted and Espinosa sent me? It's Lieutenant Governor Sandford, right? You're gonna take him down and are using his wife, Fiona, as bait, right?"

Jack was shocked. He almost jumped out of his skin when Hero leaped onto his lap and started to purr.

Maggie laughed out loud at the expression on Jack's face. "Now be nice to him."

"How'd you figure it out?" Jack asked as he reared back as the cat tried to climb his chest.

Maggie made a disgusted sound deep in her throat. "I'm a reporter, for crying out loud. I sense things, feel things, and my gut kicks in. It's what I do. It's in my blood. You guys are going to nail that slum landlord, right?"

Jack gave up being surprised. "Sandford got away with it the first time around because he's wealthy, his family is powerful, and he's the lieutenant governor. If the law won't step in, then we'll do it for them. We've got a plan, and we're going to make that skunk wish he'd never been born."

"Your . . . ah . . . plan . . . that isn't like that pumpkin plan you had back in Utah when things went to hell, is it?"

Jack grimaced. "Damn, am I ever going to live that down? In the end, it worked. But to answer your question, our plan is foolproof. Trust me."

In spite of himself, Jack found that he was stroking the skinny cat's head. Hero purred so loud that Jack laughed out loud. "Cyrus is going to pitch a fit when I get home and he smells this cat on me."

Maggie giggled. "Into each life a little rain must fall. Suck it up, big guy."

"I gotta go, Maggie. Listen, for whatever it's worth, I'm glad you're on board."

Maggie reached for the cat and cuddled it close to her chest. The little animal felt warm and safe in her arms. "Me, too, Jack. Me, too."

Maggie rolled over and groaned. What was that noise? The phone? The doorbell? She squinted at the red numerals on her bedside clock, which read 4:58. It was the doorbell! Who rang someone's doorbell at this time of the morning? An emergency? Cops? What? She swung her legs over the side of the bed and raced from the room and down the hall. She took the steps two at a time and almost threw herself at the door. She didn't even bother to check the peephole to see who was on the other side of the door. She swung it open, and barked, "What? Do you know what time it is?"

Ted didn't say a word; he kicked the door shut with his foot, grabbed her and kissed her until her teeth rattled. When he broke away, he stared down at Maggie, and said, "Say something, or I am outta here forever, and this time I mean it."

"Do that again, that thing you do with your tongue," was all Maggie could manage to say. Ted obliged.

When they broke apart the second time, Ted took charge. "It's too cold in here. I'll make a fire, you turn up the heat and make us something to eat and lots of coffee unless you want to skip all that and we head to the second floor *now.*"

Maggie blinked. Who was this guy who was suddenly in charge of her life? Whoever he was, she decided in that moment that she liked him. She turned and galloped up the steps, Ted right behind her. She flew to the bed, jumped on it as she was ripping at her pajamas. "What's taking you so long?" she yelled as Ted tripped over his own feet.

The yellow cat hopped up on the bedroom chair and curled into a ball as he tried to shield his ears from the wild whooping sounds that filled the room. Eventually, he fell asleep when the room turned quiet.

Chapter 23

Jack Emery laughed out loud when he walked out his front door at six o'clock with Cyrus to see the *Post* van parked in front of Maggie's house. Maybe this time the relationship would take. At least he hoped so. Ted and Maggie were meant for each other, in his opinion. He looked around to see Cyrus lifting his leg on the lamppost. He whistled as he clicked the remote in his hand. It chirped, and his car door unlocked. Cyrus beat him to the car and hopped in the minute the door was open.

Jack shivered in the early morning air as he scraped at the ice on the front and back windshields. He was so sick of snow and cold weather, he vowed once again to move to a warmer climate. Inside the car, he waited until the heater kicked in before he inched the car away from the curb.

Jack stopped for a bagel and coffee and Cyrus's early morning treat along with a bag of bagels for the guys, then made his way to the BOLO Building, where he tapped in the code to the new security gate. He was surprised to see that Harry, Abner, and Dennis were already inside. He was surprised because usually he was the first one there in the morning. Noticeably absent were Espinosa and Ted.

"Okay, meeting, five minutes. Someone get Bert and

Sparrow on the Web and let's get this show on the road," Jack barked.

"What about Espinosa and Ted?" Dennis asked.

Jack shrugged. He wasn't about to gossip about Ted, and he knew Espinosa would show up sooner or later. "We can always fill them in later. Someone make coffee. I bought a bag of bagels for whoever wants one." He tossed the bag to Dennis, who caught it in midair.

The guys scattered, and Jack headed for the conference room.

"Jack, did you forget the time difference? It's four in the morning in Vegas. Are you sure you want me to roust the guys out of bed?" Abner asked.

"No, no. I did forget. Guess we'll fill them in later, too. Ah, I just heard the door, so that has to mean Espinosa is here."

Abner frowned. "What about Ted? You look kind of funny, Jack, do you know something you aren't saying?"

"You mean like my seeing the *Post* van at Maggie's house when I got up this morning? Nah, I'm not saying anything about that."

Abner grinned, then burst out laughing as he booted up his laptop, flexed his fingers, and went to work as Jack started pulling out stacks of files and folders from his overstuffed briefcase and making neat piles on the big conference table. When he finished, he looked up to see Espinosa, coffee cup in one hand, bagel in the other, saunter into the room.

"Where's Ted, anyone seen him?" Espinosa asked as he chomped down on the bagel in his hand.

Abner ignored him, and Jack shrugged. "I haven't seen him." Which was true—seeing the van wasn't the same as seeing Ted in the flesh.

"I've been calling him for the past hour and either he has his phone turned off, which he never does, or he lost it. I called him nine times and nine times it went to voice mail. I sent him four different texts. This is not like Ted. I'm starting to worry."

"Then why don't you try Maggie's house if you're so worried?" Abner mumbled.

Espinosa almost choked on the bagel he was chewing. "Why would I want to do a dumb thing like that?"

"Maybe because that's where he is," Abner said slyly.

Espinosa's fingers flew over the keys like lightning. He sat back and waited. "I'm not getting a response," he groaned.

"And this surprises you?" Abner cackled. "Try this: They are together. If he doesn't respond, and she doesn't respond, what do you think that means?" Abner didn't bother to wait for Espinosa's response and answered the question himself. "It means they are together and probably doing something that's none of our business."

Dennis took that moment to walk into the conference room, carrying a tray with coffee cups and a cup of tea for Harry and a plate of bagels. "What did I miss?"

"Ted and Maggie are shacked up," Harry said through clenched teeth. "How long did you let the tea steep?"

"Four minutes precisely, just like you said. And it's flurrying outside, in case anyone cares. They're really shacked up! Wow!" Dennis said, his face beet red.

"We don't care if it's snowing. It's been snowing off and on for days, so that's nothing new. Can we get down to business here? I have a class in forty minutes," Harry said, sipping at what Jack called his shitty tea. He nodded approvingly, to Dennis's relief.

Jack whistled to get everyone's attention. "Listen up. We have five days to pull this off. Now let's all get serious here. For starters, the Sandfords and their Christmas decor will be running in the *Post* every day, along with the other entries in the local Christmas contest. Ted and Maggie came through on that, and Espinosa, I have to say, those were some real gritty pictures. You did good.

"Dennis, you're on top with Luther Jones, right?"

"Got it all locked up tight. We own him. He'll do whatever we say. He got the other gang leaders to agree to a meet, and things actually worked out. All they want is a decent neighborhood. The Christmas festivities at the church are all taken care of. We can ride in, do what we have to do, ride out, and it's like we were never there. In other words, Luther and his boys have our backs. There is only one little problem. Luther said if we don't come through for them, all bets are off. I assured him we were sincere, to which he replied that actions speak louder than words. I'm certain we have a lock on it."

"Sounds good. Any blowback from any of the girls? I'm not talking about Maggie here."

"All quiet," Espinosa mumbled as he continued to send text after text to both Maggie and Ted.

"Annie and Myra?" Jack asked.

"I can answer that," Harry said. "They've been spending a lot of time with Nellie. Elias is not doing well. Nellie is a basket case, so they're helping out and, from what I understand, will be spending Christmas with Nellie and Pearl. It's not a joyous time, so they didn't want to do all the traditional things they normally do. I got this from Yoko, who got it from someone who came to buy a tree. Is it gospel? I have no clue but have to believe it since neither Annie nor Myra have been in touch with any of us."

Jack nodded. He looked over at Abner, and said, "Speak, Mr. Computer Guru." Jack thought he'd never seen Abner look so jittery. The computer hacker was always in control. Not today, though. He couldn't help but wonder if what he was seeing had anything to do with the holiday season and Isabelle an ocean away.

"I have here," Abner said, waving a thick sheaf of papers

in the air, "all of Lieutenant Governor and Mrs. Sandford's accounts. And there are many. They are also spread far and wide. I did find them, however. There's only one glitch. I cannot crack their passwords. I used every program there is to no avail. The only way we are going to get them is if the Sandfords 'voluntarily' give them to us. That's pretty much it, guys."

Jack smiled. "Not to worry. By the time we're done with them, the Sandfords will beg us to take their passwords and their money. Trust me on that. So, what is the devil and his mistress worth?"

"A nice round $480 million. Chump change," Abner said, trying for levity.

"Well that should certainly help clean up Luther's neighborhood and pay me back the money I've already spent," Dennis said, clapping his hands together. He was grinning from ear to ear. "But just so you know, if it didn't work out this way, I wouldn't mind a bit footing the bill for all those people. I'm just glad I could do it."

Jack moved the files on his desk from one spot to the next. "Let's get down to business, boys. Christmas Eve will be here before we know it. I want to make sure each of us knows what part we're playing in our little Christmas play. Now, listen up."

Chapter 24

Jack Emery groaned and rolled over, his hand slapping at the mound of covers.

"Jack, wake up. I need to talk to you. Jack, please," Nikki pleaded. Cyrus took that moment to throw back his head and let loose with an ungodly sound. *That* got Jack's attention.

"What's wrong? Is the house on fire? What time is it?"

"The house is not on fire, and it's a few minutes before five. Jack, I need you fully awake. Here," she said, reaching for a tray on the nightstand, "I brought you coffee."

Jack struggled to sit up as he punched pillows behind his back. "Okay, okay, I'm awake, now tell me what's wrong." He sipped at the steaming brew in the heavy mug as he peered at his beautiful wife, who looked like she was going to go through the ceiling any moment. He didn't think he'd ever seen her this agitated. She looked gorgeous, in a plum-colored suit that shrieked high-dollar designer label. She was wearing makeup, but it didn't totally cover the dark circles under her eyes. He felt his stomach muscles clench. Whatever she was going to tell him wasn't going to be good. He could feel it in his bones.

Nikki licked at her crimson lips and took a deep breath. "Listen, Jack, I know tomorrow is Christmas Eve, and I know we had plans for Christmas Day but . . . I . . . Alexis and I have to leave for Minnesota today. Our flight leaves at noon. Jack, please don't look at me like that . . . one of the little kids . . . the mother called last night . . . and . . . and . . . it doesn't look like she'll make it through Christmas. We have to . . . to . . . video the child. The mother has been putting it off hoping Marcey—that's her name, Marcey—would . . . rally, but she's gotten worse. I know this sounds ghoulish and it wasn't my idea, it was the parents' . . . they want us there. It will help their case. We talked about this, Jack, and it was you who told me to get video of all the victims because that's what they are, victims. You said juries need to see the victims. Such a sad time. I don't want to do this. Good Lord, I don't even know if I *can* do this, but I . . . she's only nine years old, Jack. And her seven-year-old brother, Donny, isn't . . . he . . . the father said at best he only has a few weeks. I have to go, Jack."

Jack bounded out of bed. "Damn right you have to go. You go and do whatever you need to do, Nik. We're the lucky ones, we'll have other Christmases. Don't give me another thought. This is more important." He wrapped his arms around his shaking wife and crooned softly in her ear. He stroked her back until he felt her stop shaking. He moved his arms and held her at arm's length, then wiped the tears rolling down her cheeks. "Do what you have to do, make those bastards pay. How are the parents fixed for money? Do you know?"

"I do know. They have to file for bankruptcy but that's the least of their problems. I have to go, Jack. What . . . what will you do?"

"Me? I'll spend the time with the guys. Like I said, don't worry about me. I have Cyrus. I'm going to teach him how to bark when I sing a carol by the tree on Christmas Eve.

I'll video it for you." His words had the desired effect as Nikki offered up a wan smile.

"I'll call," Nikki said, slipping into her coat. She grabbed a small carry-on bag, and, a minute later, she was gone.

Jack sat down on the edge of the bed and stared at his bare feet. Cyrus whimpered as he hopped on the bed and stuck his big head under Jack's arm. "Yep, it's just you and me, sport. You know, Cyrus, I've been really sweating this Christmas Eve gig we have going on. I've been racking my brain worrying about how I was going to get out for Christmas Eve without telling Nik what I was up to. She just solved my problem, sad as that may be. God does work in mysterious ways, now doesn't He? Merry Christmas, Cyrus!" The shepherd barked and started racing around the room. Jack headed for the shower, calling over his shoulder, "Don't forget to make your bed! Just because Nik isn't going to be here, you still gotta do it. Nice and neat now, no wrinkles." Jack laughed to himself as he stripped off his boxers and headed into the shower.

Cyrus looked at the bathroom door, then down at his dog bed at the foot of the king-size people bed. He nosed what Jack called his toy stash onto the floor, then tugged at his yellow blanket until the big dog bed was covered. He knew what no wrinkles meant, so he walked around the four corners and tugged at the blanket. He saw the deep wrinkle in the middle, backed off, eyed the bed, then dropped one of his toys on top of the wrinkle.

"I saw that!" Jack bellowed from the bathroom. Cyrus barked once, twice, three times, which meant, *that's as good as it's gonna get. So there!*

Ten minutes later, Jack and Cyrus were in the kitchen. He opened the door for Cyrus to go outside. A wintry blast of cold air hit him like a jackhammer. He quickly slammed the door shut and set about making a fresh pot of coffee, fried some bacon, and scrambled enough eggs for the two of them. He was filling Cyrus's food bowl when the big dog scratched at the door to come in.

Jack turned on the small television on the kitchen counter and listened to the early morning news. Same old same old. The world, in his opinion, was going to hell, and he hardly needed some slick commentator giving his biased spin on things. He switched channels, but, again, it was same old same old. Obviously there was no news so close to Christmas. Some roving reporter was questioning shoppers about what they were buying and how much they were spending this year. A straggly-looking Santa was bemoaning the fact that people weren't as generous this year as other years. "So what else is new?" Jack muttered as he carried his plate to the sink. Cyrus picked up his bowl and handed it to Jack, who rinsed the dishes and set them in the dishwasher.

Jack checked the fireplace to make sure the fire was totally out, turned down the thermostat, then looked at the Christmas tree he'd put up yesterday. It smelled heavenly. For a moment he let his thoughts take him back to his childhood and the magic of Christmas morning. How long ago that was. Then his thoughts took him to a little girl named Marcey way out in Minnesota and her little brother Donny, who would never . . . Jack swiped at his eyes. "Kick their asses, Nik, make those bastards pay not just for Marcey and Donny but for all those poor kids who aren't here this Christmas and for all the Christmases to come." Cyrus nudged Jack's leg. Time to go.

Outside in the frigid air, Jack looked around. It was still dark. He could see two people walking their dogs on the other side of the street. On his side of the street, he saw plumes of smoke circling upward from cars that were being warmed up. "I hate this weather, Cyrus." Cyrus barked to show he wasn't fond of it himself as he snuggled down on the passenger seat while Jack scraped the ice from the windshield.

Jack tossed the window scraper onto the backseat. He looked up the street and grinned in the darkness. The *Post* van was still parked outside Maggie's house. "Good for you guys," he mumbled under his breath.

It was high noon when Jack looked around the conference table to see that everyone was in attendance. Abner had set up the webcam earlier, and Bert and Sparrow were on standby. A second webcam was set up on the opposite side of the room, in which they could see Avery Snowden waiting patiently for the briefing to get under way.

The group spent fifteen minutes playing catch-up, then got down to business just as Ted and Maggie appeared. Jack outlined the plan and waited for approval via the webcams. When it came, he sighed in relief. "We're good to go, guys. We're going to do a practice run in about an hour. Espinosa is going to video it and will send it on to you. We'll have an hour or so to pick it apart, assuming we make a few mistakes along the way. We'll weed those out. And then, around nine this evening, the fun begins. We do our snatch and grab, head for the landing zone, and let matters take their course. I'm not anticipating any snafus, but you never know."

Avery Snowden had a few questions that were addressed. Jack Sparrow announced that he would be taking the red-eye out Christmas night to get ready for his new job at the ugly brown Hoover Building.

Bert cleared his throat and addressed Jack. "Are the files safe, Jack?"

"You know it, buddy. When they're needed, I'll pull them out." To the others he explained what Bert meant. "When Elias Cummings was the director of the FBI, he compiled a dossier on every politician in the District, just the way J. Edgar did. When Elias retired, he turned them over to Bert, who kept them until he left the Bureau when we went to work for Global Security, about which most of you know that I have nothing good to say. He turned them over to me, and I am the guardian now." He turned to the webcam and spoke to Jack Sparrow. "No offense, pal, but until we see how you run this new show, I'm keeping these files. You okay with that, Sparrow?"

Jack Sparrow laughed. "I always thought that story was a myth, but guess I was wrong. Jack, I wouldn't have it any other way. I understand you guys need me to prove myself, and I will. We can talk about those files some other day. Just knowing they're out there is enough for me. It's the fear of the unknown that works best in cases like this."

"Okay, we're all good then." Jack looked around to see his guys nodding. He was puzzled that even Dennis didn't have a question or two. The kid was finally on the same page. Jack felt a tremendous sense of relief knowing that the young reporter was finally getting it. Before long, he'd be totally shockproof.

"Let's do one more run-through just to be on the safe side. Then we'll meet up here again and head on out. We need to synchronize our watches so we don't screw up. When I call your name, tell me what your job is."

And so it went until Maggie asked the dreaded question. "So, what's their punishment? How far are you willing to go to get those bank-account passwords? I'm sensing not too far. Like you guys don't have the stomach for . . . the kinds of punishment we girls doled out. You do realize, don't you, that you can't threaten if you aren't prepared to carry through on the threat. Now, let me hear it."

The boys looked at one another, and they all started to talk at once. Maggie hooted with laughter. "You can't be serious!" At the expressions she was seeing on their faces, she knew they were. "Wusses! Wimps! It's a good thing I'm here since I do not share your squeamishness. Children died because of that man, and all you're prepared to do is . . . basically nothing other than trying to scare them to death. I have a few ideas. Want to hear them?"

The boys looked at one another, but it was Dennis who said, "Let's hear those ideas."

After Maggie told the guys what she intended, she almost fell off her chair when the young reporter's fist shot in the air. "For sure they'll spill their guts. Can you really do it, Maggie, if it comes down to it?"

"Oh yeahhhh," Maggie drawled. She stood up, looked around, and said, "Looks like we're done here, so I'll leave to . . . ah . . . pack up my old kit bag and meet you back here at eight on the dot. I'm not saying my old kit bag is the same as Alexis's red bag of tricks, but I think I can pull it off. First, though, I have to go back to the paper and square things away. You wanna come with me, Dennis?"

Dennis grabbed his heavy jacket from the back of his chair. "You know it!"

The moment the door closed behind the duo, everyone started talking at once.

"Holy shit! She wouldn't . . . would she really . . . ?" Abner asked, as his face started to pale.

"Oh, she can do it, trust me," Ted said, a crazy, lopsided grin on his face.

"Nah, she isn't capable, is she?" Sparrow said in a tight voice.

Bert burst out laughing. "Watch and see." He was laughing so hard, he clicked off.

Jack looked over at Espinosa and Harry, waiting to see what they would say, if anything. Both men just shrugged. Jack took a deep breath. "Well, let's hope it doesn't come to that. If it does . . . oh well, the end will justify the means."

Cyrus decided to weigh in and rose onto his hind legs and howled. He didn't stop until Jack said, "Okay, we have your vote." Determined to have the last word, Cyrus let loose with a bloodcurdling bark that set everyone's, including Jack's, teeth on edge.

Five minutes later, the conference room was empty except for Jack and Cyrus. Jack looked down at the big dog lying at his feet and grinned to himself. Cyrus was almost human, at least in his eyes.

Jack sprinted for the kitchen, poured coffee, grabbed a treat for his best friend, then hightailed it back to the conference room, where he punched in the numbers for District Management LLC, which managed Tyler Sandford's properties, and asked to speak to Lionel Marks. He was surprised when the receptionist put him through once he announced his name and said he had a check for the manager.

The two men made small talk and, when Jack adamantly said time was of the essence for him and he didn't have any to meet Marks at the management-company office, arranged to meet at the BOLO Building at seven-thirty. He did apologize for the after-hours meeting when Marks complained about the hour and the fact that the banks were closed, at which point Jack reminded him about night deposits. In the end, after a little haggling, Marks agreed to the meeting.

Jack felt a little squeamish about having to open the front door of the BOLO Building, but in the end it just made the most sense. This way they could spirit the guy out the back door into the *Post* van and no one would be the wiser. Too many eyes at Marks's building, and he seriously doubted the manager ever kept late hours. Coming to the BOLO Building made the most sense. He made a mental note to himself to remember to move Marks's car after the snatch.

Before he left the building, Jack stopped at Abner's office and knocked on the door. Cyrus barked shrilly to make sure the computer hacker heard that he and his master wanted entrance to the room. Abner himself opened the door and dropped to his haunches and tussled with the big dog for a few minutes before he reached into his pocket for a treat. "What's up?"

Jack explained what he'd done. "We'll hit him with the Taser and load him in the van, then head out to Middleburg. You have *all* of his accounts, right?"

"Yep, and I was able to crack his passwords, so we're good to go with his funds. I even have copies of the deeds to properties he owns in Hong Kong and Dubai. How cool is that? The slimeball is loaded, but not for long," Abner said as he rubbed his hands together in glee. "I hate that bastard, and I don't even know him."

Jack laughed. "Wait till you meet the Sandfords."

"Ah . . . Jack . . . about Maggie . . ."

"Don't go there, Abner. It is what it is. She was right. It won't work just trying to scare these guys. The girls would never have been so successful if they didn't follow through. Maggie has the guts. It's all doable."

"If you say so. Okay, I have some stuff I have to print out. I don't plan on leaving here, so when you all get here at seven-thirty, I'll be ready to go."

"Any word from Isabelle?" Jack asked quietly.

Abner shook his head. "Like you say, Jack, it is what it is. Go on, get out of here before you see a grown man cry."

"Yeah, I know what you mean." He told him about Nikki and her trip to the Midwest. All Abner did was shake his head. "I'm cooking dinner Christmas Day, and I expect you to show up with a bottle of wine."

"I'll be there, Jack."

"Come on, Cyrus, let's hit the road. We've got things to do and places to go."

"Woof."

Chapter 25

At six-thirty it was fully dark outside. Every light in the BOLO Building was still on. The decibel level was at an all-time high as everyone tried talking over everyone else to be heard. The topic of conversation was the giant evergreen in the middle of the foyer. Sometime during the afternoon, Dennis had dragged it in, set it up, and decorated it with Rite Aid decorations. The scent was heady and wafted throughout the building.

"Nice going, kid," Ted said as he admired the young reporter's handiwork.

"Where'd you get it?" Harry asked.

Dennis scowled. "Where do you think I got it, Harry? I called your wife, and she had it all ready for me. She told me how to set it up and here we are. I even wrapped the presents under the tree. I have not been idle." He looked around, the frown building on his face. "What? So, I'm the only gift giver here? Where are *your* presents? Tell me they're in the trunks of your cars?" He was rewarded with sheepish looks. Dennis shrugged. "Shame on all of you. It's Christmas, and I know we're all wired up, but for crying out loud, the drugstore even gift wraps."

Jack stepped up to try to avert what he thought might become a major issue if he didn't calm things down.

"Christmas is at my house, Dennis. I have a tree and the presents go under *it*. We didn't know you were going to do this, right, guys?" Everyone started to babble at once, agreeing with Jack. "So, you're going to have to lug those presents to my house Christmas Day. Nice thought, though, and you know we appreciate it, right, guys?"

"Yeah, yeah," the guys all agreed. Maggie stood on her toes and kissed Dennis on the cheek. "This is just so sweet of you, Dennis. And we all needed this. We're all a little tense right now."

"Okay, okay. No problem," Dennis said, relief washing over him.

"Listen up, guys, and gal. I brought food, and I think we should chow down now. It's going to be a long night, as you all know. And we need to run through our plan one more time before Lionel Marks gets here. I don't want any screwups. This has to go off like clockwork. Everyone in agreement?" Jack asked.

When everyone agreed they were, he said, "Okay, I brought Italian and Chinese. We're drinking tea," Jack said, looking at Harry, "and soda. Orange and grape for Dennis and cola for the rest of you. We have a little over an hour, so let's get to it."

The little group talked about everything but what they were about to do in the coming hours. Maggie was the most verbal as she laid out one pitfall after another only to be shot down time after time. Or as Harry put it, "We've got it covered." Finally, she relaxed and started to clear off the long conference table. "Save or not?" she asked, looking at the leftovers.

"We won't be back here till the day after Christmas so no, don't save it," Jack said. "Cyrus does not like leftovers, and this kind of food isn't good for him anyway."

Ted looked down at his watch, which did everything but

his laundry. "Ten minutes, and your guest should be here. Should we relocate or what?"

"I'll let him in and bring him back here to the conference room. I need him to get back here under his own power without suspecting anything. Once he's here inside, it's a whole different ball game."

In the foyer, Jack eyed the ugly banana tree and the beautiful Christmas tree as he paced the room from one end to the other. Like a little kid, he dropped to his haunches and poked and shook the beribboned gifts. He looked for the one that had his name on it and smiled. Guessing was half the fun. He remembered that when he was little at times he'd been disappointed when he found underwear or a scarf in an exquisitely wrapped package. He shook the box, but nothing rattled. Probably something for Cyrus, but no, he'd seen a package with Cyrus's name on it. He finally set the package back where he'd found it and got to his feet just as the doorbell rang. He sucked in his breath and undid the one-of-a-kind security lock he'd commissioned when the building was being refurbished and opened the door. "Mr. Marks, you're on time. I like that. Time is money. Sorry to call you on such short notice, but my time here in the District is short. So, if you'll follow me to the conference room, we can finalize our business. I have everything here with me. My lawyer, Lizzie Fox, overnighted everything. Tomorrow, the banks will be open, so you can deposit the checks. That will work for you, won't it, Mr. Marks?"

Marks nodded. "What is this building? I've seen it but never knew what kind of business operated here." Managing a building like this here in Georgetown would certainly be a feather in his cap, he thought. The commission would be robust, not that it mattered at this point in time. His eyes were everywhere, mentally cataloging the cost of the furniture and the square footage.

"I just use it when I'm in town. The owners, friends of mine, decided to close for the holidays, so it worked out perfectly for me. A great bunch of guys own it. It's a high-dollar consulting business."

Lionel Marks went back to calculating the high-end furnishings and the cost of the building and the rent it would garner if he had it to rent out. Too bad he didn't have more clients at this end of town instead of in that shit hole in Southeast. He could really clean up and fatten his bank account quickly. Still, it didn't pay to get too greedy. He had this guy snookered, and if his calculations were spot-on, he'd walk out of here with 150 grand in his pocket.

Jack stopped at the conference room door and stood aside as he opened it. "After you, Mr. Marks." The minute the door closed behind him, Jack snapped the dead bolt. The sound was like thunder in the quiet room.

Marks whirled around and noticed Cyrus, who was growling deep in his throat. Then he let his gaze circle the long table and the people seated in the plush padded chairs who had their eyes fixed on him. The fine hairs on the back of his neck stood straight up. The words *set up* flashed through his mind. *I've been set up.*

Marks turned to Jack. "Who are these people? Are they the tenants living in the units you want me to manage?" Wrong. Wrong. Something wasn't right. The hairs on the back of his neck moved with the air circulating from the room's heating vent.

"In a manner of speaking. Have a seat."

Marks sat down but only on the edge of his chair. Maybe he was wrong. Maybe he was being overly paranoid. Like hell. He could smell deception a mile away because he held a master's degree in the subject of deception. Maybe he could bluff his way through whatever *this* was. "Could we speed this up, Mr. Tremaine? My family is waiting for me, and as I told you, I don't do business after closing hours. I made an exception for you since you're only in town for a few hours. Where are the contracts?"

"Well, you see, Lionel, it's like this: there are no contracts, and my name isn't Tremaine. I lied to you. The reason you're here is we want your money. All of it. Don't be shy, now, and try to tell us you don't have any because we know differently. We know about all the property you own, including those two getaways in Hong Kong and Dubai. We know that you bought a ticket this morning for Hong Kong. Your plane leaves at five after six in the morning of December twenty-sixth. A one-way ticket. No companion ticket."

Sweat beaded on Marks's forehead as his stomach crunched into a hard knot. He knew it. Goddamnit. "What the hell are you talking about?" He looked down, fear in his eyes when he saw the big German shepherd circling his chair.

"Try this on for size, Mr. Marks," Abner said as he slid a sheaf of papers across the table. "It must take many hours a day to shuffle all that money here, there, and yonder. I guess that's why you don't have time to requisition the repairs the tenants requested out there in Southeast. So what if a few people don't have heat, so what if they don't have hot water, so what if they can't flush, so what if the electric doesn't work. A busy man like you needs to tend to his finances. And I'm here to tell one and all that your finances are robust. Ooops, *were* robust. *Were* is the operative word here."

Abner slid a second sheaf of papers across the table. "Take a look at the bottom line, Mr. Marks. Zero, straight across the board."

Lionel Marks could feel Cyrus's hot breath on his ankles. He'd never been so cold in his life. And yet he was sweating like a pig. He needed to get himself together. When he saw the zero balances, he forgot about the monster dog and how cold he was, and bellowed his outrage. "You fucking stole my money! Who the hell are you people?" He was on his feet, his face red with rage.

Cyrus reared up and backed away a step as his lips peeled back, showing a magnificent set of teeth. His growl sounded deadly. Marks paid no attention as he continued to rant and rave. "You bastard, you lied to me! You came to my office and pretended to want my help! And now you tell me you just stole all my money. You just wait till I get out of here! I know important people in high places. Unlock that goddamn door and let me out of here *right now*!"

Jack sighed. "That isn't going to happen anytime soon, Mr. Marks."

Cyrus hated to be ignored. He looked at his master, who shrugged. It was all Cyrus needed. He lived for moments like this, when he could sink his teeth into something substantial. He lunged, his teeth clamping down six inches below Marks's belt.

"Ooooh." Maggie grimaced. "I bet that hurts! Oooooh."

Marks's eyes rolled back in his head. He had a death grip on the arms of the chair he was now sitting on. The room went quiet.

Jack looked down at Cyrus, and said, "Okay, let him go. You didn't break the skin, did you?" Cyrus just looked at his master as much as to say, *I know the rules. The next time is when I get to go full bore. If there is a next time.* Jack gave him a treat.

Jack fixed his stare on Lionel Marks, and said, "The next time, he'll chew them off. Just so you know. Now, we want to ask you some questions. Oh, by the way, you will not be going to Hong Kong. Nor will you be spending the holidays with your family. You're going to be spending them with your favorite client and his wife. Now, to the questions."

"I'm not telling you anything. It's client privilege. That

was part of the deal. This is kidnapping. You can go to jail for this, and I'm calling the FBI as soon as I leave here," Marks blustered.

Jack sighed. "Obviously, you haven't been listening. You aren't leaving here. Well, that's not quite true; you are leaving but not for home. You won't be making any calls to anyone. I guess you forgot about Cyrus here. Yes, we are kidnapping you. That part is true. The other true part is we are stealing your money. Ooops, correction. We *already* stole your money.

"Let's get on with it. I don't want to hear about any client privilege bullshit either. What did Sandford tell you when he signed on with you? Ah, you thought we didn't know. Get it through your thick skull, we know *everything*. We just want to confirm what we already know. What kind of deal did you have with him and his wife? I won't ask you again. What kind of deal did you have with Sandford and his wife?"

Marks looked around at the faces staring at him. He thought they looked evil, especially the Chinese guy. "If I tell you, will you let me go?"

The one-word reply was an explosion of sound. "No."

"Then go to hell, Mr. Whatever-the-hell-your-name-is."

Jack didn't respond. He just pointed to Cyrus, who was contentedly chewing on a rawhide strip. Then he pointed to Marks's groin. He folded his arms across his chest and waited for a response. When none came he watched in slow motion as Dennis got up off his chair, walked around the table, and, before Jack knew what he was doing, pulled his arm back and then shot it forward, his fist slamming dead center on Marks's nose.

Blood flew outward in a fine mist, then gushed down Marks's chin. Cyrus looked up to see if his services were required, decided they weren't, and went back to his chew bone.

"Way to go, Dennis," Ted chortled.

"I'm sick and tired of coddling him. It's getting late; we need to get ready to leave if you want to stick to the timetable," Dennis said fiercely.

Jack looked at Harry and hissed, "You created a monster." Harry actually laughed.

Maggie ripped off a length of paper towels from the sink at the bar and shoved them at Marks. She couldn't resist adding, "Don't worry about that designer suit you're wearing. Where you're going, you won't be needing it."

"What the hell does that mean?" Marks bellowed as he tried to staunch the flow of blood coming from his nostrils. "What gives you the right to steal my money? I'm calling the FBI right now. You'd better keep that damn dog away from me. And that crazy asshole that just punched me. I'll see you all in jail. You're crazy!"

"It means whatever you want it to mean, you dickweed," Dennis snarled. To Jack he said, "Look, we already know everything, so why does this dickweed have to confirm it? We're going to run late. I say we dump him, then head for Middleburg. We can question him in the van if you think it's that important. Let's take a vote." Every hand in the room shot in the air.

"I'm not going to Middleburg. Get that idea out of your head right now," Marks sputtered.

"You're right, you are not going to Middleburg, we are. You are going to the Southeast Ritz Carlton. Okay," Jack said agreeably. "Let's load up. You need to shut up, Marks. I don't want to hear another word out of you. If you so much as breathe heavy, I'm going to let Cyrus play with you."

Cyrus understood the words *load* up and *play*. He grabbed his ragged duck and raced to the back door.

"Tie this jerk up and load him into the back of the van," Ted ordered as he tossed a set of flex cuffs to Espinosa. Abner set his briefcase down in the event he was needed to help with a noncompliant Marks. In the end, cursing and yelling, Marks went limp. Ted threw him over his shoulders in a fireman's carry, and they all marched single file out to the *Post* van.

Thirty-five minutes later, the *Post* van pulled to the curb right behind Marks's stripped-down Mercedes. Luther Jones appeared out of nowhere, three of his gang behind him. He high-fived Dennis and the others as he introduced himself and his friends.

"What do you need us to do, man?"

Dennis drew Luther to the side, clued him in, then walked back to the little group. "He understands he and his friends are to stand guard until we get back. Once we dump Marks on the second floor, there is no way he's going to leave unless Marks can fly. There is no heat inside this condemned building, which, by the way, belongs to Sandford. The water is still running so they can flush, but the system leaves a lot to be desired. Sometimes it works and sometimes it doesn't. They rigged up some electricity earlier and there is a fifteen-watt bulb hanging from the ceiling. And, Luther tells me the temperature is a robust forty-nine degrees. There is no furniture in the apartment, the floors are rotted, the windows broken, and when they rigged up the light, they let loose a dozen or so rats that they had trapped over the past few days. Hungry rats!"

"That excites me," Jack said as he eyed Marks, who looked like he was going to black out at any moment. Espinosa grabbed one arm and Abner took the other as Marks struggled to free himself as he screamed at the top of his lungs for help. "Stop that right now!" Jack ordered. "If you don't stop, we'll take the lightbulb out, and you'll be in total darkness. If that happens, how are you going to see the rats? Now shut the hell up."

Marks shut up.

"Okay, boys, take him up to the second floor. We need

to get on the road. Luther, my man, we appreciate all your help. If he starts to squawk, give him a good belt. Are you sure you don't want me to leave Cyrus?"

"We got it covered, man. Go on, do what you gotta do. The dude ain't gonna go anywhere. Glad to help. By the way, my granny and some of the others want to know if you folks are coming to the church service and the party tomorrow."

"You know it," Dennis said, accepting for everyone. Another round of high fives were completed before the group started back toward the van. "Hey, Luther, we forgot to frisk him. Take his cell phone and give it to someone who needs one. If he has any money on him, it's yours."

"All righttttt," Luther called over his shoulder as he climbed the rickety, rotted steps to the second-floor apartment.

Chapter 26

The night was crisp and cold, with barely any wind. Millions of stars dotted the black night as the small group climbed into the *Post* van. Ted took the wheel, and Jack rode shotgun, with the others piling into the remaining seats. For the most part they were subdued, each busy with his or her own private thoughts.

Twenty minutes into the hour-long trip, Jack looked down at his watch. "When you spoke with Mrs. Sandford earlier, did you believe her when she said she and her husband were just making a token appearance at the mayor's annual Christmas party?"

"Yeah, I did, Jack. When I told her I was bringing her an early copy of her spread, she about turned herself inside out. When I tried to nail down if her husband would be there for sure, she assured me he had gotten to the farm at two o'clock this afternoon and, like herself, had exactly no interest in staying at the party. She said they had to make an appearance and do a little meet and greet before they headed right back to the farm. She's excited, I can tell you that."

"Security?" Harry asked from the backseat.

"She didn't say, Harry. I'm assuming not. He's in his own bailiwick and feels safe there and knows the local police have his back. That's what she told us on our initial visit, and I have no reason to think that would be any different now. There is no reason for anything to have changed in a matter of a few days. I take their going to the mayor's party as a plus. If they do it every year, for sure their not attending might throw up a red flag. I think we're good here. If not, we'll deal with it when we get there. Between you and young Dennis, we have a two-man army." Ted chuckled at his own wit.

No one said anything after that until Ted slowed the van thirty minutes later.

"I remember that old rotted tree, Ted. Go slow, there might be a light over the sign or maybe some of those reflector stickers on the other trees," Dennis called from the backseat as he tried to peer out into the darkness. "There it is, right up ahead. Whoa, slow down, see there it is. The mailbox is lit up. Do you see it, Ted?"

"I see it. Okay, everyone, take a deep breath. What time is it?" Ted asked as he crawled along at five miles an hour over the unpaved, potholed road that would take him to the Sandford farmhouse.

"Holy cow, look at those lights!" Dennis shrilled from the backseat. "Would you look at that! Damn if it doesn't look like Disney! She wasn't kidding when she said the light show was spectacular! Not that I'm thinking this is spectacular but . . . but . . . ."

"It's a nightmare light show," Abner said, as the van inched closer to the residence. "They must have bought out some electric factory to light the place up like this."

"Espinosa, you getting all this?" Ted asked, rolling down his window to get a better look at the reindeer dancing across the roof of the farmhouse. Everywhere, as far as the eye could see, were LED-lighted wire snowmen, wire Santas, wire elves, wire Christmas trees, wire sleighs filled with wire gift boxes. All the lights were multicolored. The ancient oak trees surrounding the driveway were all lit with blinking lights. Even the thick, round trunks were wired with the blinking lights. "Makes you dizzy, doesn't it?" Ted cackled. "Wait till you see the inside. Just wait." He continued to cackle.

"I think we're here. I only see a Maybach off there on the side. Was that car here the day you and Espinosa were? Or is it the lieutenant governor's car?" Jack asked.

"There weren't any cars here the day we came. Mrs. Sandford said she gave all her staff time off for the holidays, so I'm thinking it must belong to his nibs, the lieutenant governor himself. The kids aren't home, so it can't be one of theirs plus it's a Maybach, and you know what those babies retail for. It's gotta be his. Mrs. Sandford probably keeps hers in the garage, and I'm thinking they were in a hurry when they got home and just left it outside. At least we know they're home. Place is lit up like a Christmas tree, no pun intended," Ted said, bringing the van to a complete stop behind the black Maybach. Everyone exited.

As one, the group's jaws dropped as they gaped at the front porch, which was ablaze with flying, LED-lit wire angels holding trumpets. From somewhere, probably the side of the house, tinny sounds of Christmas carols could be heard.

"Now I've seen it all," Jack said, his voice ringing in awe. "Even Vegas isn't as honky-tonk as this."

"And this woman wins the first prize every year for the best Christmas decorations?" Maggie all but snarled. "I'm not getting it. Are the judges blind?"

"Maggie, Maggie, Maggie!" Abner said. "What's not to get? Her husband is the lieutenant governor. He's filthy rich. He is in line to be the next governor of this fine commonwealth. It's called kissing ass. But for all we know, the judges might really be blind. The good news is that this is the last year she'll be winning anything. Wonder who will get to take all this stuff down?"

"Who cares. Will someone please ring the damn doorbell," Ted said, "so we can get this show on the road."

Harry reached forward and punched the doorbell. Then, for good measure, he raised the prancing stallion on the door knocker. They all blinked when they heard the scratchy Christmas song about Santa coming to town playing inside the house. Maggie rolled her eyes. "Unbelievable. Absolutely unbelievable!"

"Wait!" Dennis said. "You ain't seen nothing yet."

The door opened wide. Fiona Sandford stood there, resplendent, in a billowing lemon and lime skirt with a bright orange top. She rustled when she moved. Her hair was done up in a tight pile of curls on top of her head. Long lime green earrings, possibly jade, Maggie thought, dangled from her ears. Matching bracelets clanked on her wrists. The bee-stung lips were covered in crimson gloss, and a bit of food was stuck in the left corner of her mouth. One plucked eyebrow was longer and darker than the other. Maggie looked away so she wouldn't laugh out loud.

"Mr. Robinson!" Fiona gushed as she stood aside to let the little group into the foyer of her home. Then she backed up a step, and asked, "Who are all these people and why did you bring them here? I don't think my husband is going to like this. Not even one little bit. He was against my allowing you to come out here to begin with. Well . . ."

"They're the judges. We need a picture of you with the judges. I thought I explained all that to you when I was out here earlier."

The bee-stung lips went into full pout. "Yes, yes, you did. I am so sorry. I totally forgot. My manners are atrocious. I'm Fiona Sandford. And you are," she said, pointing to Jack and on down the line, with each person stating their name in response.

"Can we get right to it, Mrs. Sandford? We have a dead-line, and we do have to drive all the way back to the District. I'm sure you and your husband have things to do this evening since it is so close to Christmas. It's up to you, do you want to share your . . . ah . . . glory with your husband? If you do, he has to be in the picture."

"Well, the truth is," she whispered to Ted, "I'd rather he wasn't in the picture, but he said he wanted to be in it, so what can I do. Like you said, this is my moment. I shouldn't have to share it with him, but he *is* my husband. I think he gets his picture in the papers often enough. It's my turn. He likes to be photographed wearing his ascot. He's such a . . . never mind. Come along people, we can do this in the den, where the *big* tree is."

She turned to Espinosa, and said playfully, "Make sure you get my good side, and you won't hurt my feelings one little bit if my husband's image is on the . . . blurry side." She reached up and tweaked Espinosa's cheek to make sure he got the point.

With a straight face, Espinosa said, "What side would that be, ma'am?"

"Oh, you little rascal! Did you forget so soon? You said my right side is my best side. Capture me completely now. Ah, here we are!

"Tyler, I'd like you to meet the people I've been telling you about." Introductions were quickly made.

"They have to hurry, Tyler, to make their deadline. We agreed to have the picture by the tree with both of us look-ing up at the angel."

Jack decided right at that moment that he really, really didn't like Tyler Sandford. He looked like what Jack's father, a very shrewd judge of men, would have called a slick dandy. It was he and Harry who were going to light up the couple's life with the Tasers in their pockets the moment they looked upward at the tacky tarnished angel atop the tree. That way, they wouldn't see what was coming, and there would be less fuss and bother. At the moment, looking at Tyler Sandford, Jack regretted that reducing fuss and bother came at the expense of causing him less terror than if he saw it coming and reacted.

Espinosa coaxed Fiona to look more to the right, and she happily obliged just as twenty thousand volts of electricity struck home.

"They call this 'riding the bull' in Taser circles," Dennis said gleefully.

"Really!" was all Maggie could think to say.

"Flex cuffs, guys!" Jack said.

The moment the couple was secure, Ted and Jack hoisted them up onto two tacky Queen Anne chairs covered with red-and-green-striped felt. Sandford seemed to be coming out of it quicker than his wife. He was groggy, but his words were sharp and clear. "Is this a home invasion? If it is, you are welcome to all this crap you see. The truth is, I'll pay you to cart it off. I don't keep money in the house. Take the car and leave us alone."

"It's not a home invasion, Mr. Sandford. We're here to steal your life and all that money you have socked away around the world. We're also here to make you pay for all those people out in Southeast. That's number one. All we need from you are your passwords, and we'll be on our way," Abner explained.

Fiona had come around just in time to have heard her beloved husband telling the people they could take all her crap. "Crap!" she screeched. "Is that what you said? You ungrateful bastard! This is not crap, this is my life's work. What else do I have? Nothing, that's what. You're saying my life's work is crap, which means I'm crap! Well, we'll just see about that." She was almost up, bent on attacking her husband, when Ted shoved her back down none too gently onto the red-and-green-striped felt chair.

"You'll get your turn, Mrs. Sandford," Dennis said as he eyed all the junk in the family room. He turned away because it all made him dizzy.

Abner sat down on a candy-cane-patterned ottoman and opened his laptop. He flexed his fingers and started to type. He clicked on a button and a list of offshore accounts appeared as if by magic. He turned his laptop around and showed the screen to Sandford. "The passwords, please." His tone was polite.

"Like I'm really going to give you my passwords. Get real, you clown. And don't think you can scare me either." Sandford turned to his wife. "Do not open your mouth, Fiona."

"Don't tell me what to do, you jackass."

"We don't have time for a family spat," Jack said. "You can ream each other out later because, believe me, you are going to have nothing else to do. Now save yourselves a lot of trouble and tell us what we want to know."

"What's that supposed to mean?" Sandford blustered. I told you, I'm not telling you anything. Take my car and get out of here, and we'll forget this ever happened."

"Now that's a lie if I ever heard one. We should forget the way you forgot about that poor family's children who died because you wouldn't fix the furnace in the building where they lived? Are you saying it's okay for little kids to freeze to death? Is that what you're saying?"

"Abner, show him the list of properties he owns." Abner obliged, then swiveled the laptop around so Sandford could see the screen again.

"So I own a lot of buildings over in Southeast, so what? You can't hold me responsible for what the property-management company does or doesn't do. My hands are clean on all of that. No charges were ever brought against me."

"Because you used your wealth to bribe people, threatened them and made promises you have no intention of keeping. Innocent children are dead because of you," Jack said as he watched beads of sweat pool on Sandford's forehead.

"I told you, I had nothing to do with those deaths. I hired a reputable management company to collect the rents and maintain the buildings. You want to blame someone, go after Lionel Marks and leave me and my wife alone."

"We did that already!" Jack said, happiness ringing in his voice. "Would you like to talk to him? Dennis, call Luther and have him put Marks on the phone.

"By the way, Marks gave you up in a heartbeat. And, wait till you hear this, Mr. Sandford, he has—had—a single one-way ticket to Hong Kong. His flight, which, unfortunately, he is not going to make, leaves at five after six in the morning on December twenty-sixth. He's truly heartbroken that he won't be able to make it."

"I told you not to trust that scumbag. He oils his hair. You can't trust anyone who oils his hair. And he takes a bath in that shitty cologne he wears. I called him the other day, and he gave me the runaround. All he was worried about was that our tenants stripped his car to a shell. I warned him. I warned you, too, Tyler, and this is the outcome. I guess this is a stupid question, but why isn't he going to make his flight?" Fiona asked. Her face was a mask of fear, and her eyes were full of tears as she stared at her husband.

"I told you to shut up, Fiona," Sandford growled.

"And I told you don't tell me what to do, Mr. Lieutenant Governor of the Commonwealth of Virginia."

"No more bickering!" Harry Wong roared.

"You should listen to him," Dennis said, "or he'll pull your tongue through your nose and out your ears. He can do it, too." He looked over at Harry, and whispered, "Did I get that right?" He handed the phone to Jack when Harry glared at him as if he were revealing state secrets.

Jack brought the phone up to his ear in time to hear Lionel Marks cursing him in every language in the book. "There are rats in here. They keep trying to eat my legs, there's not enough light, and I'm freezing my ass off. Get me the hell out of here. I'll give you whatever you want. I'll never say a word. I swear to God, I will never say a word. I'll go out there and personally apologize to those people. I just did what Sandford and his wife told me to do. I'm their employee. Go after them! For God's sake, get me out of here! I could die here from rat bites if I don't freeze first. I'm begging you, whatever your name is."

Jack clucked his tongue. "Sorry, Lionel, we already have everything you own, and, like I said, you aren't going anywhere, so get used to it. I'm going to put you on speaker now so you can tell your clients, that would be Mr. and Mrs. Sandford, the spot you are currently in. Be happy. They'll be joining you shortly." Jack clicked on the speaker and held out the phone so Marks's words could be heard by the whole room. Marks spouted a tirade the likes of which none of them had ever heard before.

"Wow!" Maggie said. "He certainly is colorful now, isn't he?"

"Yep," Ted said.

Tyler Sandford listened, then let loose with a volley of profanity the little group had never heard before either. Fiona Sandford fainted as Marks continued to scream and blame Sandford and herself for everything under the sun, ending with, "I hope they do bring your sorry ass here, and you'll see what living with rats is like. Oh, God, one of them is chewing my shoe!"

Fiona opened her eyes just in time to hear Marks's last statement. She started to wail and curse her husband. "Rats! Rats! Oh, my God! Do something. Tell them what they want to know. Look at them, Tyler, these people are evil. *Evil!*" she screeched at the top of her lungs.

"Who brought these evil people here, Fiona? You did! I had nothing to do with this; my hands are clean. You people will go to jail for this. I'll personally see to it. And you'll never see the light of day again."

"Wait just one minute here," Jack said. "Who was just Tasered? Who is tied up at the moment? Whose underling is living with rats with no heat, no water, no food, and blames you? And I'll never see the light of day again! I think you have that backward, Mr. Sandford. I'm going to ask you one more time. Give us the passwords, or I'll turn my colleague loose on you."

"You'll have to kill me then because I am not giving them to you. Go ahead, kill me," Sandford said, his face going from red to white and back to red again.

"Nah, killing you is too good for you. Once you're dead you're dead. You need to suffer, and I mean suffer. Hit it, Maggie!"

Maggie dragged her duffel bag to the center of the room, but before she could find a clear space to park it, she had to kick away four straw reindeer. Fiona started to cry when a set of ears fell off one of the reindeer.

The boys formed a circle around Maggie and the Sandfords. All eyes were on her as she slowly unzipped the duffel and drew out a pair of hedge clippers. She held them up, gave a brief demonstration showing how sharp they were by cutting a branch of the tacky white Christmas tree. Fiona couldn't take her eyes off the fallen branch. She started to wail again. Her husband told her to shut up yet again.

Jack looked at Maggie. "Maybe you should tell him what you're going to do with the clippers."

"Ya think?"

"Yeah. Ask him for the passwords, and if he doesn't come through, then you are free to go to work."

"Oooh, I like the way that sounds. Okay, listen up,

Mr. Lieutenant Governor of the Commonwealth of Virginia, and you, too, Mrs. Lieutenant Governor of this commonwealth. I'm going to be polite and ask one more time for the passwords, and if you don't give them to me, then I am going to hack off your nose, Mr. Lieutenant Governor and then I am going to hack off Mrs. Lieutenant Governor's lips. I will then chop them to pieces so they can never be reattached. I hope you are following me here." She swung around, dug in her duffel, and came up with two pictures that she had enhanced on her computer. Both were ugly pictures of the Sandfords showing gaping holes in both their faces. Fiona Sandford screamed, then fainted again. Tyler Sandford stared at the picture but remained defiant, but not before his face turned as white as the snow outside. Maggie raised the clippers and clicked them open. The room went totally silent as she made clacking sounds with the shears as she advanced on Tyler Sandford, who tried to back away deep into the chair.

Fiona struggled to awareness and screamed. "I'll give you the damn passwords if you promise to leave my lips alone. I don't give a good rat's ass what you do to his nose, but promise to leave my lips alone. I want your promise."

"I promise," Maggie said solemnly. "What is it?"

Abner Tookus flexed his fingers.

Chapter 27

"She's lying. I never gave her the passwords," Sandford bellowed.

"That's true, he never did give them to me, so I had to ferret them out on my own. This man is the cheapest bastard in the whole world. I knew the day would come when I'd need a hold of some kind over him. I guess this is it."

"Don't you dare, Fiona! I'm warning you," Sandford said as he tried to lunge for his wife. Harry reached out and shoved him deep into the chair.

Abner flexed his fingers again.

They all waited to see what Fiona Sandford would do.

"It's *reciprocity*. It's his favorite word, for some reason."

"Well, damn," Abner said as he typed in the word. A blizzard of numbers raced across the screen. "Man, this is more money than I've ever seen in my whole life. We are going to have a great time doling this out. A really great time."

"I want a big chunk to go to the Wounded Warriors," Maggie said.

"I want millions to go to no-kill animal shelters," Dennis said.

"I want to fix up the whole Southeast so people are proud to live there," Jack said.

"Millions to disadvantaged children," Harry said.

"Scholarships," Abner said.

"I'll think of something," Espinosa said happily as he smacked his hands together.

Sandford cursed long and loud as he struggled to get out of the chair, only to be restrained by Harry again.

"And to think this guy seriously thought he was going to be governor of Virginia. Not," Jack said. "Okay, let's get them out to the van and hightail it out of here. I'm going to turn off all the lighting, batten down the house, then I'll meet you outside. If that crud even blinks, hit him with the Taser."

"Where are you taking us?" Fiona yelped.

"To a place you're going to love. Your husband and you, too, own the property. It's condemned but you, Marks, your husband, and the rats will enjoy your stay, which will last through Christmas Day, at which point the three of you will be relocated. Enough talking already. Get going, everyone."

Harry hung back to help Jack. "That went well. Surprised me, though, that the wife knew the passwords. I have to say, Jack, nose or no nose, I don't think the guy would have given them up. That's just my opinion."

Jack looked at Harry. "Tell me you aren't serious. You really believe Sandford would have let Maggie cut off his nose."

"Yeah, Jack, I believe that. The wife now, women are vain, and no way was she giving up those lips. No way in hell."

"Whatever, we won in the end. I'm loving this."

An hour and twenty minutes later, Ted pulled the van to the curb. Luther and his three colleagues rushed to help unload the cursing passengers.

"Welcome home, Mr. and Mrs. Sandford," Luther said. For effect, he and his friends wore black ski masks with holes cut out for the eyes, nose, and mouth. They looked scary evil.

"How's Marks doing?" Jack asked.

"Man, that dude is something else. He's about ready to explode. That dude hasn't shut up for even a minute. I think he'll be glad for some company."

Jack grinned.

Sandford stood on his own two feet, and Harry's grip on his arm was steely hard. Ted and Espinosa each had one of Fiona Sandford's arms. Both were cursing and struggling to no avail. Maggie reached over and slapped Fiona, the sound loud in the clear night.

"God, I cannot wait to get rid of these two," Jack said as he led the way into Sandford's building. "You see anything you like here, Mr. Sandford?" The man's response brought heat to Jack's cheeks. "Okay, there is just no talking to some people. Dump him, Harry, and lock the doors. We're done with this scum."

Harry needed no urging. He dumped Tyler Sandford inside the door and gave him a shove with his foot. He stepped aside as Espinosa gave Fiona a good push, causing her to land on top of her husband. The rats started to squeal, and Marks bellowed, albeit hoarsely, about being bitten twice. Luther yanked the door closed and fastened a brand-new padlock on the reinforced door.

As one, the group looked at one another and shouted loud enough to be heard through the door. "Merry Christmas!"

A round of robust handshaking took place. Luther and his friends were all smiles when they announced that they had the dudes and *dudess* covered. "Come back tomorrow and don't forget my granny and the pastor are expecting you for the big party. Starts at six. Granny don't like people when they're late, so be on time."

Dennis assured him they would all be on time. "You guys

wrapped all the presents for everyone? No one got left out? Were there enough toys?"

"Yeah, yeah, and yeah. Way too much," Luther said.

"We're outta here, guys," Ted said as he marched over to the van, which he'd left running. "All aboard that's coming aboard!" A wild scramble ensued.

"Now what?" Abner asked as Ted pulled a U-turn. He gave the horn a soft tap and waved.

"Now we go home, go to bed, and when we wake up, it will be Christmas Eve. I have some shopping and wrapping to do. I want to talk to my wife, too. Then I have to go out and buy our Christmas Day dinner. What about you guys?" Jack asked.

"I'll buy the stuff for dinner if you give me a list," Dennis said.

"Turkey and all the trimmings," Jack said.

Ted and Maggie looked at one another. "We're going to try to get a bead on that drug company Nikki's firm is going up against. Abner is going to help. Harry has to get home to help with Lily, as Yoko is exhausted. Like Luther said, we've got it covered."

Back at the BOLO Building, the little group separated with hugs and claps on the back.

"It is soooo good to have my family back. Merry Christmas all," Maggie cried happily as she hugged everyone one more time.

"Merry Christmas!" the guys shouted. Their happy cheers rang out in the crystal-clear night.

Take Down

Chapter 28

All across the United States of America, citizens were waking up to what the weathermen were touting as a white Christmas for most of the country, thanks to a cold front swirling down from Canada. In the South, the sun was shining brightly as picture after picture blitzed across television screens showing Santa arriving on water skis, his sack of presents perched precariously on his back.

Parents, sleepy-eyed, did double time ooohing and aaahing as their bright-eyed children squealed in delight at the mounds of presents piled high under the tree, and then pointed to the empty milk glass and a few stray crumbs on the cookie plate, proof that Santa had indeed slid down the chimney, fire and all. The proof, the little ones pointed out, was the small pile of ash on the hearth. And their parents, of course, nodded sagely, congratulating their beaming children on their deductive powers.

In Georgetown, Jack Emery slept soundly. The digital clock on the nightstand read 5:10, which meant Jack had been asleep for all of two hours. It had been a long night as he and the others wrapped up their current project to everyone's satisfaction, then attended the midnight religious service in the Southeast section of Washington, D.C. No one, it had seemed, wanted the wonderful night to end, and the pastor at the church agreed wholeheartedly. This, after all, was the community's way of thanking the men who had entered their lives with riches beyond their wildest dreams. Not riches in the monetary sense of the word, but riches in food, warmth, hot water, love, and caring, which, the pastor boomed at the pulpit, just proved what he had preached all his life, give and you shall receive. And Jack and the boys, thanks to Dennis West and his inheritance, had given beyond the community's wildest dreams.

The dark night had yet to give way to the dawn that waited impatiently to surface, cloaking the house in George-town in a white mantle of snow. The silence was so total that Jack slept peacefully, his arms wrapped around his pillow as dream after dream marched through his tired brain.

Jack stirred restlessly. "Hmmnn, um, oooh," he moaned as he gripped his pillow tighter against him. "Oh, yeah, oh, don't stop. Aaah, oooh." He cracked an eye to stare at two pointed ears and two very large brown eyes staring down at him. "Cyrus!" The big shepherd barked happily as his tongue sought Jack's ear again. "Son of a gun, you gotta stop doing that, Cyrus. You got me all hot and bothered there for a minute. God, what time is it? It's only 5:15! It's not time to get up yet."

Cyrus thought differently as he tugged at the covers.

Jack yanked at the covers. "Turn the heat up. I'm not getting up until it's warm in here. Two clicks, Cyrus. I taught you how to do that. Two clicks to the right. Go!" Cyrus leaped off the bed and immediately ran out to the hallway, where he hopped up on the bench under the thermostat and looked at it. He brought his paw up, gave the button a smack, waited for the click, then hit it once more. His bark was pure joy as he spun around, jumped off the bench, and enthusiastically raced back to the bed, where he took a flying leap and landed smack in the middle of Jack's chest. Then they tussled for a few minutes, the way they always did when Nikki was away. Jack wrapped his arms around the big dog and whispered, "Merry Christmas, big guy. Thanks for waking me up. We gotta get that turkey in the oven. C'mon, I'll let you out before I take my shower. Last one to the door stinks!" Cyrus was off like a shot, while Jack shuffled in his bare feet into the hall, then down the stairs and out to the kitchen, where Cyrus was barking frantically.

"I see it, Cyrus, I see it," Jack said as he eyed the mountain of fresh snow that had fallen during the night. "Okay, in and out, and you can do the rest later."

In seconds, Jack had the coffeepot going. He struggled with the huge turkey and set it in the sink. He turned on the oven just as Cyrus rang the back doorbell to get in. The shepherd shook off the snow and saw Jack looking at the water puddling on the floor. He trotted into the laundry room and dragged a towel out of the laundry basket and dropped it at Jack's feet. "Oh, no. Your mess, you clean it up," Jack yelled over his shoulder as he raced up the stairs to take his scalding-hot shower.

Meanwhile, in the kitchen, Cyrus looked at the towel and considered the puddle on the floor for almost a half minute. Then he let loose with a shrill bark, turned around, and raced up the stairs, as much as to say, *that's not my job*.

Twenty minutes later, Jack was shaved, dressed, and ready to take on Christmas Day without his wife, for the first time in their marriage. He allowed himself a few minutes to contemplate what he was feeling before he patted Cyrus, his other true love, on the head and made his way down the stairs to start what he hoped would be a wonderful memory for his mental scrapbook.

Jack turned on the lights of the Christmas tree and smiled. He turned on the Bose sound system and was rewarded with what he knew would be twenty-four hours of Christmas music. After listening to Bing Crosby singing

Irving Berlin's immortal "White Christmas," he let loose with a heavy sigh. Today would be whatever he made of it, no more, no less.

In the kitchen, Jack poured coffee, fished a yogurt out of the fridge, toasted a bagel, then sat down, his eye on the towel and the puddle. Cyrus, having come downstairs after Jack and quietly entered the kitchen, was dancing around the towel. "You want to eat, clean up your mess. You know the rules, Cyrus. Nothing is free in this world."

Jack thought he heard the big dog sigh as he dragged the towel across the floor, back and forth. He barked again, this time shrilly, as much as to say, *this is as good as it's gonna get*. He dragged the towel back to the laundry room just as Jack opened the fridge to get out his food, which he warmed in the microwave oven. He was glad now that he had taken the heaped-up to-go plate the young pastor had insisted on when they left the parish house earlier in the morning.

"Merry Christmas, world," Jack muttered to himself as he walked over to the kitchen door to view the winter wonderland into which his backyard had been transformed. A white Christmas. It didn't get any better than that, now did it? If only Nikki were here to share it with him. If only. *Don't go there, Jack*, he cautioned himself. *Not today. Today is . . . is . . . whatever I damn well make it.*

Jack smacked his hands together to get himself in the mood, then turned up the volume on the Bose. Sound invaded the house. "Now, that's more like it!" he said to his empty kitchen. He eyed the monster turkey and vowed out loud, to his still-empty kitchen, to make the bird as delicious and succulent as one the long-absent Charles Martin would have prepared. But first he had to build a fire to complete the ambiance.

While he waited for the logs to catch, along with the kindling, Jack looked at the pile of presents he had so painstakingly shopped for and wrapped. They were definitely not up to Nikki's standards when it came to exquisite wrappings, but if intent counted, he'd aced that chore. Nikki's present was in the drawer of the china cabinet and would remain there until she came home. He'd found it by chance one day in a little shop on a narrow side street in Georgetown and immediately scooped it up because it screamed Nikki's name. From the time she was a little girl, Nikki had collected unicorns, and this particular one was not in her collection. He knew she would love it on sight. He'd also gotten her a pair of pearl earrings with a diamond bevel that he knew she would like. Nikki, like her mother, Myra, was into pearls in a big way. He smiled at the thought.

Once the fire was blazing to his satisfaction, he took one more long look at the beautiful tree, inhaled the tantalizing scent, then made his way to the kitchen, where he got his Christmas dinner under way. He decided to set the table with Nikki's favorite china before going outside and using the snowblower to clear a path for his dinner guests. The turkey would go into the oven later so that it would not have a chance to dry out before being served.

Christmas Day.

Jack's guests started to arrive a little before three o'clock, each of them carrying shopping bags full of presents. Dinner was scheduled for five o'clock since the huge turkey had not been put into the oven until eleven o'clock. No one minded the late dinner hour. It gave them all time to sit around the fire, and enjoy the canapés courtesy of Ding at the Bagel Emporium and the rich eggnog Jack had picked up at the local deli. Any discussion of last night's activities, by mutual agreement, would have to wait till after dinner. And only if anyone wanted to talk about it.

The only missing guests were Yoko and Lily, who Harry said were sick. Yoko had been fighting a cold that had turned into bronchitis, then little Lily had come down with the same thing. A visit to the medical center, shots, meds, and plenty of fluids plus sleep were called for. The doctor had told Harry they would sleep around the clock, so he felt comfortable enough to come for dinner. Besides, he said, Yoko didn't want him fussing and fretting over her and Lily. Cooper fussed enough. No one, not even Harry, crossed Yoko, and here he was. "But," he had said, "after we clean up from dinner, I'm outta here."

"So," Jack said, "should we do the presents before dinner or after dinner?"

"Let's do them now since Harry has to leave after dinner," Espinosa said. They all agreed, and it was Dennis who handed out the presents. They all laughed and smiled, poked one another at the thoughtful, silly, practical gifts everyone had shopped for. Even Cyrus had a pile that he pawed over, licked, then stashed in his basket of treasures.

The gang thanked one another, clapped backs, and hugged and kissed cheeks with Maggie doing the kissing. If there was a pall on the little group since this was so unlike Christmases in the past, it was hard to see. Life had to go on, as Ted put it, and there would be other Christmases, and this one was special because they were all together and not spending this special day alone.

They shared stories of their childhood Christmas mornings, teenage Christmas mornings, and their favorite adult Christmas mornings until they all knew everything there was to know about one another.

And then it was time to get dinner on the table. They fell to it, getting in one another's way and laughing as they squabbled over the seating arrangements, and looked for the carving knife Jack said was somewhere but couldn't be found. In the end, he carved the big bird with a steak knife, and no one cared.

Grace was said by Harry. Heads bowed and words

whispered. Cyrus, his paws on Jack's chair, lowered his big head and whimpered, his sign that he got what was going on. Then he barked, which obviously meant, *let's eat.* They all laughed as Jack set down Cyrus's special Christmas bowl, which was loaded with chicken instead of turkey, and everything else the others were eating.

The compliments flowed, to Jack's amazement, because they sounded so genuine. Maggie said she thought his turkey was better than the one Charles had made for the previous year's Thanksgiving dinner, which gave everyone pause for thought, but the somewhat uncomfortable silence, as everyone thought about that tumultuous day, lasted for only a moment.

Jack's plum pudding didn't garner any rave reviews, but they all agreed it was edible. Cyrus passed on it. Jack was not offended, saying it was his first-ever effort at plum pudding. No one complained, and they all applauded Jack's bravery.

Abner, with Dennis's help, served the coffee from Nikki's heirloom pot.

"This was an excellent dinner, Jack," Ted said. "Thanks for inviting us."

"Now can we talk about last night?" Dennis asked.

"Sure, kid, what do you want to talk about?" Ted asked.

Dennis had finally given up getting upset about being called a kid. He'd decided, with Harry's input, that he needed to accept it as a term of endearment, which he had come to do.

"Like what happened to the Sandfords and that guy Lionel. I'd like to know."

"Well now, Dennis, here's the thing: When a mission is over, it's over. We just walk away and let things happen as they will. We absolutely do not, as in never ever, ask questions. Once we have done our part, the exfiltration is something to be left to others. In other words, last night never happened. End of story," Ted said.

"Yeah, well, how do we know it's really the end of the story?" Dennis persisted.

"Because Ted said it was," Jack snapped. "We have moved on. Tomorrow, we meet up in the office, ten sharp, so we can get started on Nik's class-action suit. We need to move fast on that. I want my wife back, and Espinosa wants Alexis back. So if any of you have any after-Christmas plans, forget about them. We are going to need to pull out all the stops and take down the guys whose greed started the whole mess. Just so you know, we're going to split into two teams, so we can handle both of those cases. The third one Nik's firm can handle on its own. We work solely on the leukemia drug and the dog-food-processing plant. It is not going to be a walk in the park, I can tell you that right now. We are going to need this to be airtight, no screwups, and above all, absolute, total secrecy. No whistle-blowing on this one; no reports in our esteemed *Washington Post*."

"I gotta go, Jack," Harry said, glancing at his watch.

"I thought you were helping with the cleanup," Dennis said, looking at the table. Harry eyed him. "That's okay, Harry, I can do your share," he said hastily. "Do you want me to help you with all Lily's gifts?"

"That would be so sweet of you, Dennis." Harry smiled. Dennis shivered as he got up from the table. "How about if I put all of Cooper's gifts in one bag, Lily's in another, and yours and Yoko's separate?"

"Perfect!" Harry laughed.

"You really have the kid trained, Harry," Jack said, grinning from ear to ear.

Harry looked like Santa himself as he helped Dennis load up his car. He turned to wave at his friends, who were clustered in the doorway and on the stoop. Tough guy Harry was glad no one could see how his eyes had misted over. Friends forever.

Everyone shouted "Merry Christmas" at the same time,

and the sound rang out in the clear, frosty air. Not to be outdone, Cyrus tossed his head back and howled long and loud.

Their arms around each other, the gang trooped back into the family room, where they gathered around the tree, not caring that they were standing in a pile of ribbons, tissue paper, and foil. It was Abner's idea to sing "Jingle Bells," which they did. Not a single human person cared that they were shrill and off-key. But Cyrus, music critic that he was, was much less tolerant and ran as far as he could go and hid.

And as Jack said later, when the last guest was gone, "Merry Christmas to all and to all a good night. Let's hit the sack, Cyrus, and make sure you stay on your side of the bed."

"Woof." Translation . . . in your dreams.

Chapter 29

Jack Emery was winded, sweat dripping down his face even with the freezing temperatures outside. He'd just finished carrying eleven banker boxes into the BOLO Building and depositing them on the floor in the conference room. They all contained material copied and "borrowed" from Nikki's office in the dead of night. It had taken him three weeks to copy all the files, working four hours each night and getting by on two or three hours of sleep. He eyed what he thought was the solution to all of his and Nikki's problems, and, of course, those of the loved ones of the unfortunate victims who had used the drug Anmir and died because of Andover Pharmaceuticals' greed.

Jack straightened out the boxes and headed to the kitchen, where he made coffee for the gang, which was due to arrive momentarily. He'd stopped at a Dunkin' Donuts and loaded up with two bags of the sugary delights.

His stomach in knots, Jack paced the kitchen. The mission that he and the guys—and Maggie, too—were embarking on was as serious as it got. Add Nikki's return late tonight, after attending a ten-year-old child's funeral, plus the wicked weather out of the Midwest, and he was left with what he thought of as a recipe for disaster.

As always, Cyrus heard the cars in the alley before Jack

did. Jack let loose with a sigh of relief. He needed company right now, and support from his colleagues. While yesterday, Christmas Day, had been all things wonderful, considering the circumstances, today was a new day, a business day. A day when they had to map out a strategy to take down Andover Pharmaceuticals and its three greedy owners, all members of the Andover family, who had unleashed disaster on a vulnerable population. Jack intended to make things a little more right in the world they were all living in.

Jack held the massive door so that the others could enter the building along with the frigid air. He wondered if it was magic, the way they more or less all arrived at almost the same time, considering that they'd traveled from very different parts of the District. To Jack's weary gaze, his colleagues looked bright-eyed and ready to take on anything Jack brought to the table. He struggled to look positive and fervently hoped that he was carrying it off, because he did not feel all that confident about this matter.

"You guys go ahead, I'll do the coffee thing," Maggie said cheerfully. Ted offered to help. He looked so sappy, Jack fought the urge to smack him. He was instantly sorry for the thought. Ted and Maggie deserved all the happiness in the world after everything they'd been through.

Jack was the last one to enter the conference room, but he could hear the moans and groans of those who had entered before him as they eyed the banker boxes. Everyone grabbed a seat, eyes glued to the boxes, but no one said a word. Abner flexed his fingers, as though itching to get to work. Espinosa stared at the Jackson Pollock painting on the wall, his thoughts, Jack knew, on Alexis's return with Nikki at some point that day if the airports out west hadn't shut down. Harry had a dreamy look on his face, his thoughts probably on his daughter, Lily, and how she'd reacted to Christmas even though she and Yoko were sick.

In his opinion, there wasn't a better father in the whole world than Harry Wong.

Dennis was sitting the closest to the stacks of banker boxes and inched his booted foot forward to move one of them. Jack could tell that the reporter in the young man was just itching to dive into the boxes to go through their contents.

"Coffee's here!" Ted bellowed as he set the heavy tray down on a sideboard under the Jackson Pollock painting. Maggie set the tray of doughnuts alongside and offered to pour. For some reason, Ted and Maggie's cheerfulness set Jack's teeth on edge. He was too uptight, and he knew it. He had to loosen up or he was going to make a hash of this entire presentation. It was Nikki's situation that was bothering him. Big girl or not, he knew she could take care of herself, but she had no control over the weather and flying through a storm, if she even got off the ground. Cyrus nudged his leg, a signal that the big dog was picking up on his master's mood. He reached down to rub the shepherd's head and immediately felt calmer for some reason. Cyrus always had that effect on Jack.

Abner clapped his hands. "Okay, let's get this show on the road. Time is money, gentlemen and one lady."

Jack set his coffee cup down on a coaster and looked around at the expectant faces observing him as they all waited for the enlightenment he was to provide them. He immediately obliged.

"Okay, in these boxes, which I lugged in here this morning, are the files for Andover Pharmaceuticals. I have spent the last several weeks copying Nikki's files in the dead of night. I also went through her briefcase at home, while she was sleeping. We have here in our possession every note, every scrap of paper relating to the class-action suit against that nest of corporate vipers. We need to wade through it all before we make our move. That's to assure all of us that what we're about to embark on is okay with each and every one of us. If, for any reason whatsoever, one of you doesn't want to participate, now will be the time to back out. This is, after all, vigilante justice."

Abner was the first to offer up a comment. In the past, the computer genius had always worked behind the scenes in his own little high-tech world. He broke the law a hundred different ways in the interest of seeing that people got their just deserts, but he'd never been in on the physical end of dispensing their particular brand of justice. "So you just marched into the law firm and stole all the records, is that right?"

Jack grinned. "Well, no, I actually did not steal anything since I left all the files the way they were. What I did do was make copies of everything. And, since I have a key to the place, there was no breaking and entering. So, with that understood, do you have a problem with what I did?"

"I don't, but the FBI might," Abner said. Everyone laughed uproariously.

"Guess who is going to be the new director of the FBI in a few more days!" Ted said.

Abner slapped his forehead. "Ah, forgive my stupidity. Jack Sparrow, of course. Okay, I'm good."

"Anyone else have any comments, questions?" Jack asked.

"A quick overview I think would help," Dennis said. The others agreed.

"Sure. As you all know, Nikki and Alexis are in the great state of Minnesota. They left before Christmas because one of the children took a turn for the worse, and they had to . . . to get it on video. I know how that sounds, but the parents insisted that the girls go out there because the little girl wasn't expected to make it through Christmas. I'm sorry to say she did not. The funeral was this morning. She was only ten years old. The drug, which Andover calls

Anmir, was touted as the drug that would stop leukemia in its tracks. Anmir stands for Andover Miracle. Some miracle.

"Moving right along here, three years ago, somehow, someway, the drug was shipped before the FDA gave its final approval, but that was pretty much swept under the rug. They had been touting Anmir as the miracle it was supposed to be. The company, as you know, is privately held by the three Andovers. With all the hype, the stock market went crazy with speculation about their issuing an IPO and cashing in, probably becoming instant billionaires. Of course, they never did, expecting that the company would just get more valuable as Anmir sold more and more.

"And things looked good for the first year, but then the dark stuff started hitting the fan. By that I mean that a significant number of patients went from bad to worse. Deaths started to mount up. Private lawsuits were filed but never got to trial, where the very nasty truth might come out, because Andover always settled out of court. For millions. I saw a memo in there somewhere that the powers that be felt it was better to pay out a few million here or there rather than let things get out of hand with their billion-dollar drug.

"The doctors, the scientists who worked on the drug, were either fired or left on their own. From the records we have, it appears that Nikki was not able to track any of them down. There were three. One was a Pakistani doctor, another was Japanese, and the third one was an American, from Rhode Island. A new team of doctors was brought in, but Nikki was unable to make any contact with them. She tried the subpoena route, to no avail. Andover is buttoned up tight. They also have the resources to fight her tooth and nail, and that's what they did and are still doing. The bottom line is the side effects of the drug. So far, if what I read is right, nineteen children have died in the last year and a half. Very painful, horrific deaths. Children. No parent should have to bury a child. I did see documents in the files from various doctors who said if the children had *not* been given the drug, they would have had a longer life span."

Maggie made no attempt to wipe away the tears rolling down her cheeks. The others blinked away their own tears, their faces solemn.

"Who is the person or persons responsible?" Harry asked through clenched teeth.

"According to the files, there are three people who own and run the company: Otto Andover, Philip Andover, and Martha Andover Gellis. Otto is fifty-nine, Philip is fifty-seven, and Martha is fifty-five. There are three grandchildren, but obviously they have nothing whatsoever to do with the company.

"Nikki was really excited about a week or so ago when she found out that Otto has two grandchildren, ages ten and twelve. Martha has no grandchildren, and Philip has a five-year-old grandchild he seems to dote on. All three families live with serious security, even Philip. The ten- and twelve-year-olds are driven to a very private, upscale academy by a chauffeur who packs heat. I don't know how Nikki found that out, but somehow she did. If I read it all correctly—and I admit I did so on the fly, as I was copying everything—the security really didn't start to get serious until the fourth lawsuit was filed."

"Is the drug off the market?" Ted asked.

"Hell no!" The words exploded from Jack's mouth like a gunshot.

"How can that be?" Maggie demanded.

"I don't frigging know, Maggie. How about the thousands of other people who took the drug who *didn't* die? All the talk about the company's going public died fairly soon after the lawsuits were filed. You see, if the company tried to go public, it would have to release all the information it was trying so hard to sweep under the rug. Nikki said that, to be sure, doctors stopped prescribing the drug. But it's still on the market."

"And those three have never issued a statement of any kind?" Dennis asked.

"Not to my knowledge. I didn't see anything in the files, but that doesn't mean it isn't in there," Jack said.

"How did this class-action suit start?" Abner asked.

"It's my understanding that there is an organization online—a support group of sorts, I'm thinking—of parents whose children have leukemia. The parents share photos of the kids, talk about what they and the kids are going through, the progress or lack of progress they're making with the ongoing research, that kind of thing. They bolster one another's spirits in their collective fight against the disease. Nikki said the kids participate, and it's a good thing. Terribly sad, especially when one of the children passes on.

"But to answer your question, one of the parents whose child died researched the drug, didn't like what she found out, talked with a number of oncologists, then talked ad nauseam to the others online, and someone gave her Nikki's number. The woman lives in Falls Church. So she went to see Nikki, and the rest is history. She gave Nikki the names of the parents who had settled privately. Nikki went to talk to all of them. All four sets of parents told her they would willingly testify if she needed them, even though they had signed nondisclosure agreements as a condition of the settlements. They all said they were willing to give back what they called the blood money they had been paid for what basically was their silence. Anything else?"

"So that drug . . . it was all about money, the bottom line. Those three Andovers who call the shots were only interested in how much money they could make. How much did they make before things bottomed out?" Harry asked.

"Billions!" Jack said, bitterness ringing in his voice. "I forgot to tell you this: The day after Nikki filed the class-action suit, the two oldest Andover grandchildren began homeschooling. Abner, I want you to hack into the academy where those kids went to school and get their pictures from the yearbooks. Can you do that?"

"If they have yearbooks, then the answer is yes. What about the five-year-old? Does he go to a play school or kindergarten?"

"I don't know. What I do know is that we need pictures of all three of them. In the files, Nikki compiled a gallery of the kids who . . . didn't make it." Jack was so choked up, he got up from his seat and walked over to the sideboard to pour more coffee that he didn't want, just to give himself a moment to pull it together. He looked up at the splash of color on the Jackson Pollock painting, drew in a deep breath, then turned around. "We need to get those bastards. And we have to bring down their company."

Cyrus threw his head back and howled his agreement. The others nodded silently.

"Whatever it takes," Dennis said softly. "Whatever it takes," he asserted a second time, to make sure everyone knew he was definitely on board.

"Okay, then, this is what we're going to do: Abner, you know what we need, so you can get to work. If you run into any problems, let us know ASAP. Ted, you and Espinosa are assigned to Otto Andover. He's their big gun." Jack referred to his notes. "All his stuff is in boxes two and three. Maggie, I want you to do Philip; he's in box four. Dennis, you get Martha; she's in box five. Harry and I are going to go through the . . . the files on the kids, the deceased children. At some point, we're going to have to come up with a PowerPoint presentation, and I'm not the best person for that. I know Nik and Alexis were working on one, but they haven't done it yet. When we take out those bastards, I want to ram it down their throats in living color. And I want pictures of their grandchildren included in that. I want to see how they deal with the contrast between their healthy grandkids and grandnephews and grandniece and the kids they helped to kill."

"Do we have a time limit, Jack?" Dennis asked.

"We do. I want to put this to bed before the New Year. That gives us six days, counting today. I want this done before Sparrow takes office. And by the way, I scheduled a webcam meeting with Bert and Sparrow for later this afternoon, so make sure you're all back here if any of you are planning to leave."

"I just have to check in at the paper; then I can stay the rest of the day," Maggie said. "This is our easiest week of the whole year. That means the paper runs itself more or less, rehashing the year, yada yada yada."

Everyone said they were good and could spend the day.

The banker boxes were opened, the doughnuts disappeared, as if by magic, and the work started in a sea of paper and comments as the boys and one gal got to work with a vengeance.

Cyrus found himself boxed in under the table. He barked and backed out, then headed for more neutral ground, the kitchen, where he started to work on a Greenie that would clean his teeth and freshen his breath, his ears tuned to any and all sounds that were the slightest bit unusual.

Chapter 30

Jack looked up from what he was doing and glanced at his watch. He could hardly believe it was already past noon, but his stomach was telling him it was definitely time for lunch. He looked around at the others, all of whom were diligently making notes or reading files. He walked out to the kitchen and called the Bagel Emporium to order lunch: pastrami on rye all around, with tubs of potato salad and coleslaw. He was told it would be forty-five minutes before it could be delivered. To pass the time, he brewed some fresh coffee and tried once more to call Nikki. He was stunned when she picked up after the second ring. His heart fluttered. That had to mean she was still on the ground, stuck somewhere.

"Where are you, Nik?"

"Kansas City. We're grounded. There is no chance, we're told, of getting out today, so Alexis and I are going to go to a hotel and hope we can get an early flight in the morning. How's everything?"

Jack sighed. "You know, same old, same old. Christmas is over. We missed you. It wasn't the same, but we were together; the guys, I mean. And Maggie. How was yours?"

"God, Jack, don't even ask. If I live to be a hundred, I will never forget this disaster of a Christmas. Never!" she said vehemently. Her voice was so shrill, Jack blanched. "Do you believe those creepy bastards at Andover sent some . . . some flunky to the funeral? They sent a ton of flowers and a . . . and a . . . goddamn teddy bear. A teddy bear. Do you believe that? Oh, and they sent a fruit basket to the house. A fruit basket!" Her voice was so strident coming through the cell phone, Cyrus reared up and howled.

Jack struggled to find some comforting words, but they wouldn't come. It didn't matter since Nikki wasn't listening anyway. "You know what else, Jack? Those bastards are not going to settle. I know that now for sure. We're going to have to go to court. These families are worn out. All their fight is gone. Like Molly's dad said, once you see your child go into the ground, it's all over. And he's right. I want to pack it in myself. So does Alexis. But if we do that, then those bastards win. Tell me what to do, Jack. Please, tell me what I should do."

Jack wished there was a deep hole he could fall into right that second. What to say, how to say it? The best he could come up with was, "I know it doesn't seem possible right now, but it's all going to work out, Nik. Trust me on that, okay?"

There was so much bitterness in his wife's voice that Jack longed for the deep hole. "No, Jack, it isn't going to work out. I'm losing this suit. You know it, I know it, and so do those skunks at Andover. It's been almost two years, Jack, that I've been at this, and I'm no further along today than I was a year ago. Damn it, Jack, they're going to drive me into the ground. I'd like to get my hands around the neck of that Otto Andover and squeeze till his eyes pop out of his head. Listen, Jack, I have to go. Something is happening at the ticket counter, and Alexis is calling me. I love you. I'll call you later, okay?"

"Yeah, sure, do what you have to do. Love you, too," Jack said as he ended the call. He stood for a long time, just staring at his reflection in the stainless-steel refrigerator, until Cyrus nudged his leg ever so gently. Jack looked down at the big dog with the soulful brown eyes and whispered, "We're gonna make it right for her, Cyrus. We are. And I think I'm going to push up our timetable before Nik crashes and burns on me." Cyrus whined low in his throat.

Jack was a whirlwind as he roared down the hall and into the conference room, his arms outstretched and palms outward. "Stop! Listen up, everyone. New plan. I just got off the phone with Nikki." Five minutes later, the group had been apprised of what had transpired and Jack's reasons for advancing the time on what he was calling the take down of Andover Pharmaceuticals.

"Jack, do we even know if the Andovers are in the country? Don't people like that go to Gstaad for skiing or someplace warm for the holidays? Maybe cruising the Med? One of them—Otto, I think—owns a big yacht," Harry said.

"Get on it, people; find out where they are. I'm sure they all have unlisted phone numbers. Someone get Abner in here so he can hack into the records. We need a story line to get them all together. C'mon, c'mon, I want you all to think. Time is of the essence."

Almost exactly an hour later, it was Maggie who came up with the best idea. They all listened as she expounded on it, their eyes wide as Maggie slammed her gold shield down in front of her, then looked around. "We pretend we're FBI or CIA. We call the big guy, Otto, and tell him we need to get the three of them together at some designated spot because there is a terrorist threat on their company, and if you don't like the word *terrorist,* come up with something better. We call, but we're standing right outside the door when we do it, so he can't alert anyone else except his siblings. We can get the protocol from Bert and Sparrow. You know, how all that is done, so we don't screw it up. We dress like FBI: dark suits, shades, high and tight haircuts like the military, speakers in our sleeves and collars, aviator sunglasses. We waltz them out the door to an unmarked van and take them to wherever we want to go to . . . um . . . finish them off."

"I'm okay with everything but cutting my hair," Harry said.

"I don't have a gold shield," Dennis said.

"Where are we going to take them?" Espinosa asked. "And how are we going to get them extracted? Did anyone call Snowden?"

"I'll call Snowden in a minute. I was thinking of the farm. Annie and Myra left for Vegas very early this morning, before the weather got so bad, so there's no one there. Bert told me when I called him earlier in the day. He said they would be wheels down by late morning, and the plan is for them to stay until the New Year. And Myra's dogs are at Nellie's. The place is empty. The farm, I'm thinking, is our safest bet. Anyone disagree?" Jack said.

No one disagreed, but Abner did have a question. "If they find out, then what?"

"Then we deal with it at that time. Right now, we can't worry about that. Aside from Nikki being my wife, she is also Myra's adopted daughter. I don't think Myra will kick up too much of a fuss with us taking care of business for Nikki. I grant you, they are going to be seriously ticked off, but that's for another day. And, anyway, their biggest complaint will probably be that we didn't include them in this enterprise. Did you get anything, Abner?"

"I need another hour and I'll have some very serious information to contribute. Can I get back to work?"

"*Go!*" Jack bellowed. "Okay, we now have a plan," he said, gleefully smacking his hands together. "Nice work, Maggie.

"Okay, Dennis, here is your first job. I want you to get Ted and Espinosa's measurements, then go to Brooks Brothers and get them each a suit that screams FBI. Pick up two pairs of aviator glasses, some gizmos from RadioShack, so they can talk into their sleeves, and any other shit you think they might need. Chop chop, kid. Every minute from here on in counts. On second thought, pick up a suit for yourself. I'm thinking three agents is better than two. Oh, and go to a gun shop and pick up some under-the-arm holsters. We can get guns from Myra's house. Did I forget anything? Why are you still standing here?"

"Wait a minute," Dennis said. "I thought we were going to get shoulder holsters and guns from Bert and Sparrow in Vegas. Or did I miss something, and there was a change in plans?"

"No, you're right, Dennis. I'm beginning to think I would forget my head if it weren't on my shoulders. Forget about the holsters," Jack said.

"Should I get a high and tight haircut while I'm out?"

Jack grinned. "See, kid, now you're thinking. Absolutely. Ted and Espinosa will go for theirs tomorrow."

"So, then, it's three pairs of aviator glasses?"

"Yeah, Dennis, three. No, wait a minute. Make it five, just in case we decide that everyone other than Harry, who is too well-known, and Abner needs to join the FBI."

Cyrus whooped with delight when Dennis let out a long whoop of his own.

"Oh boy oh boy, we could go to the federal pen for impersonating FBI officers. Jeez, this is exciting."

"Subdued suits, Dennis," Ted called out.

"Nothing flashy, but cut well," Espinosa shouted.

"I got it, I got it! Okay, I'm outta here."

"Hold on, Dennis, I'll give you a ride. I have to check in at the paper. See you guys. Be back in a flash," Maggie said.

Jack let his gaze go to the far wall, to the Jasper Johns painting. He glared at it before he got back to work. *I'm doing it, Nik. I'm gonna make it work for you. I never break a promise. We're going to make this right. Or die trying*, he added as an afterthought, hoping it wouldn't come to that.

Chapter 31

It was shortly after four the following afternoon when several things happened. Nikki called Jack to tell him that her flight was still grounded and that they were saying the airports were not scheduled to open till the following day, December 28. As the gang converged on the conference room to impart what information they had gleaned, the high-tech smartphones everyone carried started beeping a weather bulletin about the nor'easter headed up the Eastern Seaboard.

Jack clicked his phone off and said, "At least the girls are safe on the ground," more to Espinosa than anyone else. Espinosa's face showed relief. "And since there is nothing we can do about the storm, we'll just have to ride it out. We have cots here and enough food so we can cope with anything. Plus, we have the Bagel Emporium across the street. It might be a good idea to call over there and place a to-go order when we finish up with what we have to do here. Now, let's get down to business. Show me what you have."

"Quite a bit, actually," Ted said. "I took the social side of Otto Andover, and Espinosa took the business end. The short version is the guy is a prick in every way that you can imagine. I'm not sure I've ever run across a more thoroughly objectionable character than dear old Otto. He is, of course, the oldest of the three siblings. He squeaked through college by paying people to do his research papers and taking his tests whenever he thought that plain old cribbing from someone's exam would not work. He cheats at golf and poker. I got all of this from several people who know him. Apparently, to know him is to despise him. My cover story was that the paper was thinking of naming him Man of the Year. That went over like a lead balloon, and all three guys I spoke to told me that they would cancel their subscriptions to the *Post* if we did that. No respect, no love, no admiration.

"He married well, has three children, two boys and a girl. Nothing that could be substantiated about any extra-marital affairs. All his kids live in the Virginia area. None of the kids work at the company. The two boys are partners in a software consulting firm and doing quite well, with incomes in the middle six figures. The girl married her childhood sweetheart, who is a heart surgeon. Otto does appear to dote on the two grandkids. That seems to be as warm and fuzzy as he gets. But from what I could learn, he does not spend all that much time with them, considering that they both live so close.

"The man is a power-hungry egotist who loves to be the center of attention. Not surprisingly, he rules with an iron fist, holding people to standards that he himself has never been able to meet his entire life. His motto is, No One Is Irreplaceable. He has plaques and signs all over the building to drive his point home.

"He is not close with his two siblings, or even with his two sons. I get the impression that his son-in-law cannot stand him, so Otto and his daughter rarely see each other. I had to piece together comments, stuff in our archives, and, of course, the comments from the three guys I talked with to come up with that assessment.

"Otto donates a lot of money to charitable causes and loves to get his picture in the papers. I'm afraid that Abner will have to crack into their computers because I couldn't really find out anything concerning Nikki's case—you know, internal memos, settlements, those kinds of things. Oh, and the guy likes to sail. He has his captain's license and loves to dress up in the cap, double-breasted blue blazer, and white duck pants. Very snazzy. I don't know how Andover put a lid on all that, but they did. The class-action lawsuit, I mean," he clarified.

Then it was Espinosa's turn. "Okay, here goes: Not only does Otto own a sailboat but he or the company owns a yacht as well. A really big one. He only invites high rollers, people who somehow, someway, can help him feather his nest. I found at least fifty pictures of him attired in his yachting gear. Quite the dashing gentleman, as Ted mentioned. The company also owns a helicopter and a Gulfstream. The guy jets all over the place and takes the helicopter up to New York, sometimes two or three times a week. He has an American Express Black Card." Espinosa looked down at his notes. "But now it's called the Centurion Card, is made of titanium, and there is no limit on it. I'd like to see an audit done on that guy, as well as one on the company."

"Speaking of audits," Ted interjected, "one of Otto's friends—and I use that term very loosely since he seems to have no real friends—said that the sister, Martha, is the chief financial officer and is the one who has direct control over the money, not Otto.

"He told me that a long time ago—he thinks maybe as long as fifteen years ago—something went down in the family. He was quick to say it was only a rumor, something that was just whispered about, but he was convinced that it was interesting enough to pay attention to. Something about Martha threatening him if he didn't give in and make her the CFO," Ted said.

"What was the rumor?" Dennis asked.

"He was kind of reluctant to share that, kid. But by being the astute investigative reporter that I am, I deduced that quite possibly there is a child out there who was born on the other side of the blanket and might have a claim on Otto's share of the company.

"I know, I know, I said there was no indication there were any infidelities, but as the guy said, where there is smoke, there is fire, and old Otto has the bucks to hush anything up. Can we prove any of that? Not right now, at least. That's pretty much it, unless Espinosa has anything else."

"I don't have anything else, but I did download all the pictures, and we can look at them later."

Jack looked at Maggie. "You're up, Maggie. What do you have on Philip Andover?"

"Not a whole lot, Jack. Philip is, I guess, what you would call the black sheep—or would that be the white sheep?—of this family, but in a nice way. He appears to be a gentle, soft-spoken family man. He's a bit of a dreamer. Plays in chess tournaments, takes family vacations, likes to bird-watch. Has four daughters, all married, all with careers. One write-up said that the four all speak daily, no matter where they are or what they're doing. He's not into material things, the way his brother and sister are. His wife is a master gardener. He goes to church regularly and tithes. He has three dogs and two cats. The wife drives a Chevy Blazer, he drives a five-year-old Saab. The whole family likes to fish, and until the girls got married, they would go fishing just about every weekend. He and his wife still do. They rent a boat. He's not a fashion plate and usually looks rumpled, and from time to time he forgets to get a haircut. He's in charge of development at the company. Couldn't come up with a single negative on him, but my nose tells me that what appears on the surface is too good to be true.

"The few interviews I was able to bring up have the people working under him saying what a kind, thoughtful boss he is. I couldn't find a single thing where he was directly involved with either Otto or his sister. He works in his own little area and leaves the rest to them. It took me all day to come up with this."

"He has to know about the drug if he's in development," Harry said.

All eyes turned to Abner. "I'm on it. If you guys don't need me, then how about I go back to work?"

"Go!" Jack said.

Abner literally ran from the room.

"Maggie, you want to place a dinner order with Ding? I'm all for pulling an all-nighter if you guys agree. Time is of the essence here, unless any of you has to leave."

"I'd like to take a run home to check on Yoko and Lily, if you don't mind. I can either come back or stay home and return in the morning. My time is yours, what with the dojo closed this week," Harry said.

"Play it by ear, Harry. Just out of curiosity, where does Yoko think you go when you leave?"

Harry laughed. "The Pentagon. I'll leave after I hear what Dennis has to say, so I can be mulling this all over while I'm home."

Jack looked over at Dennis and said, "Let's hear it, kid."

Dennis looked around the room. "Well, Martha Andover Gellis is a mean, mean woman. I know this is not nice to say, but she is not even one little bit attractive. She's overweight. She's a tyrant and cracks a mean whip. She wants everything done yesterday or the day before. I found an article in an accounting magazine; she's a CPA, by the way. Anyway, some accounting student hoping for a good grade wangled an interview with her and some of the people who work for her. Two of the people she interviewed were let go at some point after the interview took place for what Gellis described as *goofing off*. I called the magazine, got the number for the student who did the interview, and she gave me the name of the two people fired, and I was able to talk to both of them.

"Boy, man oh man, talk about deep hatred. If those people had their way, Mrs. Andover Gellis would be spending the rest of her life in a small room being tortured in every way possible."

Dennis looked around to make sure he had a rapt audience. He did. "One of the people who was let go said she was Gellis's personal slave. A gofer, but she still had to keep up with her job at the company, and it was too much. She said she never left the building before nine at night and had to be in at seven. No overtime. And Gellis fought the girl's unemployment, which she did not get in the end. Like Otto Andover, she motivates people exclusively by using the fear factor. All this went down when the economy tanked, and people needed their jobs. The second person she fired was a man who had been with the company twelve years. He told me on the phone that the only reason he lasted so long was that he kept his head down and just did whatever she said. That worked until he had a serious operation; he had to have a kidney removed. She wanted him back at work right away, and his doctor said no. She fought his disability, but she lost that round. He now works from home doing medical billing and is as happy as a clam to be out from under her control. Unfortunately, the money is not as good as what he was making at Andover.

"He said that she's just plain evil and doesn't do a damn thing to hide the fact. He also said that when the first lawsuit on the drug was filed, the three Andovers had so many private meetings that he couldn't keep up with them. He said that for some odd reason she lived in fear that she would be held personally responsible for the Anmir fiasco, which she insisted was all Otto's doing because he was so greedy. She tells everyone who will listen that they should have just come clean and discontinued the drug when the first problems arose.

"Now, here is the best part: This guy—whose name, by the way, is Jamie Farrell—said he took some records with him when he left. He said he didn't know why he took them, he just did. And guess what they were? Anyone?"

Dennis looked around at his audience, enjoying the spotlight. When no one ventured a guess, he continued, "They were the settlement agreements with the children's parents, the four children who died, that's what they were. He said he would turn them over to us if we needed them, as long as we didn't say where we got them.

"I just sent him a text message and asked him to fax everything to us. I said we did need them and promised him money. Told him a very generous check would go in the mail today. Tomorrow now, I guess. He deserves it; he has a family to support and he's just getting by. He didn't ask, I volunteered. Jamie said that once the decision was made to sweep everything under the rug, Gellis fought Otto, saying he was paying too much to the families, that they could have paid out half the amount to secure their silence, to which Otto responded that that kind of thinking was why he was the CEO and not her.

"The siblings only speak when it is absolutely necessary. There are two armed camps within the company, each with its own spies. And even Philip, though a noncombatant, has his spies to keep tabs on the other two. They're all mentally ill," Dennis said, disgust ringing in his voice.

"Are you saying she is the one who actually makes payments but only on Otto's say-so? That he has to approve all expenditures other than for routine things?" Harry asked.

"Yep. And Gellis hates it. She's under his thumb. And it

isn't just that he has control that she hates. She also hates
Otto himself, Jamie said. I'm not sure what her feelings are
for Philip. Jamie did say she referred to Philip as Mr.
Switzerland and even called him Swiss behind his back.
Meaning, of course, that Switzerland is neutral, and so is
Philip. Nonetheless, as I said, he has his spies, too, so he
has to know what the other two are doing. It's just that
he doesn't make waves, stays out of the limelight."

The front door buzzed. Everyone looked up until Maggie
said, "It's Ding with our food. Be right back." She was as
good as her word, returning carrying two shopping bags.

"Harry, you might want to think again about leaving.
It's really snowing out there, and the wind is starting to gust
something terrible. Call Yoko to see if you absolutely have
to leave. You came on your motorcycle, and that's not
good," Maggie said.

"You can take my car, Harry, if you have to leave," Jack
said.

Harry held out his hand for Jack's keys. And that was
the end of that.

Chapter 32

"You guys finish up here and I'll set us out a picnic in the lobby. Coffee, beer, or soft drinks?" Maggie mentally cataloged the order and left with the food. Fifteen minutes later, she had a picnic set up on the floor, using a blanket throw for a tablecloth. Colorful cushions served as chairs as they sat Indian fashion.

Dennis opened the plantation shutters so they could see the snow falling on the city. "This is just great," he babbled. "We were all together on Christmas, and yesterday we were all together to make a miracle for Nikki, and today we're together again with a plan to take down one of the most lucrative privately owned companies in the country. Someone for sure is watching over us," he said, excitement ringing in his voice.

As the group munched and chewed their way through their winter picnic, they talked about mundane things just to lighten the mood as they watched the icy snow that peppered the windows in the front of the building.

"Charles would really pitch a fit if he heard us talking business while we're eating," Ted said.

"We are not discussing Charles, today or any other day," Jack said, his face dark with anger at the mere mention of Charles Martin's name.

"So, Dennis, are you still going to the Galleria to pick up the suits?" Maggie asked.

Dennis laughed. "I went on their website and ordered them. They will be ready for pickup tomorrow at eleven o'clock. Then it's just the haircuts, and we'll be good to go."

"When Dennis told me where he was going for his haircut, I nixed that and made an appointment with my hairdresser for all three of you guys to get your hair done. Michael's Salon on Fern Terrace. He gave me a hard time when I explained what I wanted. Michael is a stylist and doesn't like high and tight haircuts, but he's going to do it as a favor to me. Your appointment is at noon. Don't embarrass me; make sure you guys tip well. *Then* we're good to go, and not one minute before."

"Has anyone given any thought to how we're even going to get into the Andover Building, much less to these guys' offices?" Espinosa asked. When Jack and the others had discovered that none of the Andover siblings had left the area for vacation, they'd changed plans to deal with the possibility that they would all be going in to work, and, if they did, they would beard them in their own den, so to speak, hence the concern about getting into the Andover Building.

Jack burst out laughing. "Since when does the FBI need an appointment for anyone? That shield is all you need to gain entrance anywhere in this country. Speaking of FBI, Bert and Sparrow were supposed to call in. Guess Annie and Myra are keeping them busy. Anyone think we should call them, or are we good?"

"I think we're good," Maggie said. "Am I the one who stands by the desk in the lobby when you guys enter so whoever is behind said desk doesn't alert our . . . prey?"

"A gold star to you, Miss Spritzer." Ted grinned. "We're looking for total surprise."

Maggie waved her arms. "I did all this so you guys can clean up." She looked over at Cyrus, who was sitting and waiting patiently for his dinner. Maggie had carefully picked all the meat off the side of the roast chicken that Jack had ordered especially for him. She added some vegetables and some roasted potatoes and set the plate down in front of the big dog. He looked up at Maggie, then at Jack, before he moved closer to the plate.

"He's not used to anyone else feeding him, which is a good thing. It's all yours, Cyrus, go for it," Jack said. Cyrus followed instructions and was finished within seconds. He nosed the hard plastic plate toward Maggie, not for a refill but to tidy up. Jack had taught him well.

"You got anything for us, Abner? You said you only needed an hour, so what do you have?" Jack asked.

"I'm pretty sure I have everything we need. At least on the financial end. I just have one more thing to do, and it will only take twenty or so minutes. I'll meet you in the conference room. Do you want printouts for everyone, or will a show-and-tell on my part work, for now at least? If you want copies, then I'm going to need forty minutes."

"Copies would be nice. So we're all on the same page," Jack said.

Maggie got up and closed the plantation shutters. "It's really going to town out there. Can't see anyone on the street. It's getting dark, too."

"I'm going to walk Cyrus, but we'll stay in the alley. We won't be long because he hates getting his feet wet. How's about someone making coffee?"

Dennis volunteered to make the coffee. Maggie sauntered off to the ladies' room, while Ted and Espinosa finished cleaning up the picnic and bundling all the trash. They both looked around. Neat as a pin, no sign that a picnic had even taken place.

The snow that seemed to be coming sideways beat at

Jack as he watched Cyrus meandering up and down the alley, looking for just the right spot. The snow was drifting, and the wheels of Harry's Ducati were almost covered. Knowing how Harry loved and babied his cycle, Jack decided to wheel it into the BOLO Building. He whistled for Cyrus to get a move on, then had him put all his weight against the door to hold it open so he could wheel the cycle into the back of the building. Satisfied that the cycle was now safe, Jack held the door while Cyrus beelined for the kitchen, where he lay down and rolled over and over on the carpet by the sink to get the snow off his back. Jack spread a ton of paper towels around the cycle to catch all the drips, then took more and dried it off. He hoped Harry appreciated all the trouble he was going to for him.

Jack smelled the coffee and grinned at Maggie, who had taken over coffee-making duties from Dennis. Maggie did make good coffee. "Need any help?"

"Got it covered. This is going to work, isn't it, Jack?"

Jack hated it when Maggie looked and acted worried, because she was always so optimistic.

"I am ninety-nine percent sure. Nothing is a given in this life; you know that, Maggie. Are you worried about something in particular or just worried?"

Maggie looked up at Jack, who towered over her. "Well, maybe one little itsy-bitsy thing is troubling me."

"And what might that be, oh my intrepid reporter turned . . . what is it you are at the paper these days?"

"It doesn't matter what I am. Where are we going to get FBI credentials?"

"They are on the way as we speak, courtesy of one Jack Sparrow and one Bert Navarro. It seems in Vegas you can get anything for the right price. And Sparrow got us genuine, authentic, as-real-as-they-come creds. Clips and all. They are supposed to be here in the morning, but with the storm,

I don't know. We don't move without them, that's a given. If Sparrow says they're golden, then they're golden."

Maggie pretended to wipe sweat off her brow. "Whew. I was concerned, Jack. I won't deny it."

"I think that what you're trying to say without saying the actual words is that you are comparing our little group to the sisters, and we're coming up short. How am I doing so far?"

"Well . . ."

Jack laughed. "Don't worry till we get to the finish line. If we don't cross it, that's when you can worry. It's not how we get there that matters, it's that we get across it. Feel better now?"

"Not really," Maggie said, chewing on her thumbnail. Jack threw a wadded-up dish towel at her. She caught it and tossed it right back. "You carry the sugar and creamer, and I'll take the pot. And just for that, you can come back for the cups and spoons."

"Okay." Jack looked over at the clock on the range. Abner's forty minutes were almost up.

Jack timed his second trip just right. Abner, his arms full of papers, held the door with his back so Jack could enter.

"We are in business, lads and one lassie, as Charles used to say," Abner said, dropping the stack of papers on the long, polished conference table.

Chapter 33

Abner knew that he was the center of attention as he separated the papers he'd carried into the conference room into individual packets and handed them across the table. "I can give you the highlights, and then we can go through the pages one by one so you can see everything I found and all be on the same page. Please hold your questions until I have finished. Everyone okay with that?" They all said they were okay with his proposals.

"So, Andover Pharmaceuticals is way more than solvent. As a matter of fact, it is bigger and in better financial shape than virtually any privately owned company in America, other than Koch Enterprises. To be sure, their valuation did take a hit in the aftermath of the Anmir drug lawsuits, but they have recovered quite nicely, even if going public is no longer feasible. And that is in part because they were able to keep a lid on things by settling with the parents of the children who passed away. They also dealt very aggressively with anyone who didn't want to settle. While what you are now holding in your hot little hands was printing out, I skimmed through the faxes that came through from Dennis's source, Mr. Jamie Farrell, former employee in the office of Andover Pharmaceuticals' CFO.

"By no stretch of the imagination are the Andovers nice

people. That is the bottom line. Fear and intimidation are what they live and work by. Nothing we could do to them would equal in cruelty what they have done to those who got caught up with that horrendous drug, both in terms of what happened to the kids and what happened to those who tried to expose Andover for what it has become, essentially a big-time criminal enterprise.

"They brought out their big guns, the best and slimiest lawyers in the country, to fight the class-action suit. For every negative that came out, they fought it with an over-the-top positive. When the class-action hit, it didn't get much play because Andover donated millions of dollars' worth of drugs to Doctors Without Borders, and it was their *generosity* that the cable news channels and the papers played up. Andover employs a kick-ass PR team, one that is way ahead of the curve. It's like they can anticipate bad news before it happens, and they squelch it. I tried calling their number-one guy, but he never returned any of my phone calls. That's about all I have. Other than the fact that I hacked into the head of the PR team's e-mail account. It boggles my mind how stupid some people are. Especially this PR guy, whose name is Duke Winslow, by the way, and is the one calling the shots. I made copies of all the pertinent e-mails. The guy is slick, and he commands big bucks."

"Did he do anything illegal?" Jack asked.

"It's all a matter of interpretation. Yes and no, more no than yes. But that's just my opinion. You're the lawyer, Jack, so that's your call."

"What else do you have?" Espinosa asked.

"I," Abner said dramatically, as though waiting for a drumroll, "have every single bank and brokerage account of the company, plus the personal banking and brokerage information for all three Andover siblings, and if I do say so myself, they are loaded. Between the company and the three of them as individuals, they could fund several third-world countries into the next millennium at least."

"Well, damn," Maggie said. "And to think they're fighting Nikki right here on the home front. I say we take every red cent they've got! Since their kids seem like nice people, I hope they've set something up for them and funded it already, because after we are finished, there is going to be nothing to leave them." The others agreed.

Jack looked at Abner. "Can you make that happen, Abner?"

Abner laughed. And laughed some more, as he flexed his fingers. "Oh, yeah," he drawled. "All I need is someone to sign the checks and we are good to go. So, my question to you, Jack, is can you get me that signature?"

Maggie's eyes narrowed, and she answered for Jack before he could make his tongue start to work. "You know it!" Jack's features split into a wide grin as his head bobbed up and down.

A beeping sound came from where Dennis was sitting, then the same sound came from Ted's position, followed by the identical sound from Espinosa's area.

"We all have the same alert on our phone for anything pertaining to Andover," Maggie said as she looked down at her phone. "It's kind of like TMZ or Radar Online, the gossip sites on the Net. Okay here is what it says: 'Mr. Otto Andover, CEO of Andover Pharmaceuticals, will be hosting a New Year's Eve party aboard his yacht, after which he will be leaving for a month in California. He will be taking the yacht and captaining it himself.'" Maggie looked around at the others. "Where are we going to nail these three? If he's getting set to have a New Year's party on his yacht and take off for California, I'm thinking that he, and probably the others, just might not be going into the office this week. I'm also thinking time is of the essence here. How are we going to play this? By the way, there was no mention of

Philip or Martha attending the party, which is likely to further complicate things."

"We need to find out if the three of them are at work this week. I can call to ask," Dennis said.

"Do that, kid," Ted said, but Dennis was already clicking away on his phone. They all listened in awe as Dennis rattled off a spiel about the Chamber of Commerce's wanting to do something special for Otto, Philip, and Martha to show their appreciation for all Andover did for the community. Three minutes later, Dennis was sporting an ear-to-ear grin as he shut down his phone. "I am happy to report that all three Andovers are spending the week at their respective homes, and Otto's secretary said she could schedule something the first week of February. You heard me say I would get back to her."

"That means we hit them at home, then," Jack said. "Here's the thing, though: I wanted a paper check for Nikki. What are the chances of Martha or Otto or Philip having a checkbook at home? Zip, I would think. With the other stuff, Abner can just do the wire transfers."

"Well, as long as we're pretending to be the FBI, why don't we just march into the Andover Building, which is probably being manned by a skeleton crew this week, go to Martha's office, and help ourselves. Isn't that what the FBI would do?" Dennis said.

"In a perfect world, yeah, that's what they would do. With warrants. And then everyone will get a good look at us. Remember, we are still going to be here after the three of them are gone. We need a plan. I'm thinking you need to call that guy Jamie Farrell to see if he can help us. In the meantime, I'm going to call Bert and Sparrow and walk Cyrus, who I think ate too many of our leftovers. You guys kick this around and see what you come up with," Jack said.

* * *

Jack hunkered down into his heavy jacket as the snow swirled about him. He shivered as he pressed the speed-dial button that would connect him with Bert, who would arrange to have Sparrow listen in with another click of a button. He rattled off the reason for the call as he watched Cyrus travel the length of the alleyway to find his favorite spot to do what he had to do. Today, for some reason, it was taking the big shepherd longer than usual, probably thanks to all the table food everyone sneaked to him. Minutes later, he said, "Do you think we can pull this off, Sparrow?"

Sparrow laughed. "When you say the magic words, it's like open sesame."

"And those words would be?" Jack said, his teeth chattering. Damn, it was cold.

"The magic words are, 'We can arrest you and hold you for seventy-two hours without a lawyer, and we've been known to lose paperwork on more than one occasion.' That's if anyone gives you any trouble or wants to look at you too closely. Use a light disguise, but nothing obvious. Different people tend to remember different things, which causes doubt on a positive ID. Keep it cool and professional and no one will give you any trouble. People in a situation like you describe have a tendency to look everywhere but at the agents. I'll take care of things on January 1, when I take over my new office, in case there's any kind of blowback. Like I said, the fibbies are notorious for losing paperwork."

Bert chimed in and laughingly agreed with everything Sparrow had said.

Jack saw Cyrus bounding toward him at a good clip. He quickly opened the door and repeated the same process he'd gone through earlier, when he'd taken the shepherd outdoors. His teeth still chattering, Jack ended the call just as Sparrow was saying he'd hit town tomorrow evening and give Jack a call.

The connection was terminated. Jack jumped around a

few minutes, windmilling his arms to try to get warm as Cyrus rolled over and over on the kitchen carpet, which was still damp from his previous expedition into the wilds of a D.C. blizzard. Jack let loose with one final violent shudder and marched back to the conference room, where the others were waiting, with the exception of Abner, who had retreated to his lair.

"I think we have a plan," Ted said. "We hit the office tomorrow at around a quarter to five, right before closing, then we hit the homes of the three Andovers the following day. Dennis just heard back from Jamie Farrell, who told him where in the office the corporate checkbook is located. He even had the checking account number that Abner matched up to one of the accounts. It's a high-dollar brokerage account, and there is enough money in it to cover Nikki's class-action suit. He also said there is another checkbook with a green binding that Martha uses for everything else. He said she is not a fan of online banking. He also said that in a lot of ways, she is very old-fashioned, whatever that is supposed to mean.

"We can use that account to pay Jamie Farrell and anyone else the Andovers screwed over who we want to help. Abner looked up that account and said there are beaucoup bucks in it. By the way, the checkbook you need for Nikki is bright blue. Seems blue and green are Martha's favorite colors, according to Jamie. He said as soon as he can, he's going to make a scale drawing of the seventh floor, where Martha's office is. Then he will fax it to us. An hour or so from now."

"He's doing all this and not asking questions?" Jack said in amazement. "Are we sure about this guy?"

"He's the real deal, Jack, trust me on that," Dennis said. "A guy with only one kidney who got screwed over by Martha Andover Gellis wants nothing more than for something very, very bad to happen to her. He knows he can't do anything himself, but if someone else can, he's eager to help as much as possible. And all that was before I told him we'd take care of him financially. Like I said, we can trust him."

Jack eyed the young reporter and nodded. "Okay, we'll go forward on your say-so. While I was outside with Cyrus, I called Bert and Sparrow." He summed up his conversation, ending with, "Sparrow is leaving tomorrow to return here and said to stay low and he'll take care of any blowback there might be when he takes office on the first of January. I do think we're good to go."

"Do we know where Philip Andover is?" Maggie asked.

"Home," Espinosa said. "Otto is home, too, as is Martha."

"When are we going to hit their offices for sure?" Dennis asked.

"Tomorrow at four forty-five. We hit them at home the following day. Any questions?" Jack asked. There were no questions.

"I guess Harry isn't coming back," Maggie said. "You should call him, Jack, and bring him up to date."

"You're right. I'll do that right now. Anything else I should know?"

"We're all good here," Ted said. "I want to read through this stuff line by line one more time. The devil is always in the details. We don't need a glitch because we ignored something that fouled things up." The others followed suit without being told to do so.

Jack moved off to call Harry just as his phone rang. It was Nikki. His heart kicked up a beat.

"Oh, Jack, you are not going to believe this, but the plane we were supposed to be on right now has mechanical problems. We're going to be stuck here another day." Jack could hear the tears and the weariness in his wife's voice. He tried to joke, to say as long as she made it home in time for New Year's Eve, it was okay. Nikki didn't buy into it. Instead, she burst into tears. Right then, Jack wanted to kill someone for making his wife cry. He did his best to console her by telling her about the storm that was raging outside. He talked about Cyrus and the guys until he heard a smile in her voice. By the time he clicked off, he was mentally exhausted.

Instead of calling Harry, Jack walked down the hall to the foyer and opened the plantation shutters to stare out at the raging storm outside. The snow, which was more like sleet than snow, was coming down fast and furious. He couldn't even see across the street to the Bagel Emporium. That wasn't good. He wondered how and if the FedEx driver would make it in the morning with his overnight package from Jack Sparrow. If not, things would have to get moved back a day. Anytime a glitch like that happened to a plan, chaos took over. "Crap!" he said succinctly. He closed the plantation shutters before he walked back to the kitchen to call Harry. Cyrus had fallen sound asleep on the wet carpet by the sink.

Jack sat down at the table, careful not to make too much noise and wake Cyrus up, pulled out his magic phone, and hit the number that would connect him with Harry, who picked up on the first ring. He quickly brought him up to date and ended with, "What are you doing?"

"I'm having a tea party with Lily. I'm Prince William and Yoko is Princess Kate. Lily is the queen and Cooper is wearing a special crown because he is the royal dog. Anything else you want to know?"

"Yeah. What is the queen serving?"

Harry hung up on him. Jack burst out laughing. It felt good to laugh. Really good. He walked over to the sink and slid down to the floor, where he proceeded to talk to Cyrus while he stroked the big dog's head. Cyrus wiggled and squirmed until he managed to turn almost completely around so that he could lay his head on Jack's lap. He listened intently to the tone of his master's voice and whimpered softly. He raised his head to lick Jack's chin. Undying love.

Jack smiled.

Chapter 34

Maggie Spritzer was the first to stir in the morning. She yawned, stretched, then rubbed her neck to ease the kinks out of her shoulders. It had been a while since she'd slept on a hard floor in her clothes, much less attended a picnic at the end of December. She looked around at her friends, who were sprawled in what were almost certainly painful positions. She eased herself up slowly, her muscles protesting. She was definitely out of shape. This was where she should make a promise to herself to get back onto a strict exercise program. She didn't bother, for the simple reason that she knew she couldn't or wouldn't keep any such promise, to herself or anyone else, including Ted.

Maggie gingerly made her way to the front foyer and opened the shutters to see a winter wonderland. It must have stopped snowing during the night, but there certainly was a blanket of the white stuff as far as the eye could see. It was so blinding that she had to squint to ward off the glare. Away in the distance, she could hear the rumble of snowplows, and that was definitely a good thing. She closed the shutters and squeezed her eyes shut. Then she waited a few seconds before she opened them again and took in the comforting dimness of the foyer. When she felt something warm on her ankles, she looked down to see Cyrus, who was getting ready to nibble at her bare toes.

"Bet you want to go out, big dog, huh? Shhh, don't wake anyone. Just let me get my shoes and jacket. Meet me at the back door," Maggie whispered. Cyrus trotted off, and Maggie looked around for her shoes, which had come to rest under one of the chairs. Quickly pulling on her socks and shoes, she tiptoed out of the room to head for the kitchen. She slipped into her jacket, opened the door, and did a double take at the cold air. "Make it quick, Cyrus!"

Cyrus did as he was told and was back inside the building before Maggie could count to twenty.

Within minutes, she had the big twelve-cup coffeepot singing its song. Cyrus was rolling around on the carpet at the sink, which Jack had conveniently thought to throw in the dryer and place all dry in front of the sink before retiring for the night. Maggie headed off for one of the bathrooms, wondering why Jack had had a laundry room, albeit a small one, installed in the building.

True, there was a laundry room, but no spare toothbrushes or toothpaste. There was, however, a bottle of Listerine in the medicine cabinet. When in Rome . . . With a sigh, Maggie rinsed her mouth and washed her face. She winced at the condition of her hair. With no comb or brush in evidence, she wet her hands and ran them through her thick, corkscrew curls. Looking in the mirror a second time, she winced again but accepted that this was as good as it was going to get.

Back in the kitchen, she listened to the slowly percolating coffee. Within minutes, she could smell the tantalizing aroma; and then she heard stirring noises coming from down the hall, followed by moans and groans. Sleeping on a hard floor would do that to a body that was past its gloriously limber teenage years. The cots Jack had mentioned earlier had turned out to be a joke. At best, they were spindly and impossible to turn around on. It was Ted who gathered them all up and stacked them in the kitchen, telling Jack to return them to whatever outlet store he'd purchased them from.

One by one, the five boys staggered into the kitchen, bleary-eyed and cranky. Maggie grinned to herself as she set out doughnuts and bagels, which were a little less than fresh but would just have to do. Fine cuisine was definitely not on the menu this morning. As she poured cups of coffee and looked around, she said brightly, "Guess it stopped snowing, and the plows are out. I think we'll be good to go in an hour or so. Now all you guys have to do is dig out the cars."

Jack, the last one into the kitchen, said he wasn't digging out anything because Harry had told him that the guys who'd installed the super-duper gates in the alley were also under contract to plow the alley. When they would get around to it, however, Jack had no idea. Harry had never said.

"The plows are already working the street out front. I heard them," Dennis said.

"Good, good, that means FedEx should get here by noon. Soon as I have my coffee, I'm going to go online to see if our package is on the truck and what time it's scheduled for delivery. Sparrow gave me the tracking number," Jack said as he sank his teeth into a blueberry bagel.

Maggie started to giggle and couldn't stop. "You all look like a herd of wild men. Good thing there are no ladies here aside from myself to see how fetching you all look so early in the morning." Cyrus barked just to bark, a sign that he was neutral. Maggie kept on laughing as each of the guys tried to smooth down his bed hair.

Abner appeared, none the worse for wear. He even looked groomed, which was a feat unto itself. It turned out that he always carried what he called a hygiene kit in his backpack. He poured coffee, taking it black. He reached for a jelly doughnut and scarfed it down within seconds. "Very good." But then again, Abner thought bologna sandwiches with ketchup were right up there with filet mignon. No one would accuse Abner of being a gourmet. "Anything happen in the world while we slept, aside from the storm's abating?"

"Nothing," Espinosa said. "We're just waiting to see if Sparrow's package gets here. I'm thinking we need to decide who is going to the Andover Building. We need to do a preparation run."

"That we do, that we do," Jack said, refilling his coffee cup. He was starting to feel more alive minute by minute. "I was thinking I would go in with Dennis since he spoke personally to Jamie Farrell, and if we run into any problems, he can call him right away. Or better yet, have him on an open line. I thought we'd leave Maggie in the lobby with whoever it is that sits at the reception desk, just to make sure that person doesn't alert anyone else. Call it insurance. I thought the three of us would go in the *Post* van. Harry has my car, as you all know. Does that work for all of you?

"Once we get the checkbooks, we hightail it back here and let Abner take a look at them, then we finalize our plans for the take down tomorrow. Anyone have any questions?" No one did.

Jack headed off to the lavatory, calling over his shoulder to have someone call Harry and then Sparrow, to see if his flight had been canceled.

Cell phones were whipped out and numbers punched in while updates were announced as the guys took turns with the two lavatories.

The final report was that Sparrow had made it out on time, Brooks Brothers would open on schedule, and Michael's Salon was waiting for its customers to show up. The weatherman said the sanitation department had worked through the night and the roads were drivable, and no government agencies had shut down, opting for delayed openings instead. While that was the good news, the bad news was that the weatherpeople had slightly miscalculated, and more snow would start to fall later in the afternoon.

Everyone moaned and groaned, even Cyrus, who pranced around woofing his displeasure at all the noise outside the kitchen area, where Harry's people had arrived and were clearing the back alley.

"I think we are good to go, people," Jack said. "Our package is on the truck for delivery sometime this morning. Okay, let's hear it, who is going where this morning? We're on a timetable here."

"Dennis, Espinosa, and I, along with Maggie, are going in the van back to the paper, then Dennis will pick up the suits at Brooks Brothers in his Humvee and join us at Michael's for our new hairdos. Maggie has to check in at the *Post* and make like she works there. Espinosa and I are good; we filed our stories late last night. No problems with us. We should all be back here by noon, one o'clock at the latest. We can pick up lunch on our way. Howszat?" Ted asked.

"Oops! I almost forgot. We have another stop to make. Joe called the specialty shop where Alexis shopped to replenish her red bag of tricks. He knows exactly what to buy and how to apply it all. He said he's watched Alexis enough to get the hang of it."

"Okay, that works. To be honest, I forgot about all of that. Abner?" Jack said.

Abner flexed his long, slim fingers. "I'm good, Jack. All I need are numbers and we're home free. I'm thinking someone should double-check, if that's possible, the whereabouts of the three Andovers. No one has mentioned

Snowden and the tails he has on the three creeps. We need to confirm that all our birds are in their respective nests."

"If anything was awry, Snowden would have been on the horn. But to answer your question, I have not heard from him. I'm not worried; Snowden is a pro and on top of his game. But it never hurts to err on the side of caution. Anything else?" Jack looked around when no one said anything. "Okay, move, and be aware of the time."

"What are you going to do, Jack?" Dennis asked as he slipped into his heavy jacket.

"Talk to Bert, wait for FedEx, and try to reach my wife, who the last I heard had gotten to Atlanta and was waiting for the airport to open. I have to say, this is the longest trip in the world time wise. The last time I spoke to her, she said that she and Alexis were both zombies. The airports ran out of food, the hotels were full, the gift shops ran out of toothbrushes as well as toothpaste, and she's like a bee-stung bear. Alexis, too, I guess."

The fierce look on Jack's face warned the others not to comment, so they remained silent. The moment Jack stopped talking, they all made a beeline for their outerwear. Cyrus barked his approval that things were finally moving. He ran to his basket of toys, pulled out a bright red elephant, whipped it into the air, caught it, then sprawled on the carpet by the sink, his statement made.

Five seconds later, the kitchen was empty. Jack waited a moment to hear the sound of the van starting up. When he turned around, he saw that Abner was gone, too. It was just him, Cyrus, and his thoughts.

Coffee in hand, Jack made his way to the conference room, where he sat down to go through the printout of Andover Pharmaceuticals' financials. He reached for his calculator, his pen, and a yellow legal pad. He worked steadily, making columns of numbers, meticulously adding and subtracting as he allocated and reallocated what he thought was fair for all of those who were to be the beneficiaries of Andover's munificent donation to the cause of all that was good and right in the world.

He set the papers aside and switched over to the personal finances of the three Andovers. Multimillionaires all. Well, not for long, he thought grimly.

Something was nibbling at the back of his mind, something Dennis had said earlier, possibly yesterday or the day before, but for the life of him he couldn't remember what it was. He got up to pace around the long conference table. He did some of his best thinking when he paced. What was it? He stopped under the Jasper Johns painting, looked up at it in the hope it would give him his answer. Nothing came to him. He continued pacing, then stood under the Jackson Pollock painting. No help there, either. *Shift into neutral, Jack. Let it come on its own.* Right. Easier said than done.

Then Jack remembered his intention to call Avery Snowden. The operative growled a greeting on the first ring. "We're all good here," was all he said before he broke the connection. *A man of few words*, Jack thought. Still, he felt reassured.

Five minutes later, Jack almost jumped out of his skin when he heard the door buzz at the front of the building. Cyrus was a black streak whizzing by him. *FedEx?* Jack ran after Cyrus, and told him to stay as he peeked through the plantation shutters. Sure enough, it was indeed a FedEx deliveryman. Jack could barely contain himself as he opened the door, stared at the driver as though he were the enemy, signed his name for both packages, slammed the door shut, and slipped both dead bolts into place.

Chapter 35

His heart beating trip-hammer fast, Jack headed for the conference room, where he had to try three times before he could open the thinner of the two packages. He heaved a mighty sigh as he looked at all the exquisite credentials Bert and Sparrow had managed to get for him and the guys, and Maggie, too. He laughed out loud when he read Sparrow's note, which said, *Whip these babies out and you are golden.* What really set him off on a laughing jag was a picture of a golden, happy face behind a set of bars. He looked for his own set of credentials. He was for now Special Agent Anthony Lupine. Ted was Special Agent Andrew Molnar, Espinosa was Special Agent Raoul Samoza, Dennis was Special Agent Donald Ryder, and Maggie was Special Agent Lucinda Collins. There were no credentials for Harry because everyone had agreed that an Asian might be too easily remembered, and Harry's picture had been in the papers too often, given his martial arts prowess and worldwide reputation in the field.

Jack eyed the second delivery, which wasn't a soft-sided package but a hard cardboard box. He knew what was in it, but his jaw still dropped in awe as he slid his pocketknife through the heavy tape. Five guns. All Glocks. Disassembled, and wrapped in some kind of mystery packaging to thwart the scanners at FedEx, he surmised. The gun of choice for the fibbies. No ammunition. That was okay; they absolutely were not going to shoot anyone. At least not today. The guns were just for show.

He pried at the special packing and saw the shoulder holsters on the bottom of the box. The holsters looked old, worn, and *real*. He guessed it was true what he'd heard: If you had the money, you could get anything in Vegas. He supposed it was all in knowing the right people, or knowing people who knew the right people. Anything for a price.

It took Jack exactly fourteen minutes to assemble the Glocks. "Good to go, baby, good to go," he muttered happily under his breath.

Because he had nothing else to do at the moment, Jack picked up one of the holsters and tried it on. He shoved the gun into it and practiced his draw. He was familiar with guns, had gone to the shooting range hundreds of times when he was an assistant district attorney. He'd always qualified. Thank God he had never had to draw on anyone. He also had a license to carry a gun in his real life but not as Special Agent Anthony Lupine.

Aha, the boys had slipped up. Nah. Not Sparrow. He rummaged in the box and found the licenses in an envelope that was stuck to the bottom of the plastic filler. The envelope read, *Just in case.* "Sorry I doubted you, Sparrow," he muttered.

And then he remembered what he hadn't been able to remember before: Andover's launch after the New Year with its new rheumatoid arthritis medicine. Why or what it meant in the scheme of things he had no idea. Beaucoup bucks for the Andover coffers and the three owners for sure. But why was he even thinking or worrying about that? When he couldn't come up with an answer, he shelved the thought as he had before. Sooner or later, it would come to him. If not, then it wasn't an important consideration as far as their plans were concerned.

Just as Jack started to look down at his watch, a gift from Nikki years ago, one of those watches that did everything but scramble eggs, in his opinion, his phone rang. Snowden. He picked it up, listened briefly, and hung up. Now he knew the importance of that new product launch.

Looking again at his watch, he was shocked to see that it was already three minutes shy of the noon hour. Working on those numbers had taken a lot longer than he'd thought. He was aware suddenly of how quiet it was, with only the sound of Cyrus chomping on a huge bone that was guaranteed to clean his teeth. That had to mean the alleyway had been cleared by Harry's people.

His stomach growling, Jack headed for the kitchen. He whistled for Cyrus, who came on the run. The shepherd waited a moment to see if his master would reach for the leash, which meant a sedate walk, or no leash, which meant a free-for-all run up and down the alley.

Jacket on, zipped up, and a heavy scarf wrapped around his neck, Jack opened the back door. No leash. Cyrus whizzed past the open door and tore down the alley, barking shrilly. Jack huddled in the doorway, hands jammed in his pockets as he stomped his feet up and down. It had to be only twenty degrees out there, he thought. He stood it as long as he could before he whistled to Cyrus to cut it short, just as the *Post* van and Dennis's Humvee appeared at the security gates. The minute the door to the van slid open, he could smell the garlic. They were going to dine on Italian.

When Dennis emerged from the Humvee, he was struggling with plastic-wrapped suits on hangers. Jack held the door open for him. Ted emerged from the van, carrying two shopping bags, and Espinosa carried the food. Maggie had her own shopping bag and a box of some sort. "Everything okay? No problems?"

"Good to go," Ted said, hustling through the doorway. The others agreed. Jack heaved a sigh of relief.

Ninety minutes later, lunch was over, the cleanup completed, Cyrus had been walked, and everyone was dressed for what Jack called the coming festivities. Jack had told them about Avery Snowden's call and the resulting change of plans. Now the only thing left to do before the trip to Andover Pharmaceuticals was for Espinosa to apply some of Alexis's tricks to alter their appearances.

"I'm not liking any of this right now," Dennis complained. "When Murphy's Law kicks in, plans go down the tubes." His tone went from whining to accusatory when he said, "You said, Jack, that Mr. Snowden said all was good, and we were on schedule for visiting the three Andovers *tomorrow*. Tomorrow, not today. I'm not liking this one little bit," he said.

Jack sighed. He was used to plans going awry, as were the others. "Yes, I did say that because that's what Avery told me when I called him earlier. But that was hours ago. When he called ninety minutes ago to say that Otto was leaving tomorrow morning for New Mexico to talk to some people about the new drug, he called me immediately. As you all know, he has some kind of equipment in place that allows him to pick up all phone conversations in Otto's house, and those of the other siblings as well. He's on top of things. Had he not had his equipment in place, and we went out there tomorrow, we'd be up the old proverbial creek without the proverbial paddle. Tell me you understand what I just said, Dennis."

Dennis yanked at his blue-and-white-striped tie. "I'm not stupid; I understand. I just said I didn't like it. Improvising at the eleventh hour is never good. Don't forget to factor in that wacky weatherman's prediction for snow later today. We have miles to drive, and after the snatches, we still have to head out to Pinewood. That's another long haul."

"Thank God the van has good new snow tires," Maggie said as she stared at her reflection in the glass of the wall oven. "I hope you aren't wimping out, Dennis, and expecting us to cancel. We adapt. That's spelled a-d-a-p-t. I hate wimps."

Dennis flushed a rosy pink, but he didn't say another word.

Jack eyed Maggie and Dennis and was satisfied with what he was seeing. He stood still and suffered through Espinosa's filling in his cheeks, adding latex to his chin to make it longer, and narrowing his nose with the same latex. While his hair wasn't high and tight, it was a good crew cut and didn't need anything done to it.

"You guys got all the electronic stuff secure," Ted said. "Remember now, you can mumble or talk as the case may be, either into your lapels or the cuffs of your sleeves. The sound is muffled but still good. You should probably leave now because under normal conditions it's a forty-five-minute drive to Andover, but with the weather and the roads, I'm thinking more like an hour and fifteen minutes, maybe more," Ted said. "I'm sorry that you're going to be hitting Andover earlier than we intended, but that's unavoidable with Otto's change in plans. And with the snatches today and not tomorrow, there's less time for something to go wrong based as a result of the Andover raid."

"It's going to take us that long to get back here, too, so you guys be ready to roll the minute we get back. Watch Cyrus for me," Jack said.

Maggie looked around, winked at Ted, then focused on Jack. "Let's do it!"

Chapter 36

The moment the heavy security door slammed shut behind him, Jack knew it was literally showtime. They'd talked it all up one side and down the other until they were breathless to get moving and make it all a reality. He sucked in a breath of the frigid air, then coughed. He felt naked without Cyrus at his side, and he said so aloud.

"What are *we,* chopped liver?" Maggie squawked as she looped a cherry red scarf around her neck.

"You know what I mean, Maggie. I'm just used to having Cyrus next to me. Maybe we could have brought him and given him a badge, like the cops do with the K-nines. Where's the van?" Jack asked, looking around.

"We're taking my Humvee instead. Ted moved the van out front. The Humvee heats up in a matter of seconds. Best vehicle on the road for this kind of weather," Dennis said.

Jack looked up at the scudding gray clouds racing across the sky. An hour ago, there had been a little bit of blue sky and a thin, watery sun. But now the sky was totally gray and dismal. Off in the distance, he could hear a dog barking, then the alley went silent as Dennis unlocked the door of the Humvee and climbed in. As Jack and Maggie entered the vehicle, the snow equipment at the other end of the back alley kicked in with a roar that was deafening until they closed the doors.

Dennis pressed the starter in his keyless Humvee and the engine growled to life. "I have a great GPS, so key in the address, Jack. We all good to go here?"

"We are good," Maggie said as she loosened the scarf she had just tied around her neck. Then she looked at her watch and mentally calculated the coming activities and how long before she'd be home safe and warm in her own bed. Like she would really be able to sleep anytime soon with the way her adrenaline was running. Maybe she'd never be able to sleep again and she'd wither away and die.

She hated thoughts like these and struggled to remember the last romp in the sack with Ted, after they'd left the Christmas party at Jack's. A low, purring sound escaped her lips. Jack looked up from what he was doing and grinned. Maggie was oblivious to his glance.

Dennis backed down the alley, clicked the remote on his visor, waited for the iron gates to open, and sailed out just as the car's heat came on full blast. "How's that for instant gratification?" he chortled happily.

"Nice set of wheels, kid," Jack mumbled as he continued to key in the address of Andover Pharmaceuticals. Maggie stared out at the rapidly darkening afternoon, her thoughts on Ted's sexual prowess.

"Traffic's kind of light for this hour of the day. We should make good time once we get out of town. I've been thinking: Even if Andover lets its employees out early because of the snow forecast, we still won't have a problem. Someone from Security will still be there. That in itself might work to our advantage. What do you think, Jack?" Dennis asked as he skillfully maneuvered the Humvee around several cars that were driving too slowly for his liking. Dennis West was a man with a mission, and he was not going to allow anything, including slow-moving cars, to get in his way.

"I agree. What about you, Maggie? What do you think?" Jack asked.

"I think it's six of one and half a dozen of the other. Either way, we're more than capable of handling whatever is handed to us. I will tell you what I *am* worried about, though. Look at the sky. It's getting darker by the minute. I think we should turn the guys loose and let them head for our primary targets *now*. Ted and Espinosa can take Philip. Harry should have arrived at the BOLO Building by now— he was already on his way when we left—and he and Abner can do the snatch on Otto, and the three of us can take Martha since she lives the closest to the company headquarters. Then we all head for the farm as soon as we've done the snatches and grabs. Don't look at me like that, Jack. I really think that's what we should do."

Dennis froze. "Oh, jeez, still another change in plans. That makes two. The third one will be the charm. Everyone knows that saying, but with what we're doing, I don't think the word *charm* is exactly the right one. I see this all going to hell really quickly," Dennis said in a jittery-sounding voice.

"You're dithering again," Jack pointed out. "And FBI agents do not dither. Not ever. Keep your eyes on the road, kid, and stop worrying. Maggie has a point. Points need to be addressed as they come up. I'm giving you permission to take your eyes off the road for two seconds. Look at the sky, Dennis!"

"Yeah, yeah. Okay. I get it, but that doesn't mean I have to like it. So what if I'm a natural-born worrywart? So is my mother, so I come by it honestly enough.

"Okay, okay. I see your point, but I'm still going to worry. How much farther, Jack?"

Jack pressed some buttons. "Eight miles. Straight road."

"Since you agree with me, I'm calling the guys now, Jack. If I'm wrong, tell me now, before I make the call."

"Make the damn call, Maggie."

After spending five minutes having two separate conversations with the guys back at the BOLO Building, she was ready to report to Jack. "Ted is going to take the other three and go to the *Post* to sign out a four-wheel drive for Harry and Abner to use. Harry said that your car was all over the road. He also squawked about having to wear a suit, shirt, and tie.

"Abner is going as is, Harry said, because he said he's scary-looking and no one will question him. And, anyway, he doesn't have a suit at the office. Just so you know, Harry will be the power player in that duo. It's all doable, Jack."

"Two miles, Dennis. And it's starting to snow," Jack said as he craned his neck to stare up and out of the windshield.

Dennis's voice was still jittery when he said, "I hope you are both noticing that no plows have been out this way recently."

"Maybe Andover has its own maintenance crews and they just haven't gotten to this stretch of the road. I see a sign up ahead, so slow down. I want you to pull right up in front of the building. If there is a guard station, I want you to let me do the talking, unless it's something you really want to do. Don't panic if you see me get out of the car. These guys are usually rent-a-cops, and I think I can handle them. What's it going to be, kid?"

"Hey, I'm just Special Agent Donald Ryder. The newbie who's driving. Everybody knows that the driver is always low man on the totem pole. You're right, Jack. I can see the security hut from here, as well as the fence." Dennis eased up on the gas pedal as he fumbled in his pocket for his FBI credentials. He could see that Jack already had his credentials in his hand. A quick glance into the rearview mirror showed Maggie waving hers for his benefit.

Dennis eased up even more on the gas pedal and coasted to a stop in front of the security hut. A man in uniform stepped out and held up his hand. Dennis rolled down his window just as Jack climbed out of the car to walk around to where the guard stood. He flipped open his billfold like he'd been doing it for years.

"FBI. I'm Special Agent Anthony Lupine. The driver is Special Agent Donald Ryder, and the agent in back is Special Agent Lucinda Collins. We'd like permission to enter the premises, but I need to tell you, we're going in with or without your permission. We have a warrant," he said, waving a folded sheet of paper he'd withdrawn from the inside of his suit jacket.

The guard, whose name tag said he was Arthur Spinelli, took his time looking at the credentials before he said, "I have to call Security."

"No, Mr. Spinelli, you do not have to call Security because we do not want you to do that. We can do this the easy way or the hard way. Maybe you don't understand what a warrant is. This piece of paper says I can do whatever I want when I want to do it. No one gets the opportunity to hide what we are looking for before we get in there. So, what's it going to be? The easy way or the hard way?"

"I can lose my job if I don't call you in. I need this job."

"Lucinda!"

Maggie was out of the car in a nanosecond and inside the hut, where she quickly ripped out the monitor and the phone, then demanded that Mr. Spinelli hand over his cell phone. But not before she patted him down for any weapons.

"Hey, you can't do that!"

"I just did. Now, come in here so I can tell you what you are going to do and not do. We can't have you alerting anyone of our presence until we want it known. We can arrest you right here on the spot and hold you for seventy-two hours. Think about it. What's that going to do to your New Year's Eve plans?"

Maggie looked over at Jack. "What do you want to do about him? We can open the gates and leave them open for anyone arriving or leaving."

Jack walked over to the Humvee and lowered his voice. "Does this nifty set of wheels have any kind of special locking devices? Like can we park this guy in it and feel safe he can't get out till we finish up our business?"

"Absolutely."

"What if he leans on the horn?" Jack asked as he looked at his watch.

"Jack, once this baby powers down, it's like Fort Knox. No in, no out; not until I press the code on my remote. Dump him in."

That was all Jack needed to hear. He opened the door of the hut and pushed the guard into the back of the Humvee. "Sorry about this, Mr. Spinelli, but in the interests of national security, we have to do this." He called over his shoulder to have Maggie open the massive gates. "And make sure you lock the door so no one can get into the hut." Jack was back in the Humvee within seconds. Maggie joined him within minutes.

"What's going on?" the guard asked in a shaking voice.

Jack turned around and said, in a voice filled with menace, "You should know better than to ask a question like that of an FBI Special Agent. As they say in that other agency whose name shall not pass my lips, if I told you, I'd have to kill you. Now just sit there and be quiet. When we finish here, we will release you. Tell me you understand what I just said."

"Yes, sir, I understand."

"Good."

Jack stared at the Andover Building, marveling at the massive structure. It was lit up from top to bottom. Even from where he was sitting, he could see a glittery Christmas tree in the cavernous foyer.

It was fully dark now and it was barely four o'clock. Snow was falling steadily. To his right, he could hear the sounds of muffled car engines as people warmed up their cars in the parking lot in preparation to leave.

"Showtime," Jack said under his breath as he exited the Humvee, with Maggie right behind him. Dennis was the last to exit, then made a production of locking in the security guard.

The trio marched up the three steps that led to oversize plate-glass doors. The twinkling Christmas tree was beautiful; a work of art, actually. At the door, Jack said, "Okay, everyone, take a deep breath. Dennis, get that open line to Jamie Farrell and keep it secure. Time to roll, folks."

Chapter 37

With a wild, wicked flourish, Jack threw open the door, sized up the lobby, and headed straight for a monster desk in the center of the room, where a man in a gray uniform sat behind a computer monitor that showed every floor in the building.

"Hands where I can see them, sir. FBI. I'm Special Agent Lupine, this is Special Agent Donald Ryder, and the lady is Special Agent Lucinda Collins. This is a warrant," he said, waving the paper in front of the startled man's eyes.

"Wha . . . what do . . . do you want?"

"Actually, nothing from you personally, Mr. . . ." Jack looked at the man's name tag. "Mr. Lee. Special Agent Collins will stay here with you while we conduct our business. Do you understand what I just said, and do you understand that this warrant gives me the authority to do whatever I want in this building?"

"Yes, sir, I do, sir. My favorite show is *Law & Order*. I know how it works. Glory be, I never thought I'd be in the presence of the FBI. I'm supposed to report to Security when something like this happens."

"Don't worry about it. We'll report it for you. For now, turn off all those monitors."

"I can't do that, sir. They are to be left on twenty-four/ seven. I could get fired."

"Special Agent Collins, see to things." Jack moved off toward the bank of elevators, Dennis in his wake. "You have Farrell live on the phone?"

"Yes, I sure do. He's telling me to go to the seventh floor, turn right, and Ms. Martha Wicked Witch of the World's office is at the end of the hall. Her underlings sweat in the other offices. He said no one will even lift their heads if they see us, that's how well-conditioned they are to her tirades and mean mouth."

After exiting the elevator on the seventh floor, Jack strode purposefully down what was certainly the longest hallway he'd ever seen like he knew exactly where he was going. He heard Dennis ask Farrell if the office would be locked. He waited for Dennis to clue him in. He didn't have long to wait.

"Jamie said the office is left open during the day, even when she isn't there, because the slaves have to be able to put their reports on her desk the minute they're finished. He said all the offices are locked at five-thirty on the dot. If someone has the misfortune to be inside when that happens, they spend the night until they are opened in the morning."

"Then I guess we had better hurry," Jack said, looking at the green numerals on his watch. "It would cut our time down if Jamie would tell us exactly where to look for the checkbook in case it isn't where he originally told you it would be."

"Jamie said that if it is not in the bottom desk drawer, then it would be on the third shelf in the closet, under the cushion of the chair she usually sits in to read the trashy novels she thinks no one knows about, or in the drawer of the table that the ficus plant sits on." At Jack's strange look, Dennis said, "Hey, I'm just repeating what he said to me."

Jack looked around. It was a very nice suite of offices, tastefully decorated. Everything was exactly as depicted in the drawing Jamie had faxed to them yesterday. There was the ficus tree Jamie had mentioned, several lush ferns, and two inviting and comfortable-looking chairs off to the side of the main office space. *Good lighting*, he thought. *Good carpet, too.* A magnificent teakwood desk held very little other than a phone console and a computer. He liked the feel of the carpet under his shoes. He eyed the liquor bar, the bar sink, the minifridge, the Bose sound system, and the enormous—he guessed ninety-inch—TV mounted on the wall. Nice, expensive digs. He saw the copy of *Fifty Shades of Grey* on the table between the two comfortable-looking chairs. It looked worn, like it had been handled a lot. He grinned to himself.

"Dismantle the computer; we're taking the hard drive with us. I'll check for the register. Work fast, Dennis." Five minutes later, he hissed to Dennis, "Tell your guy it is not in the bottom desk drawer or any of the other three places he mentioned."

Dennis relayed the information as he continued to work on dismantling the computer and removing the hard drive. "He said to try the small linen closet in the bathroom, where she hides her stash of cigarettes and Reese's Peanut Butter Cups, which she's addicted to."

Jack raced into the bathroom and ripped open the door. He gasped at the cases of candy and the cartons of cigarettes. He rummaged behind and under them, and finally found what he was looking for under a stack of lace-edged purple towels. *Purple towels?*

A minute later, he was back in the main part of the office, waving the small checkbook in the air.

"That's it!" Dennis hissed.

Jack laughed. "Maybe she has an aversion to big, cumbersome, hard-bound desk registers. Nikki has one like this.

According to the balance"—and Jack whistled as he flipped the pages—"this is it! You ready, Dennis?"

"I am so ready to get out of here I could scream." To Jamie, he said, "We got it. I'll be in touch in the next day or so. I'm ending this call now so we can get out of here."

They were halfway down the hall when they saw a very tall man dressed in a three-piece suit heading their way. Dennis muttered under his breath that the dude looked meaner than cat shit.

"Remember who we are and let me do the talking," Jack said.

"Who are you and what are you doing here? Who let you up here?" the big man boomed.

Jack whipped out his credentials so fast, Dennis got lightheaded. "FBI. And you are . . . ?"

"Evan Bell, head of Andover Security. How did you get in here and up to this floor?"

Jack waved the warrant and said, "This is the only introduction I need. Is there going to be a problem here?"

The big man planted his feet a little more firmly, looked Jack in the eye, and said, "If you tell me what and why, I don't see a problem. Does that warrant say you can take that hard drive I see in your partner's hand?"

"It does. It also gives me the power to take you to headquarters and hold you for seventy-two hours."

Bell reached for the bogus warrant Jack Sparrow had sent and pretended to read it. Jack knew full well the man needed reading glasses at his age, and wasn't at all surprised when Bell said, "Well, it looks in order. Do you mind telling me what's going on here?"

Jack smiled while his insides roiled. "We ask the questions, we don't answer them."

Out of the corner of his eye, he saw Dennis hit a number on his speed dial. Jamie Farrell, he thought. The kid was learning fast. He motioned for Jack to move to the side so he could talk to him out of earshot of Evan Bell.

"You *know* either Bell or the two downstairs are going to call someone about this the minute we leave the building. Jamie said that the locking mechanism for every floor is in a utility closet at the beginning of the hallway. I think we should get all three of them back into Martha Gellis's office and lock them in. At least they'll be warm. That guy out there in my Humvee, Spinelli, must be about frozen. Jamie told me how the system works. What do you think, Jack?"

"I say that's good thinking. I'll take this guy back to the office, you go get Spinelli, and tell Maggie to bring her guy up here. Go!"

Jack turned around and motioned for Bell to follow him back to Martha Gellis's office. "Have a seat, Mr. Bell."

Bell did as instructed, his eyes wary. "I don't understand any of this. I'm the head of Security; you should have come to me first."

Jack surmised that Bell was ex-military, what with his crew cut, spit-and-polish suit, and, of course, his height and weight, which was around six-four and 220. "How long have you worked here, Mr. Bell? I'm going to need your cell phone."

"Fifteen years."

"Is there anything about the people who own this company, and by that I mean the Andovers, that you'd care to tell me? By the way, do you get stock options in case Andover ever goes public?"

"I take care of Security; that's my job, and I'm very good at what I do. I hire good people. The first thing we were all told when we hired on was to mind our own business and do our jobs. We've all done that. The Andovers don't give second chances. And yes, as head of Security, I get stock options. Not that they are worth anything until there is a market for them. I keep hoping the company will go public.

When it does, I will probably retire and go live somewhere in the Caribbean."

"Care to tell me your personal feelings in regard to the Andovers? I'm just making conversation now, guy to guy."

Bell debated the question for a moment. "Hard to deal with. Look, I just work here. I came here right out of the military and worked my way up to the head of Security. Guy to guy, does this have anything to do with that leukemia drug? My wife wanted me to quit when that all came out. Said between my military pension and her job, and with Social Security only a few years away, we would do just fine, thank you very much. Then, over Christmas, we saw on the Internet that another little girl died. You guys got any openings for someone my age at the Bureau?"

"Yeah, as a matter of fact, we do," Jack said. "I think you might be a good fit for the new director. Stop by on January 2. I'll put in a good word for you."

Bell looked at Jack, trying to figure out if he was stringing him along or not. Whatever he saw in Jack's expression made him grin. "I'll do that. So, is your game plan to lock the three of us in here until tomorrow morning? If so, can I call my wife to tell her I won't be home till tomorrow? Then you can have my cell phone. You'd better cut the phone line, too. But please leave the heat on. It's supposed to go down to five degrees tonight."

"Okay," Jack said agreeably. "Anything else you want to tell me?"

"Yeah," Bell drawled, "the only one I would trust out of the three is Philip, and I'm not really sure about him."

Just as he finished speaking, Dennis showed up with Lee and Spinelli, along with Maggie. They held a brief conference by the door, with a lot of head shaking and hand waving. Maggie pointed to her watch.

The trio worked quickly to cut the phone lines and scour the office to make sure there was no way for the occupants who were going to spend the night to communicate with anyone on the outside.

"Mrs. Gellis keeps a supply of candy and crackers in the linen closet. I saw some blankets in there, and there are drinks in the minifridge. Are you all okay with this?"

A chorus of "No!" rang out. To which Maggie replied, "Tough!"

Jack didn't know why he did it, but he walked over to Bell, who towered over him when he stood up. He held out his hand and said, "Just remember, we're the good guys. And I really am sorry about all of this."

"Obviously you all have someplace you need to get to. I learned a long time ago never to sweat the small stuff." The handshake was firm and hard. Jack nodded as he followed Dennis and Maggie out the door.

"What was that all about, Jack?" Dennis asked.

"Never you mind, kid. Just do what you need to do and let's get out of here."

Dennis raced down the hall and activated the locking mechanism. He winced at the sound of the hydraulic hiss as the lock shot into place. "Oooh, we screwed up, Jack. We didn't check the other offices to see if anyone is in them."

"Oh, well, no one is going to freeze if they have to spend the night. We are good to go, so let's go. Anyone call in?"

"No. Well, yeah, they did, but they're still on the road. No one has a definite ETA as yet. Roads are bad because it's snowing harder. This is three glitches now. That's my limit," Dennis snorted as he raced for the front door. "C'mon, c'mon, why are you lagging behind? Yeah, yeah, first one out has to clear off the snow. Man, I always get the shit detail," Dennis grumbled.

"What did I tell you about FBI agents? They do not whine; nor do they dither. As in ever."

"Shove it, Jack. I'm not an official agent. Make-believe does not count."

Jack's cell phone vibrated in his pocket for the seventh time since they had arrived at the Andover headquarters. Now he could finally see who had been calling him.

Uh-oh.

"What?" Maggie said as she saw the expression on Jack's face in the light spilling out of the lobby.

"It's Nikki. She's home and wants to know where I am. Each message is a little more frantic. She said if I don't return her call in the next five minutes, she's calling the police and the hospitals."

"Well, crap!" Maggie said succinctly. "Now what?"

"Try Plan B," Dennis shouted as he gave the back windshield one last swipe.

"Just get in the damn car and drive while I figure out what to do," Jack said with a groan.

Chapter 38

It was a tense ride to the home of Martha Gellis. While Jack and Maggie marveled at Dennis's expert driving on the slippery road, they also knew he was at the mercy of other drivers, who weren't as cautious as he was. And then there was Mother Nature, who didn't seem to care who was driving what kind of vehicle. The wind whistled sharply, sending the swirling snowflakes into a sideways avalanche. The windshield wipers fought valiantly, but it was a losing battle, so all Dennis could do was keep his eyes on the tiny pinpoints of red taillights in front of him and hope that the driver knew where he was going.

"You're doing good, kid, just take it easy. Take deep breaths. This truck is like a tank. We're good here, so don't panic. According to this blabbering GPS, we're only a mile from our destination."

Dennis clenched his jaw so tight he thought it would crack. Somehow, he managed to get the words through his clenched teeth. "Okay, Jack."

"Maggie, what are the others saying?"

"Abner said they are two miles out. Their ETA at Otto's home, he's thinking, is about another hour. Very slow going, and Harry is like a wet cat on a hot griddle, according to him. But he did say he's a good driver.

"Espinosa said they are a half mile from Philip's home. He said it's snowing heavily, but they managed to get a few cars behind a snowplow and are holding steady. That's the good news. The bad news is, I don't know if we're going to be able to make it out to Pinewood after our snatch and grab. We might need an alternate location to . . . um . . . do our thing. And here is more bad news, in case anyone is interested. Snowden is not responding to my texts."

Jack pondered all of this as his cell phone continued to vibrate in his pocket. All he could think about was Nikki calling around to hospitals and the police, not that the police would care about his disappearance with the storm going on. Crap! He shifted his thoughts to what Maggie was saying. An alternative. Where? His mind raced. The only place he could think of was Maggie's Georgetown house, which was two doors away from his own. Crap again! The constant vibration of the phone in his pocket was making his thigh numb. Such a problem.

The robotic voice on the GPS continued to give directions.

"Her name is Gisella," Dennis said.

"Who?" Jack asked.

"The voice on the GPS. I wouldn't buy the car until they told me. They thought I was nuts. Hey, if someone is going to talk to me constantly, I want to know who it is. It's a personal thing. You know what else, those voices get paid big bucks to do that. You have a problem with that, Jack?" he demanded. His voice stopped just short of being shrill, indicating he was stressed to the max.

"Not one little bit, kid. Gisella it is. She's talking again; listen."

"Turn right one hundred feet ahead," Gisella instructed.

Jack lowered the window and was rewarded by a gust of stinging snow to his cheeks. "I think I can see a green sign; slow down, Dennis."

"I'm crawling, Jack. If I go any slower, I'll be at a full stop."

"I see it! I see it! Quick, make a right. Easy now; can you see, Dennis?"

"A little."

Gisella spoke again. "You are a quarter of a mile from your destination. Stay on this road; make no turns." And then, finally, they could see houses and pinpoints of yellow light. There were lampposts and Christmas lights twinkling in the swirling snow. Gisella spoke again. "You have now successfully arrived at your destination. Thank you for allowing me the pleasure of helping you."

Dennis slumped against the steering wheel. All he wanted to do was get a cup of hot cocoa and go to sleep, but he knew that wasn't going to happen. "You're driving on the way back, Jack."

The trio climbed out of the Humvee and didn't bother to lock it. Up ahead, they could see a structure that looked just like every other house on the cul-de-sac. There was a light over the door that displayed a Christmas wreath bare of any ornaments other than a red bow that looked to be soaking wet. On close inspection, the wreath turned out to be artificial.

Shivering and stomping their feet, Maggie and Dennis huddled close together as Jack gave the door knocker a resounding thump. They waited, hardly daring to breathe, for someone to open the door. When it opened, they saw a plump, pink-cheeked woman wearing granny glasses wrapped in a bright red bathrobe. She immediately became aggressive, demanding to know who they were and why they were knocking on her door in the middle of a storm. "If you're stuck, call AAA," she snapped.

"FBI, Mrs. Gellis," Jack snapped in return. "Stand aside so we can enter the premises. We have a warrant. I am Special Agent Anthony Lupine, the man to my right is Special Agent Donald Ryder, and the lady is Special Agent Lucinda Collins." When the woman refused to move, Jack repeated,

"I said, step aside, ma'am." She finally backed up a step as she clutched the cherry-colored robe around her throat.

"FBI? What do you want with me? I didn't do anything. If you want to question me about my neighbors, I have nothing to say. I barely know them other than to wave when I see them. What do you want?"

"We want you to get dressed and come with us. Special Agent Collins will accompany you, but first we want you to turn over your cell phone to us. Is there anyone else in the house?"

"My husband is somewhere. Probably in the basement, working on one of his stupid birdhouses. Why? Did he do something?"

"We ask the questions, you answer them. Do you understand that?"

"No, I don't understand that. You invade my home, so I have the right to ask why."

"Right now you have no rights," Jack said. Already he didn't like this woman and knew he would never grow to like her. He jerked his head at Maggie, who took the woman's arm and led her across the room.

"Special Agent Ryder, check the basement. You know what to do."

The plump woman jerked free of Maggie's grasp and spun around. "I *said* I want to know why you're here. I refuse to be violated. Do you hear me, I *refuse.*"

Jack sighed. He waved the warrant in one hand and the small checkbook he'd taken from her office. Martha Gellis turned pale. "That's . . . that's the company checkbook! Where did you get that?"

Jack waved the warrant again. His eyebrows shot upward, daring her to ask another question. She was too furious to more than sputter. Maggie moved her jacket to the side to let her see the gun in her shoulder holster. Of course, Mrs. Gellis did not know it wasn't loaded. Maggie motioned the nasty woman forward.

Jack meandered through the house as he waited for Maggie and Dennis to return. It looked to him just like any other house. The Christmas tree was nothing special; artificial, with ornaments that could be bought in any department store. There were no pictures of family members to be seen, but there were wall-to-wall bookshelves in almost every room. Every shelf was filled with romance novels. He thought he could smell fish. Maybe they'd had fish for dinner.

Dennis was the first to find him in the kitchen. He held Mr. Gellis's phone in his hand. "I explained the situation to Mr. Gellis. His comment to me was, 'What took you people so long?' He does not care, I repeat, he does not care that we are 'taking' his wife, as he put it, 'into custody.' He also said we did not need to worry about his calling anyone because he doesn't care and would be happy to see his brothers-in-law sent 'up the river' for the rest of their lives. Those were his exact words: 'up the river.'

"He makes really nice birdhouses and wanted to give me one. I said that would constitute a bribe, and he laughed. He sells them on the Internet."

Maggie appeared out of nowhere. "We're ready, Agent Lupine."

"Did you tell my husband you were arresting me?" Martha Gellis asked.

"I did. He said he didn't care. Your husband makes very nice birdhouses."

Martha had to be prodded toward the front door. "Where are you taking me? To FBI Headquarters? I know some powerful people. I want you to know that. When my brother Otto finds out you arrested me, heads will roll, I can tell you that."

"Your brother Otto is at this moment in the same position you are, Mrs. Gellis, as is your brother Philip. Those powerful people you mentioned will not be able to help you," Jack said. He crossed his fingers the way he had when he was a child and had hoped that he was telling the truth, at least for the moment.

They were back on the road, with Gisella leading them to the address Dennis, who was riding shotgun, had entered: Maggie's house. With the aid of a small light under the dashboard, Dennis sent out text after text. He whooped in delight when he saw that Avery Snowden finally responded. He typed at the speed of light, explaining, then asking questions. The time was coming up on six-thirty.

"Everyone is on the road back. Little to no resistance, except Otto tried to go for the gun in his study. How stupid is that? Going up against the FBI like that."

"My brother is not stupid," Martha Gellis shrilled from the backseat.

"Yeah, he is. Otherwise, why would you be sitting here right now, Mrs. CFO, and why would your brother, Mr. CEO, be in the same position you're in?" Dennis shot back.

Martha Gellis clamped her lips shut as she tried in vain to peer out the window at the snow-filled night. A feeling of panic was engulfing her. She wanted to lash out, to kick and scream, but she knew she couldn't do that. She didn't know what, if anything, she could do. What she felt in her bones was that her life was never going to be the same again. She wanted to cry. She tried then to remember the last time a tear had escaped her eye and couldn't come up with a time, date, or place. Maybe she was one of those people who didn't have tear ducts. Finally, she blurted out, "You're kidnapping me. I don't care if you are the FBI or not, you cannot go around kidnapping innocent people."

"You aren't innocent," Dennis said, loud enough to be heard in the backseat as he continued to text furiously.

"We're making better time; the plows are out. They've

sanded the road since we came through. What's our ETA?"
Jack asked.

"Gisella says it's ninety minutes to the address I punched in. Give or take thirty, and everyone should be arriving on schedule."

"Good to know. Snowden?"

"In place. Just waiting for our call."

Chapter 39

The more or less ninety minutes turned into an hour and fifty minutes before Jack parked Dennis's Humvee in front of Maggie Spritzer's house in Georgetown. He hopped out and struggled to see through the snow if Harry or Ted had arrived. As far as he could tell, there was no sign of Avery Snowden, but then again, he had no idea what kind of get-away vehicle he would be driving this time.

He turned to Dennis and said, "Listen, kid, they might tow this set of wheels. As you can see, there's no parking. You okay with them towing the Humvee?"

"Yeah. I can get it out of the impound lot. Let's just do what we have to do and get inside to wait for the others."

Maggie already had the door open and was yanking Martha Gellis by the arm. To Maggie's displeasure, the woman was resisting. "We can do this the easy way or the hard way, ma'am," she said, going for her unloaded gun. Gellis moved.

It took a good seven minutes to plow through the snow and up the snow-covered steps to the front door, where Maggie had to fumble in the dark for the key to open the door. Then there was a wild scramble for all four of them to get inside. Jack was the last as he turned his head to see if there were any lights on in his house, two doors away.

He winced at the amount of light spilling out into the snowy night. Nik must have turned on every light in the house. It was all Jack could do not to run through the snow to the house. He gritted his teeth and followed Dennis into Maggie's foyer.

Safe.

Hero, Maggie's new roommate, launched himself at her. At first, he was spitting and snarling, but the moment Maggie whispered to him, he calmed down and started to purr so loud, Jack started laughing.

"My God, a cat! I'm allergic to cats," Martha Gellis exploded.

"Tell that to someone who cares. Move your ass, Mrs. Gellis, and don't open that mouth of yours again or I'll shove a wad of cat fur between your molars," Maggie threatened as she tried to struggle out of her coat and still hold Hero, who was purring even louder.

Jack turned up the heat and immediately went into the kitchen to make some coffee, while Dennis raced to the family room, where he built a roaring fire. Jack wondered if he would ever feel warm again.

Forty minutes later, the front door of Maggie's house opened and a black streak raced through the rooms to slam up against Jack, who was leaning against the kitchen counter. "You missed me that much, huh?" Jack said, tussling with the big dog, then dropping to the floor to roll around, to Cyrus's delight. Hero took all this in before he leaped out of Maggie's arms and joined the fun. Cyrus eyed the intruder, growled, then barked. Hero hissed and snarled, then leaped back into Maggie's arms.

"Oh my God! A dog. I'm allergic to dogs," Gellis exploded.

"I thought you said you were allergic to cats," Maggie barked. "Make up your damn mind."

"I'm allergic to all animals that have fur or hair."

"Oh. Well, we don't care. Do we, guys?" Maggie said as she looked up at Ted and winked.

Espinosa shoved Philip Andover into the kitchen and told him to sit. He sat. He looked, Jack thought, like a college professor. Right behind Espinosa were Harry and Abner, dragging Otto Andover, who was doing his best to hang back.

Jack laughed out loud when he heard Harry say, "I've had enough of your crap." He gave the resisting Otto a chop to the neck, then moved, so Otto could drop to the floor. Abner stepped over him. "The guy has been a pain in my ass since we picked him up. Boil some water; I need a cup of tea."

Jack hustled to fill Maggie's teakettle and set it on the gas burner. "How'd it all go, Harry?"

"Just like you'd expect. He protested. I clipped him a couple of times, and he tried to take me on. Such a silly man. He's here, so can we move things along? I want to get home to my family." He moved closer to Jack so the others couldn't hear what he was saying.

"Is Otto afraid of you, Harry?"

Harry's eyes narrowed until they were mere slits in his face. "If he was or is, it was hard to tell. The guy is real mouthy, though. He made all kinds of threats. I had to threaten to pull his tongue out through his nose to get him to turn over his checkbook. Abner has his desk computer, his laptop, and every other device we found. The wife was watching some rerun on TV and didn't ask any questions, even when we told her we were taking Otto with us. All she said was, 'Good-bye, dear.' For some reason, I don't think they have a happy marriage. Now, will she call anyone tomorrow morning when he doesn't show up? That's anyone's guess. My guess would be no."

Ted bent down and grabbed Otto by the collar of his jacket and propped him up against the pantry door. "I think you need to wake him up, Harry, so we can get this show on the road."

Harry laughed, the evil laugh that made everyone in the room look somewhere else. "I think you're right, Ted." He bent over and, using his index finger and thumb, opened Otto's eyes. He leaned closer, but no one could see what he was doing. Within a second, Otto was blustering and spewing hateful words. Harry wagged a finger warningly, then put it against his lips to indicate he wanted total silence. Otto stopped in midsentence and leaned back against the pantry door.

Jack took the floor. He held up both his hands for silence just as his cell vibrated in his pocket. He did his best to ignore it and concentrate on what had to be done. "Is his head clear, Harry? Is he going to understand what I'm saying?"

"Oh, yeah," Harry drawled.

"All right then, people. Here's the deal: We want your money. Not just a little bit but *all* of it. When you give it to us, we're going to give it away."

Martha reared up and almost fell out of her chair. "You aren't FBI agents at all. You really did kidnap us! Otto, Philip, do something, for God's sake."

"What was your first clue?" Maggie asked curiously.

Before Martha could respond, her brother Otto warned his sister to shut up and told her that she always talked too much. Philip remained quiet. Otto's eyes were narrowed to mere slits in his face as he watched and listened.

"I have some papers here I want you all to sign. You will be agreeing to the terms of the Quinn class-action suit. You will sign a letter that we've prepared, then you will sign a check from this nifty little flowered checkbook of Martha's. Then you will graciously allow us to strip all your monies from all of your accounts. When you do that, you will all leave for . . . a vacation. How does that sound? You may speak now."

"I will never sign off on that class-action suit," Otto said coldly.

"Yes, you will, Mr. Andover. The question is, how quickly you will do it. Torture is a terrible thing. I'm thinking your threshold for pain is very low given the privileged life you've led," Jack said.

"I told you to settle the minute that firm filed the papers. I warned you, Otto, that it would turn into a nightmare, and I was absolutely right. Martha agreed with me, but oh, no, you said nothing would come of it. Well, look where we are right now. Furthermore, you arrogant ass, those families deserve the money. I have not had a good night's sleep since those papers were filed. And the reason for that is because I have a conscience, even if you don't. I'm not sure about Martha anymore," Philip said in an even, unemotional voice.

"We did pay some of those people. Then they got greedy, knowing the company has deep pockets. They wanted more and still more; then they brought more people into it. It was never-ending. We would have gone down the drain," Martha blubbered.

"What part of *their children died* don't you get? They deserve to own your company for that faulty drug," Jack said. "It's off the market now, thanks to those people. And we will not allow you to go with that new arthritis miracle that you're about to unveil after the New Year. We are going to cause such an uproar over that, you might as well forget you ever developed and patented that drug."

"You can torture me all you want, but I am not signing anything," Otto said.

"Wanna bet?" Maggie said as she moved closer to where Otto was still lounging against the pantry door. She kicked him in the groin just to have something to do. She really wanted a hot shower and to slide beneath the special sheets that *slithered* against her body, and this ass was preventing that from happening. She gave him another kick for good measure. He howled in pain.

Jack looked over at Martha. "Are you ready to sign? These papers require three signatures."

Tears rolling down her cheeks, Martha tried to push herself as deep into the kitchen chair as she could. "I can't unless Otto tells me to sign. That's the rule at the company."

"Bullshit!" Philip bellowed. "Give it to me. I'll sign it. Then maybe I'll be able to sleep again." Before anyone knew what was happening, Philip Andover wrote his name in legible script. He then dated it, with the time. He walked back over to the chair he'd been sitting on, sat down, folded his arms across his chest, and closed his eyes.

One down and two to go.

"Will you shut up, Martha? You're giving me a headache. You always were a whiny little brat," Otto said tersely.

Ah, the weak link, Jack thought. He looked over at Maggie, turning control over to her. She almost laughed out loud. These boys were such *wusses*. She walked over to Martha Gellis and bent down. "If you don't sign these papers, you will not like the outcome. I'll ask just once. Will you sign them?"

Not trusting herself to speak, Martha shook her head, her eyes on her brother.

"Okay. I was nice, wasn't I, guys?" The guys all nodded. "Wait right here; I'll be right back." Jack felt his insides start to shake. Maggie could be . . . he gave up when he couldn't come up with just the right word. He risked a glance at Harry, who just looked dreamy, like he'd transported himself someplace far away. Harry could do that, then come back to the moment refreshed. Dennis looked like he was about to explode, while Ted and Espinosa whispered to each other as though they knew what Maggie's next move was going to be. Abner played with his laptop, his eyes full of dollar signs. Abner loved giving away other people's money. Loved it, loved it, loved it!

Upstairs in her bedroom, Maggie looked longingly at her king-size bed. She walked over to it, turned on the bed warmer, then headed for the bathroom and the tools she would need to convince Martha Andover to sign the class-action papers.

Downstairs, she held up what looked like two large curling irons. She plugged both into the wall socket over the kitchen counter. "Mrs. Gellis, this curling iron is a new prototype that my hairdresser gave me to try out. This one that's all crazy curly will give pretty much permanent curls like those you see in my hair. They're called corkscrew curls. This second curling iron will remove the curls. I just love them. The longer you leave them on, the more lasting the curls. The only drawback is, they get so hot you have to be careful not to get burned. It takes a lot of expertise to master the use of them. It took me weeks."

All eyes were on Martha Gellis, whose eyes were on Maggie, her mouth hanging open.

"I told you I wasn't going to ask you again. So here is what I'm going to do: First, I'm going to curl your ears, then I'm going to curl your lips. Close your eyes and envision the outcome. Aside from the blisters, of course. Are you getting a visual here, Mrs. Gellis?"

Ted and Espinosa moved closer to the chair. At a nod from Maggie, they both reached out and pinned Martha to the chair.

"Silly me. I forgot the most important part. After I finish up with your lips, I'm going to shove the curly one right up your tight ass. Visualize *that*!"

"Do. Not. Sign. That. Document. Martha!" Otto bellowed. Martha slumped in her chair.

Quicker than lightning, Maggie whirled and clamped the

curling iron onto one of Otto's ears. The smell of burned flesh invaded the room. It took Harry, Jack, and Dennis, using all their strength, to hold Otto down. Martha fell off the chair. Cyrus growled, and Hero hissed at these goings-on. Philip Andover cracked one eye, smiled, and went right back to resting.

Espinosa gathered his wits about him. It always amazed him at how bloodthirsty women could be. His own mother was a gentle soul, as were his sisters. He had to admit, though, he got a thrill out of it. He filled a cup with cold water from the sink and dumped it on Martha Gellis's face. She sputtered and cursed. Cyrus licked at the water. Espinosa lifted her up and put her back on the chair. "This might be a good time to sign your name to those papers," he whispered in her ear.

Martha Gellis made a decision at that precise moment. She'd never been a pretty woman, and she knew it. Curled-up lips and crinkly ears were not something she wanted the world to see. She thought about her ass for a split second, then blinked. She wrote her name as clearly as she could with her shaking hands.

Two down and one to go.

"Oooh. I bet that hurts," Dennis said as he peered at Otto's blood-red ear, which had already blistered.

"Strip him down, boys," Maggie said.

Philip stirred himself long enough to clap his hands. "Finally, we all get to see you screwed up the ass the way you've screwed people your whole life. I applaud you people, whoever the hell you are. Bravo!" He clapped his hands again before he closed his eyes and went back to being half-asleep.

Otto Andover's naked body was not a pleasing sight. He was no Adonis. Nor was he even close to Hulk Hogan. He was fish-belly white, flabby, hairy Otto Andover. Maggie grimaced at the sight. "Before you bend him over, how about I give his dick a quick twist with the curly iron? I'm thinking we should vote here. I hate making decisions on my own."

"You have my vote!" Philip shouted.

Cyrus barked.

Hero snarled.

"Three's good enough for me. Hold him steady, boys, and spread those legs. Jeez, where'd it go? C'mon, Otto, let me see it!"

Harry ran to the bathroom. Dennis turned away, and Jack laughed out loud. Ted Robinson just looked at Maggie and vowed never, *ever* to get on her bad side. Never, ever.

"Crap, I'm going to have to dig for it. I need gloves." She set the curling iron on the counter and ran out to the garage, where she routed around for her gardening gloves, which had dry dirt all over them. She shrugged it off and pulled on the gloves, giggling as she did so. Wait till she told Myra and Annie about this.

Back in the kitchen, she waved her hands to show off her gardening gloves, reached for the curling iron, then bent over, where she started to poke and prod among the jewels. "Okay, since I can't find it, I'm just going to fry your balls. Last chance!"

The room went silent. Even Hero stopped snarling and hissing. Cyrus crept closer to Jack to see what was going on.

The scream was so primal, everyone in the room clapped their hands over their ears.

"Sign now or you know what's coming next," Maggie singsonged.

Dennis inched his way to Jack and whispered, "Holy shit, I thought she was just kidding. *She did it.* Do you think he'll hold out for the encore?"

"Nah."

Otto's eyes rolled back in his head, Ted slapped him a

few times, then Espinosa dumped cold water on him. He came around slowly, moaning in pain.

"Sign the papers, you dickweed," Jack said.

Otto Andover signed his name as clearly as he could.

"Someone call Snowden and help Otto get dressed," Jack said as he gathered up the contracts and the check that was going to make Nikki go over the moon.

"Abner, did you transfer all the monies out of their personal accounts? Where did you send it?"

"For now, the Antilles. We can decide tomorrow what we want to do. For now, it's perfectly safe."

"Dennis, call your friend Jamie and get his bank account number. Let Abner wire the money in now. How much do you want to give the guy?"

"Five million!" Dennis said smartly.

"Done," Abner said ten minutes later as Dennis rattled off numbers to him.

"Snowden said he's thirty minutes out. He's coming in an ambulance. He said that's the only kind of vehicle allowed on the road," Ted said.

"Well, ladies and gentlemen, I'll take my leave of you all," Harry said. "My job here is done and my family awaits me."

"Hold on, Harry. You're going to be driving right by Georgetown Messenger Service. They're open twenty-four/seven. I need you to drop this off, and pay cash. Feel free to tell them your name is Otto Andover. Just plunk down this hundred bucks and tell them to keep the change. I think the fee is seventy-five bucks.

"Maggie, you got a manila envelope?"

"In the kitchen drawer behind you."

Jack motioned for his friends to gather round. "This might be the only time in your lives—I'm sure in mine, too—that we will ever see a check for $650 million. I can't wait for Nik to see this in the morning. Remember now, any questions, you all know nothing." Heads bobbed up and down, faces smiling.

"What about all this other money?" Abner asked. "The money I sent to the Antilles?"

"Care to give us a number?" Maggie asked.

Abner laughed. "Upwards of $450 million. These three are rich. Oops; *were* rich." He laughed again. "I left enough in their personal accounts so their families can live more than comfortable lives. Their spouses will presumably inherit their stakes in the company, if it doesn't tank. We are good to go, guys."

"Bastard!" Otto spat.

Maggie's doorbell rang. She ran to answer it. A minute later, three guys as big as oak trees and Avery Snowden entered the kitchen. They picked up the three Andovers like they were rag dolls and walked out of the kitchen, none of them saying a word.

Snowden looked around. "This is gonna cost you, Emery."

"Meet me tomorrow at Ding's, noonish, and I'll have your money ready, or we can do it right now, if you want. Abner is still set up."

"Let's do it now."

The others watched as Abner's jaw dropped at the amount Snowden told him to transfer. And then he grinned. "Don't spend it all in one place."

"Wiseass," Snowden said and grinned in return. "Nice doing business with you."

When the door closed behind Snowden, the others looked at one another. The manila envelope in hand, Harry waved good-bye.

Dennis slipped into his heavy jacket and followed him out the door, along with Abner and Espinosa. "Where do you think they're taking them?" he asked nervously.

Harry shrugged. "Probably some potato farm in Ireland. Do you care?"

Dennis thought about it for a second. "Nope."

Then it was just Jack, Maggie, and Ted. Jack already had his coat on. "Tell Nikki I said hi," Maggie said.

"Can't do that. I'm going to have to come up with some story about where I've been so she doesn't chop me off at the knees. She's been calling and texting me since early this afternoon. If she calls, you guys know nothing, okay?"

"Will you go already?"

"I'm gone," Jack said, Cyrus at his side.

And then it was just Maggie and Ted and the slithery sheets that waited under the bed warmer.

"I just love it when things work out," Maggie said as she started peeling off her clothes on the way up the steps.

Ted tried not to think about the curling iron in his beloved's hands as he galloped up the steps. She would never . . .

Epilogue

Nikki Quinn unlocked the door to the offices of her firm, then quickly adjusted the thermostat. Today was going to be a nonstarter. So much snow. She'd be lucky if one, or possibly two, lawyers would make it in. Only those who lived within walking distance, the way she did, might give it a try. She shed her coat and headed for her office.

She didn't want to be here, but she'd told Jack last night that she needed to walk through these doors one more time before she kept the promise to herself that she was taking a year off and possibly selling the firm.

She couldn't do this anymore. She just couldn't. "I'm not doing it anymore," she muttered to herself as she picked through the mail, leaving a messenger-delivered envelope for last.

She ripped at a plain white business envelope that bore the name of the Stayman Pet Food Company, the firm's other class-action suit. The single sheet of paper held only two short paragraphs.

Nikki blinked, then blinked again, just as the buzzer at the front door sounded. She didn't know how she knew, but she knew it was Alexis. Then she let out a whoop of pure joy just as Alexis appeared in the doorway. "They caved!" she said, waving the single sheet of paper under

Alexis's nose. "Do you believe that? They aren't going to fight anymore. They're going to settle with us for the full amount. I can't believe this!"

Alexis sat down, shock written all over her face. "Why? Two weeks ago, they were going to go the distance and fight us till hell froze over. Such a stupid question; who cares why? We won! Oh, my God! We won!"

"You are so right, who cares why? Listen, Alexis, I need to talk to you about something. We talked about it while we were out west, and we talked about it ad nauseam while we were stuck in those airports for days, but I'm really serious now. I can't do this anymore. At least for now. I'm going to take a year off and do absolutely nothing. At the end of the year, I might even sell the firm. I am so burned-out, I can't see straight. I was so blinded by our cause, I could have lost Jack."

Alexis started to laugh and couldn't stop. "Now why do you think I braved all that snow out there this morning? I came here to tell you the same thing. If you weren't here, I was going to leave a letter on your desk. Like you, I realized people like Joseph only come along once in a lifetime. I love him. I hope he still loves me. I will grovel if I have to when I ask him to take me back. No damn career in the whole world is worth the misery I've been going through. I've saved some money, and I'm going to ask him to go with me to some sunny island where we can get our lives back on track. Please say you aren't upset with me, Nikki."

"I am not upset. I want you to do it. I'm doing it. The firm can carry on without us. The one thing you don't have to worry about is the cost of your getaway. The firm will pay for that. And if you need more than a year, take the time. Your pay will be deposited automatically in your account. You earned it. We were crazy, you know that, right? We thought we could take on Andover and make those skunks pay, and bring some closure to all those parents.

We made a dent. There is nothing more we can do. Let the second string fight it now. We did the hard part, laid down all the groundwork. Whatever happens, happens. So, let's get through all this"—Nikki motioned to the pile of mail and the Georgetown Messenger Service envelope—"then we can go home and veg out. You okay with that, girl?"

Alexis nodded as she tapped out a text to Joseph Espinosa. "You don't think he'll tell me to go fly a kite, do you, Nikki?"

"If he does, I'll kill him. The short answer is no."

Nikki ripped at the sealed envelope and withdrew another envelope. "Hey, look at this, Alexis! It's from Andover Pharmaceuticals. Sent by messenger." She ripped at the smaller envelope and the single sheet of paper that bore the Andover letterhead. Still inside the bigger envelope was a thick packet of papers. But it was the small blue-and-yellow check with butterflies on it that left her fighting for air. Alexis craned her neck to see what Nikki was holding in her hand while she gulped air like a caught fish.

"Oh, sweet Jesus. Am I seeing what I'm seeing?" Alexis practically screamed.

"If you mean a check that has butterflies on it and is written for $650 million, then yeah, you're seeing what I'm seeing. Maybe we went snow blind on the walk here. This is real, Alexis. Look, here are the signoff contracts, signed by all three Andovers. We won! My God, we won! Alexis, we won!" Nikki whooped.

"Call the brokerage house to make sure it's good! Do it now, Nikki, before I explode."

Five minutes later, Nikki's fist shot in the air. "It's real! We have to get this to the bank! We need to call all of our people. All the names on the lawsuit. Every single one of them deserves a personal phone call. But first, we're going to have a drink. I have a bottle of two-hundred-year-old brandy I've been saving like forever. A gift from a grateful client years ago."

"It's only nine o'clock in the morning!"

"I don't care! Do you care?"

"I. Do. Not."

While Nikki dusted off the brandy bottle, Alexis made a fire in Nikki's fireplace. She set out crystal snifters from Nikki's private bar and sat down, her head reeling. She was elated, over the moon about the class-action suits, but it was Joseph Espinosa who was on her mind. She said a little prayer that she wasn't too late, that Joseph would forgive her for choosing her career over him.

The two women sipped. Then they gulped. Then they guzzled, and, finally, by ten-thirty, the two-hundred-year-old brandy bottle was empty. Sitting Indian style in front of the fire, the women looked at each other and said in unison, "We are soooo drunk!"

Neither Nikki nor Alexis heard the buzzer at the front door. They were so cockeyed drunk, they saw three of Jack Emery standing in the doorway. They saw three of him send off a text to Espinosa that said, *Get your ass over here to the Quinn offices. Your woman needs you. Fly if you have to, but get over here.*

Jack walked back to the kitchen, a grin as wide as the Grand Canyon on his face. He made coffee, knowing full well that it wouldn't do all that much good. The kind of drunk the ladies were on was going to have to run its course.

The phone rang at that moment. Jack picked up the extension on the first ring. It was Myra. He quickly explained the situation.

"Just like that! Amazing," he could hear Annie drawl in the background. A shiver ran up Jack's spine.

"Uh-huh. Just like that. So, where are you two, and

what are you doing?" Jack asked, hoping to divert the conversation.

"We're on our way home, dear. Annie got a brainstorm and wants to invest in something she said is going to make us millions."

"Really! What is it?"

"Elastic!" Myra laughed. She couldn't button her slacks this morning. Jack laughed right along with her. They talked for a few more minutes, then ended the call.

Carrying the tray with the coffee, Jack made his way back to Nikki's office, only to find two sleeping beauties dead to the world. He smiled.

He did love it when a plan came together.